ACCEPTABLE RISK

ACCEPTABLE RISK

LYNETTE EASON

THORNDIKE PRESS

A part of Gale, a Cengage Company

Copyright © 2020 by Lynette Eason.
Thorndike Press, a part of Gale, a Cengage Company.

Thorndike Press® Large Print Christian Fiction.
The text of this Large Print edition is unabridged.
Other aspects of the book may vary from the original edition.
Set in 16 pt. Plantin.

LIBRARY OF CONGRESS CIP DATA ON FILE.
CATALOGUING IN PUBLICATION FOR THIS BOOK
IS AVAILABLE FROM THE LIBRARY OF CONGRESS.

ISBN-13: 978-1-4328-8174-0 (hardcover alk. paper)

Published in 2020 by arrangement with Revell Books, a division of Baker Publishing Group

Printed in Mexico
Print Number: 01   Print Year: 2020

ACCEPTABLE RISK

CHAPTER ONE

August
Greenville, SC

The pain compelled her —

No . . . *propelled* her.

It had to end.

Living this way wasn't living. She would be doing everyone a favor if she just ended it. She couldn't believe the burden she'd become to the people she loved most.

Dr. Helen Craft approached the window, tears tracking down her cheeks to drip off her chin. She touched them in wonder. When was the last time she'd cried? The day her father died? No, it was the day the Taliban had driven the van loaded with explosives into the playground at the orphanage.

She was working in the small medical clinic across the street and felt the blast like she was standing beside it. Only she hadn't suffered a scratch. Not like the children.

"The children," she whispered. Forty-five killed instantly. Thirty-three injured.

A sob escaped her and she unlocked the window.

The images clicked on an endless loop with no stop button. She couldn't even pause it without alcohol or some drug.

Operating on a child who'd lost a leg.

Digging through the rubble to find more children with more injuries than she could help at once.

A missing hand.

A missing face . . .

One operation after another.

One child dying, then the next and the next, until she'd lost count. Later, she'd learned sixteen of the thirty-three surviving had succumbed to their injuries.

"I couldn't save them," she whispered. "Why couldn't I save them?" What good was she when they all died in spite of her best efforts?

And the workers. Her friends —

She grabbed her head, the screams continuing to echo. "Stop, please stop. I just want it to stop."

She threw open the window and looked down. Down represented peace. If she went back, the torture would continue.

"Helen! What are you doing?"

She didn't turn, didn't acknowledge her sister's terrified cry, just stepped out onto the ledge . . .

"Helen, no!"

. . . and launched herself into the air. Free-falling. Until the pain was finally gone.

CHAPTER TWO

September
Helmed Province, Afghanistan

Sarah Denning sat on the dirt floor of the Afghani prison cell and shivered in the ninety-degree heat, fighting the fear that had been her constant companion since the Taliban had attacked the school yesterday. One minute she'd been a guest teacher at the request of her friend, Talia Davenport, the next, a prisoner of cruel men who would use her and kill her without blinking.

She tugged the piece of cloth covering her head lower and patted the bottom section that concealed her mouth and nose, while praying she could stay anonymous until they were rescued. If rescue was even on the way. If their captors found out she was an American . . . or worse, who her father was —

The guard gave the barred door a violent tug and she jumped, her heart stumbling into overdrive. The door held fast. She doubted he was worried it wouldn't. He let out a satisfied grunt and turned to walk down the hallway, his boots pounding the dirt floor before he disappeared from sight. Sarah's pulse slowed a fraction. The longer he was gone, the better their chances of rescue. However, how long before he returned?

"Sarah?"

The whisper reached her from the corner of the cell. "Fatima?"

"I'm coming over there." The teenager crawled on all fours, dodging her classmates, to curl against Sarah's side with a shiver. "What's going to happen to us?"

Sarah wrapped an arm around the fifteen-year-old. During her weekly guest teaching spots, she'd come to recognize Fatima as a bright, highly motivated young woman with the desire to be a pioneer in bringing change to her country. Sarah had treasured those days at the school and building relationships with the girls. "I don't know."

But she did. They all did.

"They're going to sell us," Samia said from the other side. "We're to be brides to the Taliban, aren't we?"

Brides? More like sex slaves. Punching bags. Assigned to a life of abuse and misery. And terror.

She, Talia, and the twelve students had been taken from the school and loaded into the back of a waiting van. No one tried to stop them and she didn't dare resist. Approximately twelve hours later, they'd arrived here.

Wherever here was.

"I'm so sorry, Sarah," Talia whispered, her voice cracking, her fear tangible. "I've been there for three years, and while we've had a few minor scares, there's been nothing like this."

"It's not your fault, Talia, you couldn't know."

"I don't want to be a Taliban bride." Nahal, the youngest of the girls at thirteen years old, scooted closer to Sarah, as though Sarah could keep that from happening.

Sarah had been afraid before, but the images filtering through her mind sent the horror clawing inside her to a whole new level. She pulled in a steadying breath, desperate to find a way to remain calm and be strong for the other girls in the ten-by-twelve cell, because while she wanted to fight back, any sign of defiance would only get her — or one of the teens — killed.

She shuddered and let her gaze roam their prison. It consisted of four cement walls with a door on the one opposite from where she lay. From a small barred window above her head streamed a thin ray of light, cigarette smoke, and low voices that sounded like they were arguing, although she couldn't make out the words.

Except for a brief stop at the outhouses lined up along the south wall that included lewd looks and a few comments she pretended not to hear, she and the other girls had been left alone by their captors.

Which was confusing, but welcome. However, she didn't expect that would last much longer. The one thing allowing her to keep her fear under control was the fact that they hadn't been searched. Knowing it would happen at some point, she'd seized the opportunity during a chaotic moment at the school to snag the satellite phone from the pocket of her burqa. Using the bodies crammed against her as a shield, she'd pressed the SOS button and sent out her distress signal.

Minutes passed, the only sounds being the hushed whispers and terrified weeping of her cellmates mixed with the low voices of the guards outside the window. Sarah leaned her head against the wall and watched the hallway while her hand searched through the folds of the cloth. Fatima looked up at her as Sarah's fingers closed around the sat phone. Did she dare take a chance to see if anyone had called? If there was a message? If help was on the way? All she had to do was sneak a peek.

"Don't ask why," she whispered to Fatima, "but can you sit slightly in front of me?"

"Yes." The girl moved enough to shield her from the guard's gaze should he return.

With shaky fingers, she pulled the phone from her pocket.

Talia's eyes widened at the sight of the phone. "What are you doing? If they know you have that, it won't be good."

"I know. I need to find a place to hide it."

She glanced at the screen. Nothing. No response that her plea for help had been seen. Cold dread sent a wave of nausea through her. The SOS should have gone out to her brother, FBI Special Agent Caden Denning, and to their father, Lieutenant General Lewis Denning. Even if her father had ignored the message, Caden should have been able to track the phone and have help on the way before these monsters could blink. Caden might be in the United States, but he had a long reach. As did their father. She'd thought carefully about adding him to the SOS list, but had decided to do so "just in case."

This situation was about as "just in case"

as one could get, and for once, she was glad her father was who he was — although she'd bite her tongue in half before admitting it. Then again, if admitting it would get them out of here, she'd shout it from the rooftops.

Surely, the message had gone through. She pressed the SOS button once more and slipped the phone back into her pocket. Caden would do something. Her father? The last time she'd talked to him had been when he told her he disinherited her for going into the Army. She'd laughed. "I don't need or want your money." She needed and wanted his love, but that had never been within her grasp.

Because of her ongoing conflict with her father, Sarah had kept a low profile, never acknowledging her relationship to the powerful man. Just before she joined the Army, she'd dyed her blonde hair a dark brown and decided to go by a different first name, insisting her family get used to calling her by it. The only feature that might draw attention to her was her green eyes. Otherwise, with her flawless Pashto, she should be able to pass as a native. At least, that's what she told herself.

The guard's heavy footfalls sounded in the hallway once more and her adrenaline spiked. Another guard joined him. They stood at the door, grinning and pointing, talking openly about the girls' futures. Bile rose in the back of her throat, even as the comforting presence of the phone pressed into her hip.

Please, Lord, send help.

Gavin Black spoke into the radio. Though he was no longer an official Army Ranger, his skills were still as sharp as the day he'd left the unit. From his position just outside the compound, protected only by a hill of sand, he could hear the faint hum of the plane's engine fifteen thousand feet above him. "It's a go," Gavin said into the headset. "Once you're down, wait for my signal. Over." He'd gone ahead, on the ground and at great risk to himself, to make sure the others could breach the compound in a way that would catch the occupants off guard — and give him and his team the advantage. Mere seconds would make the difference between life and death.

When the lieutenant general had called Gavin and requested his services, he hadn't been able to refuse — and not just because of the man's rank.

"My daughter's been kidnapped," he'd said, "taken by the Taliban from a school where she was a guest instructor. She, another teacher, and twelve female students are being held at a compound in the middle of the Registan Desert. The only way in without detection is to drop in at night."

Registan Desert? There was more than one compound in that suffocating place. "Which compound, sir?"

"Hibatullah Omar's. And they're saying he's behind the kidnapping."

Gavin stilled. Of course it would be *his.* "That's not possible. Omar's dead." Gavin had been a part of the raid that had led to his death. But another terrorist organization could have taken over the compound.

"Somehow he's risen from the grave. We've received satellite footage that he's up and running again. You know that compound. You lived there for over a year. Now that you're a private contractor, I need you to put together a team and get Rochelle and the others out of there."

Yes, he'd lived there. Working undercover as a terrorist, gaining the trust of one of the most horrific murderers in the Middle East. And Gavin had set him up to die. If Omar was truly alive, then he'd know about Gavin's betrayal.

Already on the ground in Kabul for another reason, Gavin had dropped what he was doing and quickly navigated his team

17

onto this assignment.

Rochelle Denning. Also known as Sarah. He'd met her in Kabul when they were deployed at the same time. Met her and found her fascinating. They'd gone out on three dates, shared an amazing kiss on the last date, and then she quit answering his calls and texts. Not one to tread where he wasn't wanted, Gavin had let it go in spite of his confusion over her sudden cold shoulder.

The general had said that Caden already called his resources with the FBI, but they wouldn't be much help in the Registan Desert.

His men would parachute far enough away to remain undetected, then make their way across the open fields of sand to the compound and to the north wall, where Gavin would meet them and lead them inside. With the night-vision goggles and binoculars, he could make out the entrance he'd used to come and go undetected when he was living at the compound.

"There's no way that's Omar," Cole Lawton said, his voice clear in Gavin's ear. "Over."

"I wouldn't have thought so either," Gavin said, keeping his voice low, "but the pictures don't lie. Over."

18

"Dude, I saw his body. He was burned to a crisp. We've got pictures of that as well, remember? Over."

"Yeah. Over." And before they could extract that body for DNA testing, they'd come under fire and had to fight for their lives to make it to the waiting bird.

He blinked against the memories. Unlike many of the people he served with, he didn't suffer nightmares often, but that didn't mean he wanted to dwell on the stuff nightmares were made of.

"You think they know who they snatched?" Lawton asked. "That she's Denning's daughter? Over."

"I sure hope not." Because if those killers knew they had the daughter of one of the highest-ranking men in the US Army, there would be no saving her. He checked his watch, then the altitude of the plane. Just a few more seconds, then . . . , "It's go time," he said. "You know what to do. Over."

"You sure this is going to work?"

"I'm sure." Mostly.

"What's Plan B? Over."

"There is no Plan B. I don't believe in them. Over." With that, he lowered the night vision lens over his right eye, while he used his left for depth perception and watched the plane. His adrenaline was at an all-time

19

high. "Three seconds," he said, mentally counting down. "Over."

On cue, the men propelled themselves out one at a time. Gavin could almost imagine he was with them, spreading his arms, feeling the wind pressing against him. He shuddered and focused back on the compound. He had to time it just right, which was why he was going in on the ground and not coming down from the sky. Among other reasons. But the most important was that he have the door open when his team arrived.

"I'm coming, Sarah," he whispered. "Hang on, I'm coming."

CHAPTER THREE

Sarah had buried the satellite phone in the corner of the cell's dirt floor only minutes before the guard had returned. Since then, he'd stayed just outside the door. Minutes had ticked past, turning into an hour, then more.

"What are they waiting on?" Fatima whispered.

"I don't know." Every so often another guard would come and the two men would exchange whispers. Then he'd turn and hurry down the hallway, only to return a while later to repeat the whole thing. "I heard the word 'delayed,' but can't make out anything else. I'm going to move to the door and see if I can hear what they're saying," she whispered to Fatima. "Stay put."

Eyes wide, Fatima nodded.

On hands and knees so as not to draw attention by standing, Sarah moved through the group, pressing a comforting hand on a

21

shivering teen's shoulder or squeezing the ice-cold fingers of another as she passed. Talia's terrified gaze met hers and she glared, her displeasure at Sarah's movement clear.

But if the phone hadn't worked like it was supposed to, they were going to have to know what was going on. At the door, she slid against the wall. The other guard should be returning any moment. As though he'd read her mind, footsteps pounded down the hallway to stop in front of the door. His radio crackled and Sarah thought she caught the words, "Search them one by one. Bring her to the conference room. We will make the video there."

Bring who?

"Get up! All of you!"

Sarah jerked at the order and slowly stood. The other girls followed her lead.

The guard who spoke looked to be in his early thirties, with a long beard and body odor strong enough to knock her out.

And a rifle gripped in his right hand.

When all of them were standing, huddled together, the guard threw open the door and lifted the rifle. He pointed it at Fatima. "You. Come with me."

Fatima stepped forward. When she reached Sarah, she grabbed Sarah's hand in

22

a death grip. The teen shook like she'd splinter apart any second.

The guard jabbed Fatima with the rifle. "What is your name?"

"Fatima."

"Remove your head covering."

Slowly, Fatima pushed the cloth away, her eyes downcast.

"It's not her," the other man said. "But I will take her for a little while." He placed the weapon against Fatima's shoulder. "Come with me."

The teen shuddered but didn't move to obey the order.

The guard's eyes gleamed. "Come, I said. Obey or die. Which will you choose?"

Still gripping Sarah's fingers, Fatima lifted her chin. "I choose to die."

A multitude of gasps sounded behind her.

He pulled the trigger. Fatima jerked and fell, her hand sliding from Sarah's grip.

Screams echoed.

"Fatima!" Heart pounding, ears ringing, Sarah dropped to her knees and pressed hard against the wound, barely able to control the rage she wanted to unleash on the guard. But the girl . . .

"Fatima," she whispered.

"It hurts," Fatima whimpered.

23

The rifle turned on Rashida. "You. Get up."

"Kinaaz," Sarah said, "come press on her wound."

Without hesitation, Kinaaz, the gentle soul who loved poetry, nature, and puppies, darted to her friend's side and replaced Sarah's hands with her own.

"Hold on, Fatima," Sarah whispered, "help's coming."

"I said get up!"

Rashida wailed and covered her head with her arms. The guard adjusted the rifle.

"Stop! Don't shoot her!" Sarah stood and stepped between the rifle and the other girls, ignoring the nausea curling in her gut. "What do you want?" she asked, keeping her head lowered, but watching him through her lashes.

His eyes glinted and raked her up and down. "I didn't tell you to interfere."

Sarah waited for the bullet. It didn't come, but she thought he considered it. "Remove your head covering."

She reached to do so and the smile that split his lips turned her stomach once more. He jerked the rifle, indicating she was to hurry up.

The guard behind him chuckled and muttered something under his breath. She

24

thought she caught, "That's the one."

Gunfire erupted from the hallway and the terrorist flinched, his rifle wavering for a fraction of a second. She lunged at the man, slamming her elbow into his throat. He stumbled back and she clamped a hand around the barrel of the rifle and rolled, jammed the stock into her shoulder, and aimed it at his face.

He charged at her and she pulled the trigger. Felt the kick against her shoulder. His face exploded into a red mist.

Bullets spit into his partner behind him. Footsteps pounded on the dirt floor. Another spray of gunfire above her head brought screams from the girls still in the cell. Fire exploded in her side and then her arm.

Just as quickly, the shooting stopped.

Ears still ringing, Sarah ignored the burning pain just under her rib cage and swung the rifle toward the hallway that opened into the area where she and the teens were being held. When she spotted the camouflage uniforms, she dropped the weapon and lifted one hand above her head. She couldn't lift the other without massive agony racing through her arm.

"Move away from the weapon!"

"Hands! Show me your hands!"

The commands rolled over her and she let out a sob of relief. "Don't shoot," she screamed. "Don't shoot! I'm an American!"

"Sarah!"

The voice came from behind the first soldier. Even in her terrified, semi-paralyzed state, she recognized it. "Gavin!"

He rushed to her and snagged the rifle from the dirt and passed it to the soldier behind him. She refrained from launching herself into Gavin's arms. Instead, she drew in a ragged breath. "Thank God."

Gavin lowered his weapon, helped her remove the rest of her burqa, and stared into green eyes he'd recognize anywhere. "Sarah."

"About time you guys showed up," she said.

"Had to stop for a burger. Knew you could take care of yourself until we got here." His words came out gruff, filled with emotion he had no right feeling at the moment. Surprised, he cleared his throat.

She huffed a short laugh that ended on a hiccupped sob. "Right." She didn't take her eyes from the man on the floor. "I killed him."

"No, you didn't." He listened to the voice in his ear. "The threat has been neutral-

26

ized." They were safe for now. Plan A had worked.

She swiveled her gaze to him. "What?"

"You missed."

"Not even. I don't miss."

"Whatever the case. We need to get out of here."

She stepped forward and hugged him. "I'm so very glad to see you."

"Same here." He gave her a quick squeeze and she gasped. He frowned, but was intent on their next move. "Come on, we've got to go before their reinforcements arrive. You ready?"

"As long as there's room for the other girls. Fatima is injured and needs a doctor."

"There's room and we have a medic with us." He turned to the girls in the cell and, in Pashto, said, "All of you, follow those two soldiers and we'll get you to safety."

His Pashto must have been good enough, because the girls hurried from the cell. He stepped over to the fallen teen and her friend who still knelt beside her, hands covered in blood, but still pressing hard. "Don't take your hands away yet, okay?"

She nodded.

"Gavin?"

He turned. Sarah's hands clasped her side. She swayed, then sank to her knees.

27

"Sarah!" He strode back to her. "You've been hit."

"Thank you, Captain Obvious. I hadn't noticed."

He slung the rifle over his shoulder and caught her just as she passed out.

CHAPTER FOUR

Sarah's own voice woke her. Terror sent blood racing through her veins and sweat pouring from her brow. She pressed a hand against her racing heart.

Another nightmare. Just another stupid nightmare. She was safe. Her captor was dead. Thanks to her. She'd killed a man and couldn't stop seeing it. No matter how much she told herself she'd had no choice, the vision of his exploding face wouldn't leave her.

"Rochelle." A soft hand gripped hers, the gentle voice propelling her toward the full awareness that she wasn't alone. "Rochelle, wake up."

She blinked and sat up, only to have the pain freeze her, rebuking her for moving too fast.

Hands eased her back into a reclining position. "Be careful now, Miss Denning, you've got a nasty wound there."

Sarah looked up at the woman. "Who are you?"

"I'm your nurse. You can call me Yasmoon."

"Well, thank you, Yasmoon, but I'm fine." Once again, Sarah shifted. Once again, pain shafted her into stillness.

"Be still, girl, before you rip out those stitches."

Stunned into obedience at the second voice, Sarah lowered her head onto the pillow and closed her eyes while she caught her breath and tried to process the presence of the man in her room.

Yasmoon cleared her throat. "I have your medication here."

Sarah opened her eyes, keeping them trained on the nurse. No way would she acknowledge her father yet.

Yasmoon handed her a little white pill cup. Her other hand held a Styrofoam cup with a straw. "Please take it."

"What's it for?"

"It will help you with the nightmares. Make you less jumpy."

Sarah crushed the cup around the pill and handed it back to Yasmoon. "I'll pass."

"Rochelle —" the general started.

"My name is Sarah," she snapped. "And I'm not taking medication I don't need."

Yasmoon bowed her head in a sign of surrender. "I'll just leave you to visit, then. Please let me know if you change your mind. The doctor will be in shortly."

Once she was gone, Sarah shut her eyes. "What are you doing here, General?"

"Making sure you aren't going to die." His hand covered hers, the action clogging her throat and fogging her thought processes.

"I'm not your daughter anymore, so you don't have to play the part of the concerned father. At least not on my behalf."

"Not my daughter — what the heck are you talking about?"

"You disinherited me, remember?" Still, she didn't open her eyes. She didn't want to see him. "Cut me off and never looked back. That means you don't need to be here."

"Rochelle . . ." He cleared his throat. She thought she might have heard an echo of hurt in the word. "Stop. Of course I'm concerned. I thought you were dying."

"I'm not. At least it doesn't feel like it." Actually, it kind of had, but the pain was bearable as long as she didn't move. Fatima's pained face filled her mind, and she gasped, eyes flying open. "Talia, Fatima, and the other girls? Are they all right?"

31

"All rescued. The one who was shot is still critical, though. She's on another floor."

Sarah fought the tears that built behind her eyes. There was no way she was crying in front of the general.

"That was a doozy of a nightmare you had there," he said.

"Yeah."

"It wasn't the first."

"I'm aware, thanks."

"You should have taken the medication."

"I don't want medication I don't need. The nightmares will fade. They always do."

He held out a wet paper towel and she frowned, then met his gaze. He shook the towel. "It's not a snake. It won't bite."

"Wasn't worried it would." But *he* might. She snatched it from him and wiped the sweat from her forehead and cheeks, taking in the hospital room, noting the equipment. "Wait a minute, I'm in Afghanistan. You were home in the States. How are you here?"

"They have these things called planes —"

She shot him a dark look and he shrugged. "I got word you'd been shot. Twice."

So, he'd hopped a plane and flown halfway across the world? For her? She squinted at him, tilted her head, closed her eyes tight, then reopened them. Yep, he was still there and he still looked like her father. "How long have I been here?" Asleep and unconscious. Had she said anything?

"Four days."

What! Four days? "And you've been here how long?"

"Two."

Which meant he'd dropped everything and flown over the minute he'd heard. She wasn't sure what to think about that — except to try to figure out how it would benefit him.

"You could have died," he said.

His gruff words jerked her attention back to the situation. She huffed. "What is it with you men and the need to state the obvious?" Why couldn't she simply thank him for coming? Because she didn't want him here. She really didn't want to be in the same room with him.

He scowled. "What I'm saying is, the fact that you came so close to dying — or worse — has taken a toll on your brain. You might have some PTSD."

"I've come close to dying before, and other than a few sleepless nights, I've never had a problem. I'll be fine." Hopefully. She refused to admit the latest round of nightmares was worse than anything she'd experienced before.

"You should talk to the psychiatrist," he said.

"I don't need a shrink, General." And if she did, she knew exactly who she'd go to. A trusted friend named Brooke Adams, not a clock-watching stranger. "I can't believe those words even came out of your mouth. You think they're a bunch of nonsense, remember?"

He let out a low sigh that morphed into a chuckle. She didn't think she heard any humor in the sound. "You're just like me, you know that?"

She cut a look at him, her heart going cold. She hoped her eyes reflected the ice flowing through her. "I'm *nothing* like you."

His almost imperceptible flinch should have given her satisfaction. Instead a deep sadness grabbed hold and she looked away.

"Right." He cleared his throat and stood. "I guess I'll leave you alone then."

"Have you heard from Dustin?" She wanted her father to leave, but she needed to talk to her younger brother.

"No, not in a while. I tried to call him, to let him know I was here and what had happened to you, but all I got was voice mail." He shook his head. "You know him. He'll check in when he's ready."

Usually with a text saying he was fine and

34

would be in touch later. It had been at least six weeks since she'd had a good conversation with him. Longer than that since she'd seen him. "And Caden?" Her older brother would be pacing the floor.

"He'll be waiting at the hospital in Greenville. You're being flown home tonight."

She tried to sit up and winced. Decided that was a bad idea and stayed still. "I'm fine — or will be. I'm not going anywhere. I have a job here, remember?"

"You're being sent home to recover and given hero status for your actions in rescuing the girls. There's talk of a medal of honor."

Her jaw dropped. "But I didn't do anything!"

"That's not what I hear. You defended yourself and the girls. Because of you, Fatima has a fighting chance. And you killed one of your captors."

Sickness welled. "I was trying not to think of that."

"The nightmares?"

"No!" Well, not completely. Partly.

"He would have killed you if you hadn't pulled the trigger, Rochelle."

"Stop calling me that. I'm Sarah. And I'm perfectly aware he would have killed me." Her breath caught in her lungs. She closed her eyes and yanked the blanket to her chin. "I think I want to rest now, thanks."

"Roch— Sarah —" A pause. A sigh. "This name thing is nonsense. I'm not calling you Sarah. It's not your name."

"My name is Rochelle Seraphina. It's got Sarah in it. Now, please, let me rest."

"Fine, but you're going home."

"I am no—"

A knock on the door popped her eyes open. So much for resting. Her father opened the door and Gavin stepped into the room. The two men shook hands, then exchanged words, but she couldn't hear them over her thundering heart.

Gavin Black. Out of all the people to come to the rescue, it had to be him. Not that she wasn't beyond grateful for his timely appearance in that compound. She would have been thrilled to see her father at that point. But . . . Gavin Black? She gave him a small wave. "Hi."

"Hi." Tattoos rippled every time his arms moved under the short-sleeved shirt, and his five o'clock shadow had morphed into a neatly trimmed beard and mustache.

"You lose your razor?" she asked.

His brows rose and a surprised laugh rumbled from him as he stroked his beard. "Ditched it. This is less trouble most days."

36

"Never figured you one for doing things the easy way."

"Always a first time, I guess." He crossed his arms, those tats flashing, green eyes flicking from her father to her. "I didn't mean to interrupt."

"You didn't," Sarah said. "The general was just leaving."

Her father shot her a tight smile, his eyes chilling. Now that was the man she knew. "We'll be flying out shortly, but I'll give you two a few minutes to visit."

He left the room and Sarah's stress level went down significantly, in spite of his reference to flying home. She wasn't going anywhere.

Yasmoon entered the room and once more tried to get her to take medication with the promise that "it will make you feel much better."

"I'm not taking it. You understand?" She repeated the statement in Pashto and then in Farsi.

Yasmoon sighed and left the room with a frown.

"You should take it," Gavin said. "It might help."

"I suspect it's an antidepressant. If I was depressed, I'd take it. I'm not depressed, so I won't take it. End of discussion." She

37

looked him in the eye. "I don't do medication. Ibuprofen and Tylenol, even some Toradol, are fine, but nothing stronger. No antidepressants and definitely no more narcotics. I hate the way they make me feel."

"I can understand that. And respect it." Gavin took the chair beside her bed and leaned forward to clasp her fingers in his warm grip. "How are you doing?"

"I'm ready to get out of here."

"I'm sure. Authorities are going to want to debrief you on everything you saw while you were in the compound."

"I know."

"The general's arranged for someone to fly home with you and do it on the plane."

"Sounds lovely, but I'm not going home."

He ignored her sarcasm and pulled out his phone. "I need a picture."

"What? Here? Now? Are you crazy? I look like death on crutches." And still sort of felt like it too. She swallowed, her throat dry and cheeks hot. Did she have a fever?

"You look . . . not quite that bad," he said.

"Hey!"

He grinned, then sobered. "You're alive. That's all that matters. But the picture's not for me. I need to prove to Brooke, Heather, Kat, and someone named Ava that you are, in fact, breathing and recovering nicely. Brooke keeps texting, demanding proof."

"Ah." Brooke Adams, Heather Fontaine, Katherine — Kat — Patterson, and Ava Jackson. "Ava's been my best friend since elementary school." The other three ladies she'd met while they'd all been in Kabul at the same time. Ava had been there, too, for a short time but had never met Gavin. "Okay, you can snap it, but tell them to delete it the minute they're satisfied I'm fine."

"Got it." After he sent the text, he looked her over. "You're fortunate you had that satellite phone."

"Fortune had nothing to do with it. Last year, it came in handy, and I've carried it ever since. I always knew something like that could happen, was even surprised most days when it didn't. But I wasn't going to be caught with no way to call for help."

"Smart."

Her smile faded to a frown. "Why is the general insisting I go home? I can recover nicely right here and then get back to work. I'm planning a trip home in about two weeks. Dustin and I coordinated that so we could be home together, but in the mean-time, I've got stories I'm working on. And now, I've got one more."

Gavin blinked, then narrowed his eyes. "The general didn't tell you?"

"Tell me what?"

He shifted and rubbed a hand over his beard.

"Gavin, what is it?"

"There's no easy way to say this, but you've been discharged from the Army. You've been diagnosed as . . . uh . . . as a danger to yourself with recommendations to return home and seek the help of a psychiatrist."

Gavin wanted to recall his words as soon as they left his mouth. He could tell when she'd finished processing. Her mouth tightened, nostrils flared, and eyes narrowed. "I'm sorry, what?"

He was furious that her father hadn't told her. "You heard right. You're being discharged under Other Designated Physical and Mental Conditions."

For a moment she didn't speak. Move. Breathe. "What's the condition?"

"Basically, they think you need a break. Time for your mind to heal."

She scoffed. "They think I'm crazy?" She paused. "They're discharging me because they think I'm suicidal, don't they?"

"You know ODPMC can apply to a mul-

40

titude of things. It's a catchall, but . . . yeah. That word was mentioned."

"You have *got* to be kidding me." Fingers knotted the blanket over her legs. "Why? How would they come to that conclusion? I've been unconscious!"

"The nurse witnessed your nightmares, as did your father. They've had to sedate you several times since your arrival to keep you from tearing out your stitches and . . ."

"And?"

"And, you may have muttered some things that could have been interpreted as a wish to die."

Her mouth opened. Then shut. "I don't remember any of that, but I certainly don't have any wish to die. And taking what I said while I was unconscious as fact isn't even ethical, is it?" She pressed fingers to her eyes. "What exactly is the official diagnosis?"

"PTSD and possible desire to self-harm."

"Unbelievable." She dropped her hand and lasered him with a hard look. "How do you know all of this anyway? I thought my medical information would still be protected even here."

"The general told me. He didn't share how he got it and I didn't ask."

"I see." She smirked. "So he left you to do the dirty job of filling me in." A scoff

41

escaped her and she looked away. However, he thought he might have seen a sheen of tears in her eyes. "He finally found a way," she whispered. "Writing me out of his will couldn't get me to stay out of the Army, so he's resorted to this."

Gavin leaned closer. "Your father didn't —"

"Make no mistake," she said sharply, "this is the general's doing. I'm no more suicidal than he is." The PTSD might be another story, but she wasn't ready to face that idea yet. She slammed a hand on the bed and winced, but that didn't stop the growl that came from her. "Oooh, I can't believe he'd stoop so low." She paused. "Then again, yes, I can. I actually should have known something was up when I opened my eyes and saw him sitting there. But I'd hoped —"

"Hoped what?"

"Nothing. I'm an idiot."

"Come on, Sarah, you know as well as I do, there has to be some basis to this. The Army doesn't just offer up discharges without some kind of documentation."

Her laugh held no humor. "They do if it comes in the form of an order from a lieutenant general. What do you think? You think I'm suicidal?"

"I'm reserving judgment, but I'm leaning toward no way. You fought too hard to live during the rescue."

"I sure did." She frowned. "Who's the lying psychiatrist that was willing to make this brilliant diagnosis?"

"Lying? I don't know that she actually lied. At least not on purpose. No physician who wants to keep practicing is going to offer up a false diagnosis. Your father —"

She held up a hand. "The name of the psychiatrist?"

He pursed his lips, then shrugged. "Dr. Emily Winslow. She's the one who took Brooke's place when she left." Brooke Adams. She'd been one of the psychiatrists for the base for a long time — and one of Sarah's good friends. However, when Brooke had been given the option to get out of the Army six months ago, she'd taken it. Gavin didn't blame her, but he knew Sarah missed her terribly.

"So, Dr. Winslow witnessed a few of my nightmares, overheard something I said, had a little chat with my father, and decided she could diagnose that I was suicidal without putting her license in jeopardy."

He studied her. "I could actually see that happening, but still, it's a stretch if you ask —"

"If the general encouraged her to make the diagnosis official, she wouldn't go against him. No one does. She could be wrong, but the documentation to support her decision is there. No harm, no foul. Except that I lose the career I've fought tooth and nail for. I lose the job I love and leave with a stain on my record."

When she looked up at him, Gavin caught his breath at the fiery rage blazing in her eyes. The flush on her cheeks deepened to a bright red. "He's not going to get away with this," she said. "I'll fight this all the way to the courtroom if I have to."

"Sarah, before you condemn the man, maybe you should ask him."

"I don't have to. I know him and that's something he would do without even giving it a second thou—"

A knock on the door interrupted her and she snapped off her words. The general stepped inside.

Sarah glared at him. "Get out."

The man blinked, and Gavin stood when he noticed the waxy look to his skin. "Sir? Sit here." When the general dropped into the chair without a word and his shoulders slumped, Gavin shot a glance at Sarah. Her expression had morphed from anger to confusion in the span of a second.

"What is it, General?" Gavin asked.

The man cleared his throat. "I just got a call." He looked at Sarah. "Did you know Dustin had checked himself in to the VA psychiatric hospital in Greenville?"

"What?" Sarah's cry shot through Gavin. "No. When did he leave Afghanistan?" she asked. "The last I heard, he was still here."

"About three months ago." The general paused. "I'd talked to him several times and he never said a word."

"He didn't say anything to me two months ago when we were coordinating our leave," Sarah said. "Or rather, I was coordinating mine. Because he was already back in the States? I thought he was just a couple of hours away from me."

The general swallowed. Looked at Sarah. His mouth worked.

Sarah's eyes widened and she shook her head. "No. Don't say it."

Gavin braced himself. He'd seen that look on too many heartbroken parents' faces. Part of him wanted to leave, probably *should* leave, but leaving in the midst of their raw grief seemed wrong. Worse than staying and being unable to do a blasted thing to help ease the pain.

So, he stayed. And let his heart break with theirs.

CHAPTER FIVE

The general rubbed his eyes, an unusually human gesture for him, and Sarah steeled herself, because he wore the same expression he'd had when they'd buried her mother fifteen years ago.

"Rochelle . . ."

"I said don't say it."

The general's gaze didn't waver this time. "Dustin was released from the hospital three days ago. He went back to the hospital for a check-in appointment but never made it to the psychiatrist's office. Instead, he went to the roof of the building —"

"Stop," she whispered. "Please stop."

"— and he jumped. He's dead."

She held the tears inside, refused to let them fall, but the heart that had been anguished and livid by her father's dictatorial actions now shattered. "Why?" she choked.

"I don't know. No one does right now."

"Get out," she whispered. "Just . . . go away."

He hesitated. "Rochelle —"

"Get out!" The shout echoed through the room.

Gavin shifted, reminding her that he was there, and shame burned a scorching path up her spine and into her cheeks. "Both of you, please. Go. Leave me alone."

"Our flight leaves in two hours," the general said. "Be ready." He left and didn't look back.

Gavin did. She turned her gaze from his, holding her body rigid. Finally, Gavin stepped back and shut the door.

Her mind reeled with so many things to consider, but all she could think about was Dustin. So . . . she would go home just in time to bury her brother, then find the strength to fight her father and the diagnosis, get reinstated, and get back to Afghanistan.

Sarah closed her eyes and allowed the sob to break free. Shivers racked her, pain assaulted her, and she wasn't sure how long she suffered alone — until Gavin returned to the room and sat on the bed next to her. When he gathered her up against his chest to simply hold her, she didn't have the strength to fight him. The tears continued to flow. Sarah cried herself into a fitful sleep, broken by alternating shudders that threatened to shake her apart, followed by a fiery heat that left her weak, sweaty, and disoriented.

Time passed. She had no idea how much, but then someone was shaking her shoulder, pulling her from her nightmares, demanding she get into the wheelchair. She refused, her heart shattered, her need to grieve overshadowing her will to cooperate.

Strong arms lifted her, settled her into the wheelchair, and wrapped a blanket around her. Her father?

"No," she cried, "don't touch me. Go away!" It was petty and childish — and she didn't care. "Gavin can push me, but you stay away from me."

She thought she might have seen pain flash in the man's eyes but refused to acknowledge it.

Gavin stepped behind her, and then she was moving, rolling through the hallways. She kept her eyes on the tile flooring. At some point, Gavin stopped and lifted her from the chair. He carried her into the plane and lowered her onto a gurney. His face hovered above her, his calloused fingers gentle when he wiped the tears from her cheeks. "She's got a massive fever," he said

48

to someone. "Maybe we should stay here until she's stronger."

"She'll be fine," the general said. "We've got a nurse on board to monitor everything. I want her out of this godforsaken country before it claims her life too."

He wanted. It was always what *he* wanted. What about what *she* wanted? It was her life.

Gavin hung the IV on the pole and gripped her hand. She was mortified that she so desperately needed his presence, knew she didn't deserve his support, but was grateful to have it nonetheless. Her eyes refused to stay open, and she dropped into yet another fitful sleep.

Once they were in the air, Gavin's phone rang and he snatched it to his ear, as though the gentle vibration could possibly wake Sarah. Although, *sleeping* might be stretching it. She muttered often, and only his hand in hers seemed to keep her from attempting to flee the sheets tucked around her.

"Hi, Dad," he said, his voice low.

"Son. Well, you answered, I guess that means you're still alive."

"I am."

His father was retired special forces. Gavin

49

kept his mouth shut about a lot of things but, for the most part, was relatively unsuccessful in keeping his dad in the dark. He knew too much because he'd lived it.

"On a plane, too, I hear. When do you land?"

Gavin huffed a short, quiet laugh. "Not for a while."

"So . . . overseas? Which was it this time? Afghanistan, Syria, or Iraq?"

"Dad, come on now. Don't do this to me."

His father laughed. "Forget it. I'm just messing with you."

"Although, you'd really like this plane. It's a private one with lots of room and a very attentive staff."

"Rich clients, huh?"

"Something like that. What can I do for you?"

"Have you talked to Kaylynn?"

His sister? "Not recently. Been a little busy, why?" More to the point, why would his dad even ask that question? Last time he was home, Kaylynn had had no interest in talking to him.

"Just curious. She's so focused on getting through her last year of college that we don't see her very much."

"She hasn't moved out, has she?"

His father chuckled. "No, she's still here.

50

At least when she's not with a friend who lives on campus."

"So, what's going on with her?"

"I'm not really sure anything's going on with her. Just thought I'd see if she'd talked to you."

"You know how we left things, Dad," Gavin said, his voice rough.

"Yeah, I know. I'm only slightly ashamed it was you who confronted her boyfriend and not me. But since I have to live with her, I can live with that shame fairly easily."

Sadness gripped Gavin, even as his lips curved into a small smile at his father's words. He wanted to make things right with his sister, but she shunned him every time he tried. She was still angry with him for chasing off her scummy boyfriend. A fact he hated but didn't know what to do about. If he'd had to do it all over again, he'd do exactly the same thing. "How's Mom doing?" he asked.

Thankfully, his father allowed the change of subject. "She's great. Still volunteering at the homeless shelter and reading to vets in hospice. I don't know how she does it." His voice roughened before he cleared his throat.

"She does it for Uncle Jordan. It's his legacy." His mother's brother, Jordan

51

Standish, had died of liver cancer after serving his country for thirty years. One year after retirement, he'd passed away, but not before establishing the Standish Literary Foundation for terminally ill vets. Gavin's mother had been one of his first recruits.

"I know. Jordan was a standup guy, but it tears her up every time she goes over there."

This wasn't the first time they'd had this conversation, and Gavin figured it wouldn't be the last. "Just keep praying for her. She knows how you feel."

"Course she does. I tell her as often as possible."

"Maybe she needs you not to be so vocal about it. Maybe she just needs you to support her. In silence."

"Maybe so, son. I don't want to talk about all that. I'm just making sure you're okay. You need anything?"

"Nope, I'm good."

"Went by your house the other day. Cut the grass and trimmed up the edges so your neighbors won't complain or sic the HOA on you."

Gavin pressed his fingertips to his eyelids. How did he get so fortunate to be born into the family he called his own? "Thanks, Dad, I appreciate you."

"I know you do."

"I probably should sell the house and just get an apartment, but when I got out of the Army, I thought I'd be spending more time at home and wanted a yard." For a dog. The dog he hadn't gotten yet.

"Things are different when you do contract work."

Gavin huffed a laugh. He'd never told his dad what he was doing, just that he was opening his own security business.

"Now, if I could just get your sister to see how awesome I am," his father was saying, "we'd be in business."

Gavin laughed. "She knows, Dad, she's probably just busy." But he made a mental note to text her and tell her to pull her nose out of her books — or whatever she was doing — for a few minutes to acknowledge her parents. He hesitated. "She's not seeing that jerk again, is she?"

"No way. I checked on him and he's serving time in the local prison for distribution."

"Well, well, he finally got caught, huh?"

"Someone tipped off the cops and he got swept up in a raid."

Gavin narrowed his eyes. "*Someone* tipped them off?"

"Yeah, craziest thing."

His father paused and Gavin frowned. "Is everything really all right, Dad?"

"Yeah, yeah. Everything's fine. I just wanted to hear your voice."

"Good to talk to you too."

Sarah groaned and cried out. Gavin squeezed her hand while the nurse checked her vitals.

"I've got to go, Dad," Gavin said. "We'll talk soon."

"Sure, of course."

"Tell Mom and Kaylynn I love them."

"Will do." His dad hung up and Gavin turned to Sarah.

The nurse looked up. "She's still out," she said, "but those nightmares are brutal. Wish she'd let me give her something to ease them."

"She was very clear she wanted nothing more than the antibiotics and whatever it took to keep her fever under control, and that's all we'll do unless her life is in danger." He kept his tone mild, but he was sure the woman heard the thread of steel in the words.

"I understand. Her fever's holding steady at a hundred four, though, so I'll admit I'm concerned."

The nurse pulled the empty IV bag from the pole, and Gavin took the full one from her, connected it, then hung it. "Come on,

Sarah," he whispered, "fight that infection off."

"That's my job, you know." The nurse eyed the bag, then him.

"Yeah, I know, but it makes me feel useful. Humor me, please?"

She offered him a small smile. "Of course. She's a lucky woman to have you. It's obvious you care very much about her."

"I do." Gavin didn't bother to correct her mistaken assumption that he and Sarah were a couple. The fact that they'd almost been that very thing still unsettled him when he thought about it too long. He didn't know why they weren't or where he'd gone wrong, he just knew Sarah had ghosted him after their third date. But all that was water under the bridge and not important. Now, he just wanted to get her home safe so she could recover.

Through lowered lashes, Gavin studied Sarah's father. The man seemed immersed in his newspaper and coffee, but every so often, Gavin would catch him shooting glances at Sarah. Every time she cried out or groaned, he'd frown and his jaw would harden a fraction more.

"Gavin?" Sarah whispered.

He leaned in. "I'm here."

"Good." She licked her lips and he

scooped a teaspoon of ice chips between them while he had the chance. "Where am I?"

"On the plane headed home."

"Don't wanna go home."

"You're really sick. You need to heal."

Her eyes locked on his. "Don't let him take me to his house. I mean it. I won't stay in the same house with him."

She was as lucid as she could be, and she really didn't want to go to her father's home. He nodded. "I'll call Caden."

"Thank you." Her eyes shut and Gavin glanced at her father once more. He didn't know whether to be angry with the man or pity him.

When Sarah woke again, it was to the dreaded familiar smell of a hospital. She frowned, vaguely remembering the flight. Gavin had been there, holding her hand because she wouldn't let him go. And he'd wiped her tears. Hadn't he?

Or had that just been a dream?

Oh, please let that have been a dream.

And the general. Had he been there as well? Memories flickered. Fuzzy and difficult to bring forth, but finally, she brought them into focus.

On the plane, Gavin had stayed with her,

56

held her hand, fed her crushed ice, changed her IV bag . . . Ugh. Not a dream. Then she remembered Dustin. Her baby brother had jumped off a building. Grief crushed her and she swallowed, desperately wanting a sip of water but unable to muster the energy to look for some.

Her eyes finally stayed open long enough to zero in on the softly snoring man in the chair beside her bed. He'd fallen asleep facing the television that was turned to a national news channel. Captions ran across the bottom of the screen. For a moment, she watched, trying to figure out what day it was. The date and time stamp in the right-hand corner finally flashed and she blinked. She'd lost another two days.

"Cade?"

Sarah wasn't sure she actually voiced his name out loud until he jerked and sat up. "Sarah?"

"Water."

He grabbed the cup and held the straw to her lips.

After two pulls, she lowered her head back to the pillow. "What happened? Which hospital am I in?"

"You spiked a fever just before the flight home — which turned out to be thanks to a raging infection. We transported you here to the VA hospital, and the doctors pumped you full of antibiotics and more." He shuddered and squeezed her fingers. "It's been touch and go for the past few days."

"Dustin . . . ," she whispered.

Grief flashed across Caden's face and he glanced away. So, that hadn't been a dream — a nightmare — either. She noticed Gavin sitting under the window. "Hi," she said.

"Hi." He leaned forward. "How are you feeling?"

Embarrassed. Mortified. Devastated . . . "Tired. Very, very tired."

"You've got visitors," Caden said. "You up to it?"

"Who?" She forced her eyes to stay open.

"Brooke, Heather, and Ava."

"Ava? Thought she was still on a boat somewhere in the Persian Gulf keeping Iran out of trouble." Ava Jackson. A certified genius.

"She got home about two weeks ago. Her mother's having some medical issues and Ava got a humanitarian placement in order to be closer to home and take care of her."

"Her father died," Sarah said, wondering why her tongue slurred the words.

"I know."

"There have been times I wish mine would." The thought shocked her. The look on Caden's face jolted her. Had she said the words out loud? Apparently. Remorse came in waves, but her father's latest betrayal had struck deep, creating a wound she couldn't fathom ever healing. This one even worse than the first. The first betrayal had been his lack of caring for her mother when she'd been dying. No, forgiveness wasn't an option at the moment.

"Sarah . . ." Gavin's voice came from a distance while the blessed blackness beckoned. The darkness tempted her to let go of reality. All she had to do was drop into it and she could escape this world of pain, sorrow, and traitorous fathers. For a moment she fought it, then gave up, letting it swallow her back into the world of painless oblivion.

The nightmare woke her the next time. And the next. Every time it was the same. And every time, either Caden or Gavin had been there to hold her hand and reassure her that she was safe.

But now, she let herself relive it, sifting through the details, trying to tell herself it wasn't real.

She was trapped in the midst of a crush of bodies. When she finally managed to break free and run, she ended up at a locked door while the bodies followed her, reaching for her, wanting to smother her. And then Dustin was stepping off the roof of the hospital, arms outstretched, face raised to the heavens. Free-falling . . .

And she was screaming, reaching through the bars of her prison cell . . . and firing the gun that killed a man. That red mist spraying, covering everything. Her hands, her face, drowning her, filling her mouth, her lungs, cutting off her air . . .

She shuddered and threw the covers off. Gavin and Caden were both gone, and for some reason, being alone terrified her. Sweat beaded her brow in spite of the cool hospital room. When she sat up, her stomach growled. The rumble took her by surprise, and she realized she was starving. A good sign she was on the way to getting better? Hopefully.

Light filtered in under the door from the hallway, and a scream reached her. Then another. Sarah swung her legs over the side of the bed and her bare feet touched the floor. Yet another wail sent shivers racing over her skin, and she wondered if it was the same person she'd heard last night about this time. Ignoring the dull throb in her side, Sarah grabbed the IV pole and stood. While weak, she decided she could make it to the door.

Once there, she opened it a fraction. The yells had subsided to sobs that came from the room next to hers. The palpable angst twisted her heart into a sympathetic knot.

Sarah carefully slipped out the door, and walked five steps to her neighbor's room. When she pushed the door open, the crying intensified.

Stringy blonde hair lay limp around a pretty heart-shaped face and tears tracked down flushed cheeks. Blue eyes lifted and locked with Sarah's, and Sarah sucked in a sharp breath. For a moment, the cries faltered. Sarah's gaze dropped to the restraints around the thin wrists with enough lead to let her reach the bathroom. But she definitely couldn't leave the room. The pitiful woman whimpered. "Please let me go. Please help me."

"What's your name?" Sarah asked, moving closer.

The eyes darted to the door, then to Sarah. Back to the door. Tears continued to fall and drip from her chin to the bedcovers. "Bri— Brianne."

"I'm Sarah."

"Take them off," Brianne whimpered, holding up her shackled wrists. "Please take them off."

Sarah bit her lip. "Why are they on?" She

61

couldn't help asking.

"Because I know too much. We all do. They're killing us," Brianne whispered. "They're going to kill us all!" She shook her hands, a violent convulsing that rocked her whole body and dug the plastic into her tender skin. "Get them off! I need to get out of here before they kill me!"

The woman's stark terror sent waves of unease through Sarah. Obviously, she was mentally ill, but just as obviously, she clearly believed someone was out to kill her and she needed comfort or something to calm her down.

"It's a conspiracy." Brianne grabbed her head with her hands and began to rock.

"What's going on in here?"

Brianne screamed. Sarah stumbled backward. Hands settled on her shoulders, steadying her. She spun, pain snagged her side, and she pressed it as she came face-to-face with Dr. Kilgore. Her doctor and obviously Brianne's as well. His brown eyes flicked from her to Brianne. "Sarah? Brianne?"

"I heard her crying," Sarah said. "No one was helping her."

Dr. Kilgore dropped his hands. "It's okay, I'm here. I'll help her. Go on back to your room."

"No!" Brianne cried and once again set up a violent struggle to get loose.

Blood seeped from under the restraints, and Sarah started forward, only to have Dr. Kilgore's hand clamp on her bicep and pull her to a jarring halt. "You can't, Sarah. She's dangerous. Go back to your room."

"Where's Max?" Brianne cried. "Max! Help me, please!"

Footsteps hurried in the hallway.

"Dangerous?" Sarah asked. "More like hurt, frustrated, and confused, but not dangerous."

The doctor's eyes hardened. "You don't know the situation here. Go back to your room. I'll be in shortly to check on you."

That was the third time he'd made that statement. This time it sounded like an order. What would he do if she refused? She was tempted to press the issue, but the pain in her side had intensified to the point that nausea churned.

A nurse rushed into the room, holding a syringe.

"No! No more drugs! Please, make them stop! They're trying to say I'm crazy and I'm not. I'm not. What have you people done to me?" The last two words were drowned in sobs.

Sarah's heart thudded, and if she could

have ripped the drugs from the nurse's hand, she would have, but the doctor was ushering her out of the room and into the hallway. She lasered him with a frown that had intimidated many, including her two brothers. "What's wrong with her?"

"I'm not allowed to discuss that with you. Any more than I'd discuss your issues with her."

Okay, that was a fair answer. Sarah sighed. "Right. Sorry. I just feel so bad for her."

His eyes softened. "I understand. She's in a sad state right now. In the morning, she'll feel much better, I promise."

"Of course." The initial adrenaline rush Brianne's screams had sent coursing through her had faded. Now weakness invaded her. "I think I'm just going to get back in my bed." Before she fell flat on her face.

"Good idea. I'll have the nurse bring you something to help you sleep."

"That's all right. I'll pass."

Sarah returned to her room under the watchful eye of the doctor. He really was a nice man and he was right. She didn't know what was going on with Brianne, but she'd rather have the nightmares than put drugs in her body. She shuddered. That was one thing she could relate to.

When the nurse stepped into her room, Sarah shut her eyes and pretended to be asleep, and the woman left without administering the medication. Sarah let out a low sigh of relief.

She lay there and let the minutes tick past, unwilling to drift back off — mostly because she didn't want to dream, but also because Brianne's desperate cries continued to echo in her mind. More time passed and she wondered where Caden and Gavin were. She wanted one of them to check on Brianne and make sure she was really okay.

She stilled and drew in a breath. Then again, she'd never been one to wait around on someone else to get something done. Once more, ignoring the pain, Sarah pushed herself out of the bed and made her way to the door.

CHAPTER SIX

Gavin had stepped out of Sarah's room intending to call his sister, only to find the general in the hallway.

"Follow me, son. We need to talk." Curious, Gavin followed him down the hallway and through a door marked Private.

"Sir?"

"You might want to sit down for this."

Gavin had taken a chair but soon found himself on his feet, pacing as the general laid out his thoughts. He stopped near the door of the conference room and turned, while Sarah's father stood ramrod straight, his hard, green eyes watchful, missing nothing. "You want me to act as her security?" Gavin asked. "*Secretly?* If she finds out, she'll be spitting mad."

"I don't plan for her to find out. And if you're creative enough, you can stay by her side without too much trouble. Heck, pretend like you're in love with her if you have to. Just keep her safe."

Gavin flinched at the mercenary statement but chose to ignore it for now. "What about Caden?"

"He babies her. Caters to her every crazy whim. She has him wrapped around her little finger, and he will be of no use to me in this regard. Besides, he'd flat-out refuse."

"Right." Which was exactly what Gavin planned to do.

He opened his mouth to do so, when the general clasped his hands in front of him, the only sign he was running out of patience. "Look, I'm trying to keep her alive. She barely made it out of Afghanistan this time. If she goes back, it'll be a one-way trip. I need you to make sure she doesn't do something stupid like fight to prove the diagnosis in her medical —" He stopped.

Gavin felt sure the man's definition of "Sarah stupid" differed from his. "So. Sarah was right. You had her diagnosed with PTSD and discharged."

Only for a moment did the man look uncomfortable before his expression smoothed back into his unreadable façade. "She knows?"

"Once I told her about the diagnosis and discharge, that was the first conclusion she jumped to. It might have had something to do with the fact that you were there and dictating that she would be flying home instead of staying in the country." He held the man's gaze — and his own tongue. He wanted to say something to the effect that that information should have come from the general, not Gavin. "I'd say she knows you pretty well."

The general winced. "I see." He cleared his throat. "Well, it doesn't matter. She's not thinking straight. She can hate me as long as she stays alive — which is where you come in."

"Why are you being so dogged about this? She's a grown woman — and regardless of what you think, she's quite capable of making her own choices."

"But that's just it. She's not. She's suffering debilitating nightmares." He swallowed and looked away, even while his impossibly straight shoulders stiffened another fraction. "I saw her in the midst of several. She's not well."

"Sir —" He really couldn't argue that. He'd seen the nightmares himself and they weren't pretty. His heart had broken each time she'd awakened screaming and thrashing against an unseen force.

"And there's one other thing," the general said.

"What's that?"

"Her kidnapping in Afghanistan may not have been a complete coincidence."

Gavin went still. "What do you mean?"

The general blew out a low, almost inaudible breath. "I've been receiving threats," he said softly. "Against myself only, nothing about my family. But . . ."

"But you'd rather be safe than sorry."

He met Gavin's eyes. "Yes."

"Again, what about Caden?"

"I have someone watching him as well."

Gavin hesitated, then asked, "What about Dustin? Could his death have been anything other than a suicide?"

The general's granite features hardened even further. "No. There's security footage from the roof that clearly shows Dustin jumping. But . . ."

"But?"

The general hesitated. "I don't know. All evidence clearly shows suicide." He shook his head. "I think I'm just questioning it because I don't want to believe he could do something like that."

"Are you investigating?"

The general shook his head. "No. That boy's always had issues. I tried to help, but . . . no. He jumped. End of story."

Gavin frowned. It was like the man was

69

trying to convince himself.

A knock on the door interrupted them. The hospital chief of staff stuck her head in. "I'm sorry, General, but we need the room now. I hope that's not an imposition."

"Of course not. We'll be finished in five minutes. Is that all right?"

"Perfect. Thank you."

She ducked out again and the general turned back to Gavin. "Well? Can I count on you to help?"

Gavin gave a silent mental groan and nodded. The general smiled his satisfaction, but Gavin frowned.

Sarah was going to kill him if she ever found out. When she found out. Because she would. He stood. But if Sarah was truly in real danger, then he'd do whatever he could to keep her safe. "She deserves to know all of this, General."

"Maybe so, but not now. When she's stronger. I have some phone calls to make." He strode toward the door. "Get me a coffee, will you?"

"Sure. I could use a cup as well."

He and the general parted ways, and Gavin found himself in the coffee line, pondering the idea of acting as Sarah's secret bodyguard. Then he pictured her finding out and shuddered at the imagined reaction. Yeah, that wouldn't be pretty.

With a cup in each hand, Gavin approached Sarah's hospital room by way of the nursing station. Sarah's nurse looked up and shot him a frown. "She's sleeping right now. I think it's best not to disturb her."

"Don't plan on disturbing her." He planned to sit next to her and watch the door. He glanced at Sarah's door. "Is her father in there?" The general had been headed to her room twenty minutes ago.

"No, I haven't seen him."

That didn't sound right. If the general was so concerned about her safety, why would he leave her alone?

Then he spotted the man at the far end of the hallway next to the exit sign with his back to Sarah's room. Wireless earbuds in the general's ears and his stiff posture made it clear he was on a call and disturbing him wasn't an option.

But he'd left Sarah wide open for trouble should the threats be real. The truth was, Gavin wasn't fully convinced the threats on the general had anything to do with Sarah's kidnapping. That's what terrorists did over there. They terrorized. One of those methods was kidnapping innocent women and girls. He walked to her room and, using his hip, pushed his way inside.

He stopped at the sight of the empty bed. "Sarah?" Gavin set the cups on the counter near the sink and knocked on the bathroom door. "Sarah?"

No answer.

He tried the handle and it opened easily. Empty.

He frowned and returned to the nurses' station, where he found Sarah's nurse exactly where he'd left her. This time he noted her name tag. Donna. "She's not in her room."

Donna's head snapped up to face him. "Not there? Of course she's there."

"Trust me, the bed and bathroom are empty."

Donna darted from behind her station and jog-walked to Sarah's room. Gavin followed. Donna pushed open the door and stopped so fast he almost ran her over.

"She's not here," she said.

Gavin raised a brow. "Really?"

She glared at him. Then did an about-face and stormed past him.

Sarah stood in the immaculately clean room, leaned against the wall, and waited for everything to stop spinning. She wasn't sure this was one of her more brilliant ideas, but she had to reassure Brianne that she'd help her.

Somehow.

Only Brianne's room was empty, smelling of bleach and pine cleaner, with no indication someone had occupied the room just forty-five minutes earlier. Had she stumbled into the wrong room by mistake?

No, it was the one right next door to hers.

She'd been rattled, but not *that* rattled. Confused, she checked the bathroom. Same story.

"Unbelievable." *So, go ask where she went.* Sarah turned to leave the room when her eyes landed on a cell phone near the sink. Just as her fingers closed around the device, voices outside the door caught her attention.

". . . consent . . . her family . . . questions."

"She's better off where she is now."

Better off? Who? Brianne? That was Dr. Kilgore, but who was the other man?

"Has she been taking her meds?" A different voice, another man's.

"Of course."

"Take her off of them."

"But —"

"Just do it."

"But you know —"

73

"I know," the unknown man snapped. "I know."

"Right."

"We'll figure it out." They fell silent, but footsteps drew closer to the room and Sarah's nerves twitched. "There's still no sign of the package," the stranger said.

Dr. Kilgore sighed. "It'll turn up. I've got people watching for it."

Package?

"What about the other girl? What do you think she knows?" Again, the unknown voice that was . . . familiar. Sarah strained to hear.

"We'll have to keep an eye on her," the doctor said, "but she's been so drugged up, I doubt she'll remember much."

Sarah swayed. *What other girl?*

"And if she does?"

"I'll take care of it."

"You'd better. We're too close to have anything go wrong now."

Close to what? Her brain might not be firing on all cylinders at the moment, but even in her weakened, woozy state, his words made her shiver. No, not his words, his *tone*. It scraped along her nerve endings and raised the hair on the back of her neck.

"I'll be in touch," Kilgore said. "I think I left my cell phone in the room. The last

74

thing I need is that falling into the wrong hands."

Sarah jerked and looked down at the phone. What was the doctor so worried about? She tucked the device into the pocket of her robe.

"Might not be there by now. They just finished cleaning the room."

"It's there. Cleaning staff said they left it in case someone came back for it. I'm back."

Sarah grimaced and guilt slammed her. Was it still stealing if it was done for an altruistic purpose and she planned to give it back?

Probably. But what if there was something on the phone that she could use to help Brianne? A woman she was starting to wonder if she'd created or had been a figment of her fevered imagination.

No. Brianne was as real as she.

But, yes, it was stealing.

But, yes, she really *would* give it back. After she sneaked a peek. After all, her father may have derailed her military career, but that didn't mean she couldn't look for her next story to sell. Nothing wrong with that, right?

More guilt.

A silent sigh slipped past her dry lips.

She couldn't do it. She might be a reporter, but she had her standards. Besides, he probably had a password she couldn't crack. And then there was the whole phone finder app thing. It wouldn't take him long to locate it anyway. Sarah slid the phone from her pocket and started to put it back on the counter, only to freeze when the door to the room squeaked on the hinges.

Having standards was all well and good, but for some reason, she didn't want to be caught in the room. Not by Dr. Kilgore anyway. Quicker than her battered body liked, she scrunched into the small double closet and pulled the doors shut.

Less than a second later, confident footsteps entered the room and strode in her direction. Pain throbbed through her at the uncomfortable position, but she didn't dare move. Or breathe.

The more she thought about it, the more certain she was that "they" had done something with Brianne. *Better off where she is now.* Where could that possibly be? If they were even talking about Brianne. If not, then who? A shudder racked her, and she bit her lip against the moan that rose in her throat. She truly felt awful.

More footsteps. A string of curses. Sarah shivered and heat radiated from her. A wave of dizziness made her glad she was already kneeling with her knees against the side of the closet. Her breaths came in low, silent pants through dry lips.

Was she being silly? Hiding in the closet while her brain spun crazy theories? From what she knew of Dr. Kilgore, she liked him. He'd been kind to her and helped her. So why was she afraid of him now?

She's better off where she is now.

Where was that? Probably home or in the psychiatric ward.

Another round of curses and a hard thud against the cabinet made her jump. He really wasn't happy. Her fingers curled tighter around the device. What would he do if she stepped out of the closet and handed it to him?

There were so many things wrong with that mental picture. Wouldn't that fuel her father's quest to ruin her career and have her declared mentally incompetent?

The darkness in the closet grew even blacker. The light filtering between the cracks faded and Sarah blinked hard. *Don't pass out. No passing out allowed. At least not until he's gone.*

More banging. More footsteps that stopped in front of the small closet. She squeezed her eyes shut. *Don't open it, don't open it, oh please, don't op—*

"Doctor?"

"What?" The snapped word cracked like a whip, and Sarah's eyes flew open to find the door still shut. Her heart thudded and she pressed a hand to her chest, afraid he'd be able to hear it pounding.

"Um . . . I'm sorry. I was asked to find you and let you know that Ms. Denning is missing."

Stillness. As though he was having trouble processing the statement.

"What do you mean she's missing?"

"She's not in her room and no one can seem to locate her."

A scoff, then a hard thud against the closet door. Sarah flinched.

"Of all the incompetent —" His deep breath reached her ears through the doors. "I'm coming."

Sarah wilted, her thundering heart slowing from warp speed to runaway train. Once he was gone, she unfolded herself out of the closet and set the phone on the counter where she'd found it. Now, to make it back to her room without passing out.

Gavin had been all over the floor looking for Sarah and had come up empty. He returned to her room to find Dr. Kilgore and Nurse Donna in a heated discussion they snapped off when he stepped into view. Donna cleared her throat and Dr. Kilgore smoothed his facial features into an expression of reassurance. "I know this is disturbing," he said, "but the doors to this floor are locked. She's most likely wandered into another patient's room and —"

"I understand, Doctor. She's not a child. She can leave her room if she wants, but she's been spiking a fever and I'm concerned she could fall and reopen the wound."

"Of course, of course. Where's her father?"

"At the end of the hall on a phone call. I don't think he's aware Sarah's gone AWOL."

Dr. Kilgore released a short chuckle with no humor. "I'd like to keep it that way, but I suppose we need to tell the man."

"I'll stay here in case she comes back," Gavin said. "Why don't you see if anyone else has located her?"

"Good idea."

The doctor slipped out of the room and Gavin raked a hand over his head. "Where are you, Sarah?" he whispered. "What are you doing?" He paced her room from one end to the other while he checked his phone. Nothing. Not a call nor a text. He stilled. Did she even have a phone? Probably not.

He stepped out into the hallway once more. Looked left, then right. And thought he saw a sock-encased foot peek out of the room next door before pulling back inside. He hurried the few steps to the entrance to find Sarah leaning against the wall, her face pale except for the bright flush to her cheeks. "Sarah!"

She swayed and he caught her against his chest. She blinked up at him. Focused. "Gavin," she said. "Thank goodness."

"What are you doing in here? Are you okay?"

"No, get me back to my room, please." She tugged the belt of the robe tighter. "Hurry."

"You shouldn't be out of bed."

"I promise I'm trying to get back in it." She pushed away from him and took two wobbly steps.

Gavin gripped her arm, concerned when she leaned heavily against him. "Sarah . . ."

"Don't let them know I was in here," she whispered.

"Who?"

"Dr. Kilgore." She swallowed and panted. "She's in trouble," she said, her voice low and weak. "They've done something to her."

"Who?"

"She begged me for help. But now she's not there. Need . . . to find . . . her, but I think I'm going to pass out." Her last word ended on a whisper just a split second before she slumped. He caught her before she hit the floor and lifted her into his arms. Not seeing anyone at the nurses' station or in the hallway, Gavin scurried back to her bed to deposit her gently on the sheets. She groaned and he noted the heat radiating from her.

"What's going on?"

Gavin looked up to find the general in the doorway with a frown on his face. "I'm not sure, sir." Well, that was the truth. "She said someone needed help."

"Who?"

"Beats me. She passed out before she got that far. She's definitely got a fever again."

"I'll get the nurse."

CHAPTER SEVEN

Lewis Denning walked into the café like he did every morning he was in town and found the table he paid to have reserved, whether he showed up or not. With his back to the wall and an unobstructed view of the entrance — and his two discreet bodyguards whom he tolerated — he picked up the cup and took a sip of the coffee made just the way he liked it.

He'd been coming here for five years and had gotten to know every server who worked in the place — unless there was someone new. And even then, it didn't take him long to train them in his preferences — they knew exactly how and when to serve his coffee.

The second cup remained empty and would be filled the instant the man he was meeting walked through the door.

No sooner had the thought crossed his mind than his friend, former unit member, and fraternity brother stepped into the restaurant. Lewis lifted his chin by way of greeting and Marshall McClain nodded in return.

Just as Marshall was halfway to the table, the young waitress stepped up and poured steaming coffee into the empty cup, then set three sugars and two creams on the table next to the saucer.

"Thank you, Jenny," Lewis said.

"Of course. I'll be back to take your order in a few minutes."

"You know what I want."

"Sure thing. I'll have Zoe start cooking it."

"You're a keeper."

She smiled and walked away, stopping to refill cups as Marshall took the seat opposite him.

His friend fixed his coffee and Lewis blew out a low breath.

Marshall glanced up. "How are you doing? Really."

"I'm not going to lie. It's tough."

"I'm sorry."

Lewis narrowed his eyes. "You don't look so great either. What's going on?"

"One of our employees was killed in a car wreck a couple of weeks ago."

"What? I didn't know. I'm so sorry."

"Thanks." Marshall scrubbed a hand down his cheek and shrugged. "It's been tough. He was a good friend, not just to me, but to many in the company. It's going to be hard to replace him." He took a sip of the steaming brew, then shook his head. "Some days I think I'm crazy to have gotten out of the service to open my own company."

"It's what you've wanted for a long time. The Army might have paid for your education, but you were never meant to stay there forever."

Marshall pursed his lips and nodded. "Thanks. I needed that pep talk." He paused. "The employee who was killed?"

"Yeah?"

"He lost his son about two months ago. And now this? It's inconceivable."

Lewis winced. "You just never know what life is going to deal you or when it's going to deal it to you."

Marshall let out a small groan. "Listen to me going on and on about an employee when you're struggling with losing Dustin. I can't find the words to tell you how sorry I am."

"Thank you."

"The funeral was a fitting tribute to him, though."

"There shouldn't have been a funeral." Lewis pressed his thumb and forefinger to his eyes and gathered control of his emotions before they were reflected on his face. "I don't understand. He was doing better. Caden took him home the day he left the hospital and then saw him a few days before he . . . well, before. Caden said he looked better than he'd seen him in a very long time. He was on the new medication and it seemed to be working."

"Was he taking it like he was supposed to? Because if he stopped taking the pills or . . ." Marshall shrugged. "You know how that goes."

"How do I know? Once he was out of the hospital, who knows what he did?"

"But the medicine was definitely working while he was under supervision of the hospital?"

"Seemed to be. I don't know what happened. No one does."

"What about Rochelle? How's she doing?"

"I don't know. She doesn't speak to me these days." He took another sip of coffee.

"Do you blame her? From what you said, you played dirty pool with her and her career."

"It was for her own good." But the hate on her face and in her eyes the last time he'd seen her sat heavy on his heart. "I never wanted kids, you know."

Marshall stilled. "I didn't realize. You've never said."

"I mean, I was never home and wasn't going to be home anytime in the foreseeable future. But *she* wanted them."

"Tara."

He nodded. "And I wanted to make her happy. When Caden was born, I have to admit, it was life changing. I mean, I had a son."

"Let me guess. You decided you wanted kids after all?"

Lewis laughed, a harsh sound that he cut off quickly. "No, not hardly. But, in time, he grew on me. They all did." He shrugged. "Of course, I didn't see them all that much, but . . . yeah." He paused and broke off a piece of the biscuit Jenny had set in front of him. "I've never asked you this before, but . . . you've never married or had children. Do you regret it?"

Marshall raised a brow and blew out a slow breath. "I've been so focused on my life's work that I haven't had time to think about marriage or kids." He stopped, then shook his head. "No, I don't regret it. At least not right now."

"You're doing good stuff."

His friend smiled. "That's the idea anyway."

Lewis rubbed his eyes. "I should have done more," he said, his voice soft, "for Dustin."

"What more could you have done?" Marshall set his spoon on the table and lifted his cup to take a sip.

"I don't know what, but just . . . more. Something. Anything. I knew he was having issues. I knew he was in trouble and fighting to keep his sanity. I knew about the panic attacks, nightmares, and that he was an alcoholic. I just didn't know he was so close to the edge." He rubbed his eyes again. "How could I not know?"

"You did everything you could, my friend."

"I should have stepped in and gotten him out earlier or delayed his release. Something." He had no idea what would have been the right thing to do. "But I didn't. And now look where we are."

The waitress arrived with refills for their drinks and Marshall waited until she left to raise a brow in Denning's direction. "So, that's why you tanked Rochelle's Army career."

Again, his daughter's enraged face flashed to the forefront of his mind. She wasn't go-

87

ing to forgive him very easily or quickly. But she would. Eventually. Hopefully.

"I might not have wanted them to start with," he said, "but I can't lose another child, Marshall. I can't."

His friend eyed him, his gaze sad. "There's more than one way to lose a child."

Rays of sunlight filtering through Caden's guest bedroom window woke Sarah, and she wished she'd told him to make sure they were shut after he'd taken her tray of food last night. Then it occurred to her. She'd actually slept without a nightmare interrupting her rest. Hope sprouted that she was well on the way to recovery — both mentally and physically. She grimaced. Probably more so physically than mentally. Just because she had a few hours of sleep nightmare-free didn't mean they were gone forever.

But hopefully, her fever was. She'd had a slight relapse at the hospital — a fever spike and a couple more days in and out of awareness until Caden had finally been able to bring her home with him. She stayed in the bed for three days, except for the debrief that finally happened yesterday afternoon, short walks to the bathroom, and the occasional nap on Caden's deck off the sun-room.

Yesterday, she noticed a big improvement in her energy level, and today, for the first time since getting her stitches out, she'd sat up without the piercing pain in her side.

It was down to a dull throb to match the one in her head. She refused to take the stronger medication tempting her with more oblivion. And the only reason she'd conceded to take that was because Caden promised her he'd be there while she slept. True to his word, every time she awakened screaming, he was there to help chase the nightmares away. Now that her mind was clearing, questions were surfacing. Questions that she'd had to put on hold while she healed.

Whatever had happened to Brianne? What had Dr. Kilgore and the other man meant by their conversation? Had they actually been talking about Brianne or someone else entirely? Who *was* the other man?

She still wasn't completely sure and had, during her more lucid moments, bugged Caden to find out about Brianne. This morning she'd learned he'd come up empty.

Had she simply dreamed all of that in her fever-induced state? Dreamed that, along with the nightmares of her kidnapping and

Fatima's shooting and Dustin's suicide?

She had a brief flash of the hysterical woman in the room next to hers. Weeping, pulling against her restraints so hard her wrists had bled.

No. Those screams echoed, reverberating in her head. The woman had been real, all right. As real as Dustin.

Before the grief could once more consume her, Sarah shoved thoughts of her brother away while taking a physical inventory of her injuries. Her shoulder was sore, but the graze had scabbed over and the itch was more annoying than painful. Her side was healing. Her emotions had a ways to go.

"You're awake," Caden said.

She turned to see him standing in the doorway. "Really? I hadn't noticed."

He raised a brow. "And grumpy. This is the thanks I get for taking you in? I don't share my guest room with just anyone, you know."

Sarah grimaced, then swallowed the lump that rose in her throat. "Thanks for letting me stay here and for taking care of me." She rubbed her eyes. "I guess I need to move home at some point."

"In spite of your grumpiness, I'm not in a hurry for you to leave, but we could go by there and grab some clothes and whatever else you need if you want. Although, I can't think of what that might be. I got your suitcase full of stuff you had with you overseas, so I think you're good for a while."

"Thanks," she whispered. Clothes were really the last thing on her priority list. And, truthfully, so was going home. "Please tell me I've just been trapped in a really bad nightmare."

"I wish I could."

The huskiness in his voice seared her and grief slammed her all over again. "Why'd he do it, Cade? Why would he kill himself?"

"I don't know. It doesn't make any sense to me either."

She swiped a stray tear. "Why do you say that?"

"I picked him up from the hospital the day he was released and took him home." Caden walked over to sit in the chair next to the bed. "He was upbeat and happy. Said he felt like the sessions at the hospital had really helped and the drug protocol was working. He'd also been sober for three months and was working out, getting in shape." Caden shrugged. "He said everything was looking brighter and he had hope that the future held good things. Less than forty-eight hours later, he's dead? I don't get it."

91

"Why didn't you tell me? Tell the general?"

"Dustin told me to keep my mouth shut. He wanted it to be a surprise."

Sarah huffed a harsh laugh. "Well, guess what? I was definitely surprised."

"Stop, Sarah. He wanted everyone to see how good he'd done for himself. That he was doing better and getting his life together."

"So he was lying? Putting on a good show for you and the doctors in order to get released on time?"

"The thought occurred to me, but I don't think so."

"Then he was bipolar and you caught him in the manic stage?"

Caden blew out a low breath. "Maybe." A guilty look flashed across his face. "But I don't think that was it either."

"For an FBI agent, you have the most expressive face. What are you hiding? Come on, spill it."

Caden rubbed a hand down his chin. "I looked at his medical records."

She raised a brow. "How'd you manage to do that?"

"I was suspicious after I saw him so . . . up. I tracked down his psychiatrist — Melissa McCandless. Told her about the whole thing, and she said while she couldn't talk about Dustin's medical information without permission from Dustin, she seemed to think Dustin had turned a corner and was expecting great things."

"But how'd you see his medical records?"

He flushed.

"Caden . . . ?"

"I . . . uh . . . sort of sweet-talked a nurse into finding me some creamer for the cup of coffee she'd offered. She might have left her laptop open and I *might* have happened to see her type in the password, so . . ." He shrugged.

And with his unique ability to remember just about anything he saw or heard, he hadn't had any trouble retaining the password. He could probably still tell her what it was. Caden didn't often use his good looks and charm to do something like that, so he must have been feeling pretty desperate. She let it go without teasing him, not in the mood to bother. "Then . . ." She lifted a hand in confusion. "I don't understand. What happened?"

He shook his head. "I don't know. It's all I've been able to think about in between making sure you weren't going to die. I went to see Dustin once more after that — a couple of days after he was released — and he was still doing great. With the help of one of the counselors at the center, he had a job lined up and a place to live. He said getting out of the Army was the best decision he'd made in a long time. He seemed happy, Sarah. Really happy about everything."

She frowned. "Then you missed something."

He stood and slammed a fist onto the desk behind him.

"Cade!"

He whirled back to face her. "Don't you think I've thought of that? I keep going over it and over it in my head, wondering what I missed. How could I not pick up on that he was so depressed he was thinking of killing himself? How?" Tears stood in his eyes.

"No, no, no. I didn't mean it like that. It's not your fault." She pressed a hand against her side, keeping the pain from her expression. If Cade thought she was hurting, he'd change the subject.

"But that's just it," he said. "How can it *not* be my fault? As far as anyone knows, other than the hospital staff, I was the last one to see him alive."

Sarah closed her eyes. "It's not your fault. It's not my fault. I'm not even sure it's the general's fault, but I'm okay with blaming him." She swallowed hard and opened her eyes. "Only I can't. As much as I hate to say it, this is Dustin's fault. He's the one who made the choice."

Caden pressed his fingers to his eyes, then sat down next to her. "Yeah, but what did we miss?"

"We could do this all day, making ourselves crazy, trying to find a place to put the blame. I, for one, would prefer to look for answers."

His gaze sharpened. "What do you mean?"

"I mean, I want to talk to the people who were treating him, the people at the rehab center where he was getting help for his alcohol addiction, the nurses and doctors that worked with him on a daily basis, the counselor who helped him get the job and apartment. Everyone."

"Sarah —"

"No. Someone missed something — not you, not me — but the professionals who're trained to work with people like Dustin. *They* missed something." She paused and looked away. "Have you searched his home yet?"

Caden grimaced. "No. The general told me to take care of it, and I haven't been able to bring myself to go over there yet — or found the time, what with nursing my sister back to health."

"The general," she muttered. "I don't want to hear about him."

"He asks about you every day."

"He can ask all he wants, he'd just better not show his face in my presence."

He blinked. "Sarah, that's not like you."

She flinched and memories better left buried flooded back. Caden must have read every one of them. He gripped her fingers. "That was a long time ago, Sarah. You're not that rebellious high schooler anymore. You've moved on from that."

"I thought I had," she whispered. "But old feelings are being fueled. Old behaviors are wanting to rear their ugly heads. How could he do this to me?"

"Do what? I know you two have your differences, but you're on a whole other level right now. It's almost like you hate him."

Hate? That was a pretty strong word. And emotion. Did she hate her father? Not sure she wanted to explore that question, she waved a hand. "Sit back and let me fill you in, because I'm going to need your support if this goes to court."

By the time she finished, Caden's face had paled. Fury and pain flashed in his eyes and he shook his head. "Unbelievable."

"I've used that word a time or two."

"Wow. I can see why you're so upset." He

96

paused. Looked at his hands, then back at her. "I know you don't want to hear this, but he really does want the best for you. He just doesn't go about it the right way."

Sarah bit her lip on the retort she wanted to fling and simply said, "I don't want to talk about it anymore. Let's go back to the topic of Dustin's place. I want to go with you. Promise me you'll wait until I can go."

"Sarah . . ." He sighed. "Yeah, sure. We'll do it together."

"Thank you." She paused. "What if his death wasn't a suicide?"

"What do you mean?"

She shrugged and met his gaze once more. "From all you say, it doesn't sound like he was depressed. You looked at his records and there's nothing about bipolar or any other mental illness in there. So . . ."

"So?"

"So, what if someone killed him and set it up to look like a suicide?"

"But . . . why?"

"I don't know. Maybe he was involved in something he shouldn't have been? Who knows?"

"Don't hate me for saying this, but I think — sometimes — you look for a story where none exists."

"You just said you don't understand it,

that Dustin seemed happy and upbeat and —"

"And there's security footage of him jumping, Sarah. No one pushed him. He walked to the edge of the roof . . . and jumped. It was suicide."

She rubbed her eyes. "Then —"

The doorbell rang and Caden jumped like he'd been shot. "Good grief. Let me see who that is."

"Sure."

Caden left and Sarah dropped her head back onto the pillow. She didn't know why she'd thrown out the possibility that Dustin hadn't committed suicide. It had just popped into her head, but Caden's description of his last time with Dustin didn't sound like the personality of someone who was planning to jump off the roof of a hospital.

Voices from the foyer reached her and she thought she recognized Gavin's. And just like that, her pulse skittered into overdrive. Why did he have that silly effect on her?

She swung her legs over the side of the bed and waited for the room to stop rocking. When she finally felt steady, she started to rise, then noticed the end table for the first time. Really noticed it. It looked like a pharmacy. She opened the top drawer and swept the medications and bandage material into it.

She'd only taken the pain pills at night in order to sleep, unwilling to chance becoming dependent on them. Now, she was done with them. Especially if they made her so loopy she couldn't distinguish a dream from reality. And if Gavin decided to walk down and pay her a visit, she sure didn't want him seeing them.

Why it mattered, she couldn't say. It just did.

Gavin followed Caden into the den and took a seat on the couch. "How's she doing?" He finally asked the question that had been burning a hole in his brain since he'd followed her and Caden home from the hospital three days ago.

"She's healing. And she's struggling," Caden said.

"With?"

"A lot of things. We had a long chat and she told me what our father did." He shook his head. "He really got her discharged on ODPMC? Saying the PTSD makes her a danger to herself and possibly to others?"

Gavin nodded. "Yeah, she wasn't too happy about that."

"That's an understatement. She's mad as

fire and plans to fight him — even said something about suing him and the diagnosing psychiatrist."

"Suing?"

"Libel. HIPAA violations, malpractice. She's still thinking." He paused. "I wouldn't say this in front of her, but I understand my father's actions on a certain level. He's a dictator for sure, but what Sarah doesn't understand is that he really loves her and I know he just wants to keep her safe." Gavin narrowed his eyes and Caden held up a hand. "However, I'll be the first to admit that wasn't his call to make. If she finds out he's hired you to be security for her, she'll send you packing."

"I know." Gavin sat forward with his elbows on his thighs, hands clasped between his knees. "But I'm surprised you know. The general said he wasn't going to tell you about any of it."

Caden let out a laugh that sounded more like a snort. "I'm surprised he thought he could keep it from me. He finally confided in me three days ago when I questioned the security around my home and at Dustin's funeral. He muttered something about incompetents and fessed up." Caden shook his head. "He's been getting threats for his stance on the war in the Middle East and

100

the attack he ordered on a terrorist. The man's wife, three young children, parents, brother, and two sisters were hit. It was thought it had taken him out as well, but . . . apparently, it didn't."

"And he's vowed revenge."

"Exactly."

"I know this terrorist," Gavin said. "Know him better than I'd like to admit."

Caden studied him with sudden realization. "You were a part of the strike."

"I was." He'd been so much more than that, but he'd let that explanation suffice for now.

A short huff escaped Caden. "The general didn't tell me that part, but it explains why he wants you as security for Sarah. You know the man and how he works."

"I do." Boy, did he ever.

Caden raked a hand over his head. "Sarah wonders if someone got to Dustin. I wonder what the general thinks."

Gavin nodded. "When I talked to him, he was certain it was suicide."

"I know. It was. I watched the security footage. He just walked over to the edge and jumped. Didn't even hesitate like he was having second thoughts." He swallowed for a moment and closed his eyes. When he opened them, the raw grief sliced at Gavin's heart. "But . . ." Caden sighed. "I told the general about Dustin's mood and everything he'd accomplished during his stay in the hospital. He was doing so well. The general finally confessed to the threats. He also admitted that while he knows what the security footage shows, he keeps wondering if the two — the threats and Dustin's death — are somehow related. That Dustin was set up or there's something missing from the security footage and Dustin didn't really jump. Or . . . something. Then he shakes his head and decides that's impossible." Caden threw up his hands. "I don't know. Sounds like we're all in denial, if you ask me." A pause. "But I can't help wonder too. Could Dustin have been working on something that got him killed, and the killers simply had the sophisticated skills to pull it off?"

Gavin pulled at his beard while he wondered how much to say.

"You don't agree the two could be related," Caden said. Gavin started, and Caden shot him a tight smile. "I'm trained to read people, remember?"

"And I'm trained to not be read." Gavin sighed. "Must be getting soft," he muttered.

"Why don't you agree?"

"It's just a theory. Doesn't mean it's right."

"So, let's hear it."

"Omar's a killer," Gavin said. "He doesn't try to make things look like a suicide. If he was behind Dustin's death, he would have sent a suicide bomber and just blown up the hospital floor that Dustin was on. Or an assassin to put a hole in his head. He doesn't go to the effort to plan his murders to look like suicides." Caden flinched and Gavin wanted to bite his tongue. "Sorry, man. I shouldn't have been so blunt."

"It's all right. I'm not one to dance around the facts." A pause. "So, you don't think Omar could have had anything to do with Dustin's death?"

Gavin thought about it once more, trying to find a way to make it work. "No, I don't. At least I can't come up with a reason he'd choose to do it that way. It's simply not the way he operates — at least it wasn't when I was with him. It's been a little over a year since that bombing." He rubbed his eyes. "I suppose there's an infinitesimal possibility that he changed the way he works, but I wouldn't bet anything on it."

For a moment, Caden simply stared at the floor and Gavin let him process. The man would speak when he was ready. He took the moment to text his sister.

Hey. Could we find some time to talk, please? Text or call me.

Footsteps sounded to his right, then Sarah appeared in the doorway. As always, she made his heart thud a little faster and a little harder just by being in his presence. He'd almost find it amusing if it didn't disconcert him so much. Their one and only unforgettable kiss surged to the forefront of his mind, and it took effort to make it go away. Again.

"Hi," he said, finally finding his tongue. Because he was all about making a good impression with his brilliant conversational skills. He gave a mental roll of his eyes and she quirked a smile at him.

"Hi."

"What are you doing out of bed?" Caden asked.

"Being very careful." She pressed a hand to her side and walked over to sit on the sofa next to Gavin. Once seated, she let her gaze touch on him, then Caden. "Don't stop talking. I want to hear."

"You just got your stitches out, Sarah, don't push it."

"I'm not. Now, what are you talking about?"

Caden rolled his eyes and she stuck her

tongue out at him. Gavin couldn't help the grin that wanted to break out but managed to smother it, even though he thought Sarah might have noticed.

Then she turned serious. "I need you to find her for me," she said to Caden.

"I've already tried, Sarah. She's not in the system — they're saying she wasn't even there."

"What? Of course she was there. You're FBI, Cade, try a little harder. I *need* to know she's okay."

"If she was a patient, I would have to use my FBI status to get information. I asked them to ring her room and they said they didn't have a patient there by that name."

"So, maybe she went home?"

He sighed. "And you don't remember her last name?"

"No. She never gave it to me. I saw her. She said her name was Brianne. Dr. Kilgore and the nurse came in, and I was sent back to my room. Approximately forty-five minutes later, Brianne was gone and her room had been sanitized." She stilled. "Where's this hesitation in helping me coming from?"

Caden shrugged. "You're obsessing over a complete stranger. I'm not sure it's healthy."

"I'm not obsessing, I'm concerned. And if you'd seen her, you would be too. Now,

105

please, go do your FBI thing and track her down." She flicked her hand, waving him away.

Gavin's gaze ping-ponged between the siblings, his regret growing at the distance still between him and his own sister. Kaylynn often appeared like a meek little mouse and used to cry if he so much as looked at her cross-eyed. Which was understandable, he supposed. Even women he'd served with had often given him a wide berth before they'd gotten to know him. Now, Kaylynn didn't cry. She just avoided him.

Much like Sarah had done. It had taken him aback so much that he'd actually tracked her down to make sure she was all right — and had found her eating and laughing with friends at one of the restaurants on base.

Hurt and confused, he'd left before she saw him.

The whole thing had bothered him because he had a feeling that she'd behaved in a manner completely contrary to the character of the woman he'd been getting to know.

The one who stood her ground and had no trouble voicing her opinions during their many conversations. He'd have thought she would have gone toe-to-toe with him if she felt strongly enough about something.

106

Like finding out her father had hired Gavin to be her personal secret security team.

Yeah. She'd feel very strongly about that one.

When Gavin focused back on the conversation, Sarah was saying, "You'll find out if she's okay and if she needs help."

"Yes."

"And you'll be sneaky if you have to, because you're apparently really good at that when you choose to be."

He rolled his eyes. "If it will put your mind at rest."

"Good. It will help." A pause. "Thank you."

"Welcome." He turned to Gavin. "She's stubborn."

Gavin wondered why the man had even bothered to put up a protest. "Why doesn't that surprise me? From what I can tell, it's the strongest gene on *your* DNA strand, so I can see it being a sibling trait."

Sarah gave a light snort of laughter while Caden's lips quirked. "That's probably true," he said. "Dustin was the same way."

They fell silent while they battled their grief all over again, and Gavin looked away to give them the shared moment.

Caden cleared his throat and stood, pulled

107

his phone from his pocket, and waved it at Sarah. "If it's got you this worked up, let me see who else I can talk to that might know more than the last person. Shouldn't take me too long. And then I'm going to order pizza. Gavin, you can stay and join us if you like."

"Uh, sure. Thanks." Well, that was one way to keep an eye on Sarah without too much trouble. And besides, he was hungry.

Once Caden left the room, Gavin turned to Sarah — who'd slumped against the back of the couch. "You okay?"

"I'm fine," she said. "Tired of answering that question, but . . . yeah."

"Right. Sorry."

She grimaced. "I'm also in a cranky mood, but I shouldn't take that out on you."

"I can handle it."

Silence fell between them. "I don't re-member his funeral," she finally said softly.

"You were there."

"Barely."

"You insisted. Threatened to walk if that's what you had to do." It had been the day she was released from the hospital with her fever finally under control but apparently back on some heavy-duty painkillers some-one had snuck into her IV. She was livid when she finally came to. Gavin recalled the

108

tongue-lashing she'd given Caden when she realized what had happened, and Caden promised to take her home immediately. He'd promised she'd be given no more drugs unless she okayed them.

"I have a picture of the graveside playing in my mind. You rolled me in the wheelchair," she murmured.

Her gaze was distant, her vision turned inward with her effort to remember. "Uh, yeah. You insisted on that too. You told Caden you knew his driving skills and felt safer if I was the one behind the wheel — so to speak."

"I remember that." She closed her eyes. And just like that, fell asleep.

CHAPTER EIGHT

She really had to quit waking up with no memory of having fallen asleep. Sarah frowned and mentally scrolled back to the last thing she remembered. Zonking out while talking to Gavin. Great. Why was it always Gavin who was the one to pick up the pieces?

Between passing out *twice* — and having Gavin save her from what could have been serious injury should she have hit the floor with her head — and falling asleep when she least expected it, she was going to have to start chugging some caffeine or something.

With a sigh, she sat up. If she remembered correctly, she'd also been waiting for Caden to find out about the woman in the room next to hers — Brianne. And wondering how Dustin could have committed suicide. So many questions begging for answers.

She climbed out of bed again with the

whole déjà vu thing happening, noticing that she was still in her yoga pants and a long T-shirt. Her stomach rumbled and she took note that she was starving.

And in need of a shower.

Twenty minutes later, with some effort but not as much pain as she'd feared, Sarah made her way to the kitchen where she found Caden and Gavin once again deep in conversation. They stopped talking the moment they saw her.

"Haven't we done this once today?" she asked.

Caden lifted a brow. "What? Have a conversation while you sleep your life away?"

"Something like that."

"No. That was yesterday."

"What?" Sarah was horrified. "I've lost another day?" No wonder she was so hungry. She'd missed the pizza. And breakfast.

Gavin shifted. "You were shot twice, Sarah. You've got to give yourself time to heal. I tried to wake you up to feed you, but you told me to get lost."

"I did?"

"Yep. The fact that you slept this long should be a signal for you."

She touched her still bandaged arm. "This was barely a graze." Her fingers moved to her side. "And the other . . . well, I can heal later. Now, please, what did you learn about Brianne?" The two men exchanged a glance and she held up a finger. "Oh no, no, no. You don't get to do that."

"What?" Gavin asked, innocence radiating from him.

"That," she said flatly. "No looking at each other and communicating in your silent bro-language."

Caden snorted and Gavin cleared his throat. "I'm sorry, what kind of language?" Caden asked.

"You know what I mean. Spill it."

His amusement faded. "All right. I finally went to the top link of the chain at the hospital and was told there wasn't anyone by that name on the floor, and the room had been unoccupied for the duration of your stay."

Sarah blinked. Then blinked again. "Uh . . . what? You're kidding me."

"I wouldn't," Caden said. "Not about this."

"It's simply not true," Sarah said. "Why would they lie about it?"

"I also talked to Dr. Kilgore, and he said he didn't have any patients by the name Brianne during that time period."

Disbelief held her stunned. "He's totally

lying. They're all lying." She needed to write down the conversation she'd heard between the two men before she forgot it. There was something about it that made her skin crawl.

"Why?"

"I don't know." She stood, feeling more steady on her feet than she had since the shooting. Finally. Maybe she'd needed that extra sleep, but she'd bite her tongue off before admitting it in front of these two.

Gavin handed her a bagel slathered with strawberry cream cheese, and she took a bite.

"Thank you," she said around the food.

"Welcome."

She swallowed. "Did Dr. Kilgore treat Dustin too?"

"No, why?"

"Just wondering. What was Dustin's doctor's name?"

"Melissa McCandless. She's a psychiatrist, not a doc who treats wounds like you had."

"Right. Of course. That was a stupid question." She stood and headed for the door.

"Where are you going?" Caden asked.

"To change clothes." She left them sitting in the kitchen and marched — okay, more like walked carefully — to Caden's guest room. After her lovely, refreshing shower, she'd dressed in a clean pair of yoga pants

113

and one of Caden's T-shirts. Now, she chose a loose-fitting pair of navy-blue pants with an elastic waist and a white-and-navy-striped T-shirt.

After her stay at the hospital in Kabul, her things had been delivered to her father. Caden had picked them up the day of her release and brought her — and her luggage — to his house.

While she was grateful for his care and devotion, she missed her small one-bedroom apartment. Somewhat. Her father had nearly stroked out when she moved into the building located in one of the sketchiest neighborhoods in the city. She could tell he'd actually come close to losing that vise grip he held on his legendary control when he showed up on her doorstep demanding she move home. She'd simply shut the door in his face.

The memory made her smile.

Then she frowned as guilt pierced her. She shouldn't press his buttons so gleefully, but . . . she did. Getting a rise out of him had become second nature to her in high school.

She pressed her fingers to her eyes. She'd thought she was past that stage in her life, that she'd moved on and put all that rebellion behind her.

114

I have. I don't live there because it bugs him. That's just an added bonus.

She had several reasons for choosing to live in that cramped, crime-infested building. The fact was, she liked her apartment and knew he'd never understand her reasons for wanting to live there. So, she didn't bother to explain them.

Shoving aside thoughts of her father, she brushed her hair and tried to think of a reason the hospital would deny Brianne had been in the room next to hers. She could understand them saying they couldn't release medical information, but to deny her very existence? That was just weird.

Once she decided she looked presentable, Sarah made her way to Caden's office and lifted his spare truck keys from the top right-hand drawer of his desk.

"Going somewhere?"

Sarah's heart jolted and her head jerked up. Gavin leaned against the doorjamb, lips quirked into that lopsided smile she found herself liking way too much. "Yes. Why?"

"I didn't think you could drive yet."

Rats. She dropped the keys back into the drawer and sighed. "I'll call an Uber then."

"Why don't you just ask someone for a ride?"

"Because if you're referring to the two

115

someones in this house, I know they'll try and talk me out of it."

He narrowed his eyes and crossed his arms. The T-shirt pulled across his chest and the tattoos rippled with the movement. She found it fascinating. "Come on, I'll take you," he said.

She blinked. "You will?"

He shot her that one-sided smile again. "You're a big girl, Sarah. I figure you can make your own decisions. If you want to go to the hospital to ask about Brianne and probably Dustin too, I don't mind taking you."

She caught her jaw before it swung open. "Are you a mind reader?"

"Of course not. It's just a little deductive reasoning. Caden's questioning and lack of answers didn't satisfy you, so you want to go get your own." He shrugged. "You're an investigative reporter. It's what you do." A pause. "It's what I'd do if I were in your shoes."

"But . . ." Why was she protesting? "Okay, thank you."

He did a one-eighty and headed down the hall with an "I'll be in my truck whenever you're ready" thrown over his shoulder.

Sarah hurried after him. "Hey, I'm ready now."

"Don't you need a purse or something?"

She wrinkled her nose. "I have my phone. It's got a credit card and my driver's license in the little pocket attached, so it's all I need."

His brow lifted, but he simply held open the door for her and she slipped through. He followed her to his truck and waited for her to get in the passenger side. "Where'd you get the phone? Caden?"

She nodded. "He pulled some strings and got a copy of my license for me and then gave me one of his old phones." She shifted and winced, but tried to cover it by pressing her lips together.

"Are you sure you're up to this?" She shot him a black look and he nodded. "Right. Seems like you're pretty fluent in bro-language yourself."

"It's a matter of survival some days."

He laughed and shut the door.

Sarah leaned back and closed her eyes, already tired from the walk to the car, but she couldn't put this off any longer. Dustin's death had left so many unanswered questions rolling around in her head. And that poor woman's cries were haunting her. She had to see if there was anything she could do to help her.

Assuming she could even find her.

And she wanted to know who Dustin's last visitors had been, what they'd talked about, if he'd made any phone calls, gotten any emails or text messages. Because if Dustin had truly jumped off the roof of the hospital under his own power, she had to know what the trigger had been to make him do it.

Caden stood in front of his father's desk in the house he'd grown up in, once again feeling like a twelve-year-old and trying not to show it. He waited until the general looked up with a raised brow. "Can I help you with something?"

"You got her discharged from the Army."

"I did." The man didn't even blink and Caden bit off a scoff.

"Why?"

"She doesn't have what it takes to make the Army her career. I managed to save her reputation by getting her an honorable discharge."

"Her reputation didn't need saving. She's one of the most highly respected journalists over there. She speaks the language, she has a relationship with the locals — and she writes the facts. People who don't trust their own family members trust her. And she's not suicidal."

"She has PTSD."

"Yeah, well, you would too if you went through what she's experienced, but using your clout to get her discharged wasn't your call — and not really something I thought you were capable of."

"I was trying to save her life!" The words burst from his father's lips, a momentary loosening of his iron-clad self-control.

"It's not your life to save," Caden said, purposely lowering his voice. "She's an adult. A very smart and capable one, if you'd open your eyes and take a good hard look at her."

"You know how she was in high school. She's not capable of looking out for herself. And since you baby her, I have to take measures to make sure she's safe."

"I accept her. Sarah *is* who she *is*. She's not who she *was*. That was a long time ago. She's forgiven herself for all of that. At least I think she has. But if you ever want her to speak to you again, you need to undo what you've done."

The general ran a hand over his graying head, and Caden realized for the first time that his father was starting to look older. Not old. Just . . . older. At fifty-five, he was still in excellent health. Running five miles a day was a habit he'd had since Caden was a boy. And he'd never once invited Caden or Dustin to go with him. Resentment stung and Caden swallowed it.

"Get out of here, Caden. What's done is done and I'm not going to undo it. Couldn't if I even wanted to try."

"Bull. I don't believe that and neither do you." Caden held on to his temper with effort. "Dad, I've always done my best to treat you with respect whether I felt the emotion or not because that's what Mom asked me to do. So, I'm only going to say this once. It's time you stop thinking that just because you're a lieutenant general in the Army, you can rule your family like you do your soldiers — because one day you're going to look back and wish you'd made some changes." He paused, taking advantage of the man's shocked silence. "Mom would be terribly disappointed in you."

Caden did a perfectly executed about-face and walked out of his father's office.

CHAPTER NINE

Gavin pulled into the hospital parking lot, put the truck in Park, and let it idle while he watched Sarah sleep. She'd conked out about three minutes into the twenty-minute drive and hadn't stirred. For the next thirty minutes, he let her sleep while he answered a few emails on his phone, checked in with her father via text and feeling like a rat the whole time — and set up a security detail request for a visiting politician who'd be arriving in town next week. Lastly, he texted his sister.

Come on, Kaylynn. PLEASE TEXT OR CALL ME. I'm SORRY for handling the situation the way I did. It's been a year. Can we please talk?

He waited.

No three little dots indicating a return text.

Nothing.

He sighed and shook his head. What else could he do?

Finally, Sarah shifted and opened her eyes — which landed on him. She groaned. "I fell asleep again, didn't I?"

"It's okay. I was productive while you snoozed." He waved his phone at her.

She rubbed her eyes. "I feel guilty sleeping while poor Brianne may need help."

Putting things off was just stressing her even more, but he had a question that had been burning a hole in his gut for a long time.

She placed a hand on the door handle, and he touched her shoulder, stopping her movement. Her brow rose.

"Sarah . . ."

Wariness flickered in her gaze. "Yes?"

"When we were in Kabul and went out a few times . . ." And shared a bone-rattling kiss he still thought about. "Why did you . . . disappear on me?"

Her eyes slid from his and a flush darkened her pale cheeks. "It doesn't matter, Gavin."

"It matters to me. Why?"

She finally met his gaze. "I shouldn't have ghosted you. I'm sorry."

"Thanks, but I'm not looking for an apology. I was kind of hoping for something along the lines of an explanation."

Her eyes searched his for a moment before flicking back to the building. "I . . . don't know if I can explain it in a way that makes sense."

"Try me. Was there someone else?"

"No." She spit the word out on a huff of humorless laughter. "No, not at all. It wasn't that."

"So, is this where you tell me it wasn't me, it was you?"

She shook her head. "No, because it *was* you." He huffed a humorless laugh, and she bit her lip.

"Wow," he said. "It's a good thing I have a pretty healthy ego. Or at least I used to. Okay then. It was me. 'Nuff said."

"Partly you. And partly me."

He stilled and waited.

"It was just a combination of things, I guess."

"You realize that's clear as mud?"

She sighed. "I . . . I had some . . . issues in high school that have, unfortunately, followed me into adulthood."

"What kind of issues?"

She blew out a slow breath. "Boy, that's a loaded question. And one that I don't know I can answer adequately right now."

He studied her, then gave a short nod. "All right, then. Ready to go see what we can find out in there?" She didn't move. "Sarah?"

"No." Her fingers curled into fists. "That's not fair to you. It wasn't fair when I refused to answer your calls or texts. I was horrible and I do owe you an apology whether you want one or not."

"You've already apologized."

"What it boils down to is . . . I was scared."

Three little words had never wounded like those. His fingers flexed around the wheel. "I'd never put my hands on you to hurt you, Sarah." He glanced at her.

"What?" She blinked at him. "Oh, I wasn't scared of you physically, it was more of an emotional thing."

Okay, now he was just confused. "How so?"

"That last date after our kiss —"

"That was a really good kiss, by the way."

She laughed and rubbed a hand over her eyes. "Yes. Yes, it was. But that was beside the point. I think it was . . . you just reminded me too much of my dad that night." She grimaced. "Minus the kissing part."

"Ouch. Thankful for that anyway."

A short laugh bubbled from her lips.

124

"How can you make me laugh when I'm talking about things I'd rather not?"

"It's a gift."

She looked away but didn't seem quite as tense as she was at the beginning of the discussion. "Being reminded of my father brought up other memories that brought to mind . . . other stuff that I didn't want to think about."

"And we've moved from mud to tar."

She groaned. "I'm sorry. It's just really hard to talk about it."

"Then at least tell me how I reminded you of your father." He had no idea what she was talking about but knew that reminding her of her father was bad. Very bad. "What'd I do?"

"I told you a little about the story I was working on. The drug ring that was operating on base."

Oh yeah. He remembered that.

"You said, 'That's not something you want to mess with, Sarah. It's dangerous and will come back to bite you. You need to back off before you get hurt, and back off now.' "

He frowned. "I remember that. I also remember thinking, 'I'm just getting to know this amazing woman and I want it to continue.' I thought about what you were investigating, *who* you were investigating,

125

and I was scared to death something would happen to you." He cut his gaze to hers. "I guess I came across as a bit of a dictator?"

"Just like my father."

"I see." He cleared his throat. "Well, thank you for clarifying."

"I'd also like to clarify one more thing."

"What's that?"

"The truth is, I know you're really not like him. You've demonstrated that over and over in the last few days. I know you're Caden's friend, so I guess I've just chalked your presence up to that." She gave a small laugh. "I suppose, as much as I don't have the right to wish it, part of me was hoping you might be sticking around because you wanted to."

Hope inflated, even while he shut his mind to the real reason he was sticking tighter than superglue. "I'm definitely sticking around because I want to." A completely true statement. He squeezed her fingers. "Now, are you ready to do this?"

"Ready as I'll ever be." She still didn't move.

"So?"

"So, I'll tell you the rest of it one day."

"Soon?"

"Yes, soon." She punctuated the promise with a nod.

"Then I'll be ready to listen when you're

126

ready to talk."

Stepping back into the hospital sent chills down Sarah's spine, and she couldn't help the flash of memory from when she'd entered Brianne's room to find the woman in such agony. A shudder rippled back up her spine.

"You okay?" Gavin asked.

"Yes, why?"

"You shivered and went all tense when we walked in."

Observant, wasn't he? "I'll be all right." She walked past the information desk without pausing.

Gavin stayed with her. "Not going to announce you're here, huh?"

"I think I'll just see if I can find the nurse who was on that night. Donna."

"She might not be working this shift."

"I know. But first, we need to make a stop." Hand pressed against her side and moving carefully, she made a beeline for the gift shop located on the first floor across from the elevators.

"What for?"

"Flowers." With their conversation fresh in her mind and wishing she had time to process it further, Sarah pushed open the door and made her way back to the floral

127

arrangements. Fortunately, there weren't a lot of premade choices to consider, so that made the decision easier. She chose a vase with an assortment of pink and yellow calla lilies.

"That's one of our most popular arrangements," the woman to her right said.

"I can see why. They're gorgeous. I'll take them."

"Wonderful."

Sarah paid for the flowers. While the woman worked, she glanced at Gavin from the corner of her eye. She'd been truthful when she said he scared her off a bit when he'd gone all dictator on her, but there was more to it than that. She bit her lip when she realized she wanted to be fully honest. How would he react if she told him of her past? The things she'd done — and the reasons she'd done them? What if she spilled everything?

Once again, pushing the thoughts aside to deal with at a more appropriate time, she nodded to Gavin. "Now, I'm ready to go find Donna and thank her for her excellent care."

They made the elevator ride to the third floor in silence while Sarah mentally prepared herself for battle. Brianne had *not* been a figment of her imagination and she'd go toe-to-toe with anyone who tried to convince her otherwise.

In a nice way, of course.

With Gavin slightly behind her, Sarah made her way to the nurses' station where three medical personnel sat in front of laptops. The older woman with short and stylish gray hair and a name tag that said Camilla looked over her bifocals at their approach. "May I help you?"

"Yes, hi. I was a patient here a couple of weeks ago and there was one nurse who was really kind and I just wanted to say thank you." She lifted the flowers, and Camilla smiled, the corners of her eyes crinkling.

"Who was your nurse, hon?"

"Donna."

"Sure. She's with a patient right now, but I'm happy to give them to her." She held her hands out.

"I appreciate that," Sarah said, "but I'd like to deliver them myself, if that's all right."

"Of course." Camilla dropped her hands. "Just hang out here. She'll be around shortly."

Camilla went back to her laptop and Sarah leaned against the counter. Five minutes ticked by and her fatigue grew with each passing moment. She was pushing too

129

hard, too soon. Weakness slipped through her.

Great, she was going to face-plant right there in front of Gavin and everyone else. She spotted a chair outside the nearest room and walked over to it. Gavin followed her.

"You okay?" he asked.

"I'm fine." She lowered herself into the chair, hoping the strain didn't show on her face.

"But you need to sit so you don't keel over and draw attention to yourself?"

She wanted to refuse to be amused, but the corner of her lip twitched before she got it under control. "Exactly."

"Which is why you probably should have stayed home, but I'm aware that wasn't an option, so I won't bring it up."

"I'm glad you've got a clear understanding of things."

"Stubborn," she thought she heard him murmur. If he only knew. Again, she almost laughed but didn't have the energy.

Two female nurses walked past them, but Sarah didn't recognize them. Then a door opened midway down the hall and a young woman stepped out. Sarah perked up. "That's her." She stood and Gavin slipped a hand under her elbow. She raised a brow,

130

but decided it was better to lean on him than land on the floor.

Donna walked their way, and her eyes met Sarah's. For a brief moment, confusion creased her face before her eyes went wide and her nostrils flared. Just as quickly, her expression cleared and she offered a smile. "Rochelle Denning. How are you doing?"

"I go by Sarah, but I'm doing much better, thank you." She tilted her head. "You remember me?"

"Of course. I remember all of my patients — at least the most recent ones anyway." She gave a small laugh. "Don't ask me about the ones who came through last month."

"Good, because I have a question about a patient of yours who was here the same time I was. But first" — she passed the flowers to the woman — "thank you for taking good care of me."

"Oh, they're beautiful, thank you so much." She sniffed them and smiled. "Which patient did you want to ask me about?"

"I don't know her last name, but she was the one next door to me. Brianne."

Donna's brow furrowed. "I'm sorry, I don't seem to remember having a patient by that name."

"Well, that's really weird, because I was in the room when she was screaming and you rushed in with her medication."

Donna huffed a short laugh that held no humor. "I don't think so. I remember you were out of your head with a fever and wandering the halls, but the room next to yours was empty. I think the combination of the drugs and the fever must have caused you to hallucinate." Her eyes softened. "You were really sick, hon."

Sarah held onto her patience with effort. "That's true, I was, but not so sick I was out of my head. I know there was someone in that room."

The woman blinked. "I see. Well, even if there was — and I'm not saying there was — there are laws protecting the patients here, including you. By law, I couldn't tell you about this Brianne even if I remembered her."

Okay, that was a valid argument. However . . . Sarah caught sight of Dr. Kilgore at the end of the hall. Brushing past the nurse with a hurried "Excuse me," she headed for the man. "Dr. Kilgore."

He turned. "Rochelle?"

"Sarah."

"Right, sorry. How are you? I didn't think

132

we had another appointment until next week."

"I'm healing and we don't. I'm here looking for another one of your patients. She was in the room next to mine. Her first name is Brianne and she was terribly upset the last time I saw her. I . . . I guess I just wanted to know that she was okay and got the help she needed."

"I told her there was no patient here by that name," Donna snapped from behind her. "Now, it's time for you two to go."

"I really don't think I can leave until I get some answers," Sarah said, keeping a smile on her face.

The doctor frowned. "Brianne? Wait a minute. Someone called up here looking for a patient by that name, and I told him I didn't know who he was talking about."

"That was my brother, Caden."

"I see. Well, nothing's changed since I talked to him. I still don't know who you're looking for." He tucked the file in his hand under his left arm and pulled a phone out of his pocket. "Now, I really must get to the next patient. I'll see you next week, Sarah." He turned on his heel and headed down the hall.

Sarah barely managed to hold in a frustrated growl. Why were they giving her the

big runaround? Why deny the woman ex-
isted?

"Dr. Kilgore, wait! Please."

"Sarah —" Gavin touched her hand.

"I see you found your phone," she blurted.

The doctor froze. And slowly turned.
"What?"

"You'd left it in the room and came back
for it. You were talking with another man.
Who was he?"

Dr. Kilgore's smile flattened. "I'm sorry, I
have no idea what you're talking about. I
really have to go. I'll see you next week."
With that, he turned and headed into the
next room.

"Now, will you two leave?" Donna asked,
shifting the flowers to glance at her watch.
"Believe it or not, we have more patients
than we can handle and never have enough
time to get everything done. I'm falling
behind as we speak. Please, go."

Gavin's hand gripped Sarah's upper arm
in a gentle, but firm hold. "Of course," he
said. "We understand. Thanks for your
help."

Sarah started to object but caught his look
and snapped her lips shut. He wasn't shut-
ting her down, he was up to something.
"Well, anyway, enjoy the flowers," she said.

"That was very kind of you. I appreciate

134

the thought." Somehow, the words didn't hold the gratitude the first thank-you had.

Once they were in the elevator, the doors started to shut and Sarah whipped around to face him, wincing in the process of moving too fast. She pressed a hand to her side. "What was that all about?"

"I have contacts. Let's do this the easy way — or at least *easier* way."

"You mean your way."

"Since that's turning out to be the easy way, then yes, that's probably what I mean."

135

CHAPTER TEN

"I didn't dream her," Sarah said.

He helped her into the passenger seat of his truck and shut the door. Once behind the wheel, he turned to her. "I don't think you did."

Gavin had already been working on an idea of how they could find Brianne — assuming Caden hadn't already done so — and now after the weird response they'd gotten from Nurse Donna and Dr. Kilgore, he was even more determined to follow through with it.

"You really believe me?" she asked.

"Yeah, I really do." Her narrowed eyes, pale cheeks, and lines around her mouth told him this little outing had been too much, too soon, but he also had a feeling she was perfectly aware of that. "Something's off. They completely deny her existence when all they had to do was say, 'She went home. Sorry I can't tell you anything else.' "

"True," she said, dragging the word out as she considered that. "If they'd said that, I probably wouldn't have questioned it further."

"I don't know about that. Knowing you, you still would have wanted to see for yourself that she was okay, but it does make way more sense just to say she was discharged than to say she wasn't even a patient there."

He caught the flare of surprise in her eyes, followed by a flash of amusement at his offhand assessment of her personality.

"Caden already called to ask about her," she said, "and they told him the woman was never there — maybe thinking that would be the end of it — but it wasn't. We showed up. So, do you think they just had to stick to their story that Brianne was never there?"

"Sounds reasonable. Who was the first person to deny she was in the room?"

"I'm not sure. Probably just the person at the information desk, but we'd have to ask Caden. I know he talked to several people who sent him up the chain, saying they couldn't find a record of her being there. He didn't have a warrant or anything for the information — and wasn't going to use his badge on unofficial business — so he couldn't really do much better than you or

I would have. Then he finally talked to Dr. Kilgore, who told him the same thing."

Gavin stroked his chin, pulling on the hair while he thought. "So, what about this scenario? The first person to answer a query about Brianne would be the receptionist taking calls on the main line."

"Right."

"If that person said she couldn't find a record of Brianne, then it's possible Brianne was just completely removed from the system."

"Which meant Donna and the doctor couldn't admit she was there or say she went home without someone questioning why she'd disappeared from the database — or whatever they use."

"So . . . they had to get their stories straight in case someone came around asking questions," he murmured. "If there's a story to get straight. You realize this is all pure speculation."

"So, how do we find out for sure?" She spoke the words out loud, but he had a feeling she didn't expect him to answer. She was working on the solution all by herself.

"I have an idea," he said.

She blinked. "Oh. Okay. What?"

"We check the security cameras."

"They're in the hallways for sure," she

said, "but not in patient rooms."

"She had to go through the hall to get to the room, right?"

"Yes. But there's no way Caden would agree to use his badge to get that footage."

He pursed his lips. "Well, thanks for the vote of confidence, but I don't need Caden or his badge."

"You don't?"

"I don't."

"Well, all right then. You can work on that while I see if I can talk to Dustin's doctor. The mental health unit is on the opposite side of the building. Can you take me over there? I'd walk, but riding sounds much better."

He shook his head and cranked the truck. "Stubborn."

Gavin drove around to the psych ward and parked, noting the gray sedan that pulled into a parking space not too far away from him.

"What is it?" she asked.

"Nothing, just keeping an eye on things."

"Once paranoid, always paranoid?"

"Something like that."

"Do you have —" She broke off and looked away.

"What? PTSD?"

"Yeah."

"No, not really. I have a bad dream every once in a while, but I'm one of the fortunate ones."

She frowned. "Why do you think that is? I know you saw some stuff over there no one should ever have to see."

"Same as you."

"Exactly."

Gavin shook his head. "I don't know how to explain it. I'm more watchful than the average person, I get a little tense in traffic — especially when I have to stop for a red light. I jump at sudden loud noises, but I'm not triggered into a flashback and I don't suffer anxiety or panic attacks. Or many nightmares."

"I hope you know how blessed you are."

His eyes caught hers and he wished he could take away the pain she kept trying to hide. Physical and emotional pain. "I do." He paused. "What are you going to do, Sarah?"

"About?"

"Your father. The Army. All of it."

She shook her head. "I don't know. I'm still trying to process that I'm actually no longer *in* the Army. I guess I'll need to find a job at some point — at least until I can get reinstated."

"A job doing what?"

"Investigative reporting. What else?" She shrugged. "It's all I know how to do. And I love it."

"My sister, Kaylynn, talked about that as a career for a while."

"Is she pursuing it?"

"No, she changed her major to communications. Or something. I think." He shook his head. "I need to ask her."

They found the mental health unit, and Sarah, walking even more slowly and holding her side, approached the speaker on the wall outside the locked double doors. She pushed the button.

"May I help you?" The voice from the little box echoed in the white concrete hallway.

"I'm Sarah Denning, here to see Dr. McCandless if she has a few minutes."

"Do you have an appointment?"

"I don't, but she treated my brother and I was hoping to talk to her for just five minutes, please."

"I'm sorry. You'll have to make an appointment."

Impatience flashed across Sarah's features followed quickly by frustration. She took a deep breath, then let it out slowly. "Look, I know this is a little out of the norm, but I really need to speak to her."

"Then I suggest you schedule an appointment. Now, if that's all, I hope you have a good day."

"No, that's not all —" She stopped and bit her lip as she stepped back from the speaker. "That went well," she muttered.

About like he thought it would. "I don't want to sound like I'm being a know-it-all, but —" No, he shouldn't say anything.

"But what?"

"Never mind."

"No, say what you were going to say."

"I was just going to say I think you're pushing too hard," he said softly. "I know you're a big girl and don't need me reminding you that you're still recovering."

"But?"

Was she mad? "But I recommend going home, making an appointment with Dr. McCandless, and then resting until it's time to come back."

She scowled. "You're right. I am a big girl."

"Uh-huh."

"You also make sense."

"I do? I mean, yeah, I do."

She nodded. "I'm ready to go."

"I can go ahead and just carry you and save us both the trouble of catching you when you pass out again if you like."

142

The look she shot him should have dropped him six feet under.

The strain of the visit had obviously rattled her brain, because the idea of Gavin carrying her was not terrible at all. And it should be because she didn't *want* to be attracted to him. However, she wasn't in denial to the point that she refused to face reality. The truth was, she was very attracted to Gavin and had been since she'd first laid eyes on him. But . . .

There was always a *but*. She wouldn't let herself fall for him now for exactly the same reason she hadn't let herself while they were in Kabul. Yes, in that one instance, he'd reminded her of her father, but that hadn't been the complete reason she'd shoved him away and run. She also knew he deserved better than her. Someone who didn't have her insecurities and emotional baggage. Someone who didn't have a past she couldn't change — no matter how much she might wish she could. She wouldn't put that on him, so she needed to simply keep her distance.

Her priority was her brother and figuring out what had gone wrong with him. If the medical staff were negligent, she needed to know that. If they weren't, and Dustin had somehow slipped over the edge for whatever reason contrary to Caden's observations, then she had to know that too.

And she needed to know about Brianne. For her own peace of mind. So, a romance with Gavin wasn't the most important item on her to-do list at the moment. And probably never would be. *But . . .* she couldn't quite squelch the wish.

Gavin drove in silence, lost in his own thoughts while she fought to stay awake. Honestly, this lack of energy was going to drive her insane. Being out of commission was so rare for her that she simply didn't know how to handle it. Getting more rest would probably help, but she was tired of resting. Sarah pulled her phone out of her pocket and called Dr. McCandless's office. After learning she wouldn't be able to get an appointment for three months, she hung up and shook her head. "I'm on the waiting list."

Gavin snorted.

"That's a crime," she said. "What if I was truly suicidal?"

"You'd have to get in another way. Like via a referral from a doctor saying it's an emergency."

Sarah huffed. "All right, then that's what I'll do."

"Do what?"

She dialed Dr. Kilgore's number and requested the referral from the woman who answered. "They said I couldn't get in for three months," she said. "And I know in the scheme of things, that's fairly quick, but I just feel like I really need to talk to someone. The dreams are bad and I don't know how much longer I can hold on to my sanity. Brianne said you might be able to work something out for me."

"Brianne Davis?"

"Yes, ma'am." Her heart thudded. And just like that, she had a last name.

"Are you having suicidal thoughts?"

"I . . . don't know. I mean . . . sometimes I —"

"All right, we need to get you in immediately. I have access to the appointment book. Hold on just a moment, please. Let me see . . ." The keyboard clicked and Sarah ignored Gavin's frown. Finally, the woman came back on the line. "Can you be there tomorrow morning at 10:45?"

"I — I can. Thanks. But I'm not —"

"Do you have someone you can stay with tonight?"

Guilt slammed her. "I do, but listen, I'm just really calling because it's so hard to get an app—"

145

"If you get overwhelmed, please go to the emergency room or call 911."

The concern in the woman's voice touched her and she almost felt guilty for lying. Then realized she wasn't completely lying. The bit about the dreams and holding on to her sanity was all truth. "I will."

"Thank you for your service, Sarah."

Her throat went tight. "You're welcome," she managed and hung up. She looked at Gavin. "Her last name is Davis."

"What?"

"Brianne Davis."

"You're sure?"

"Pretty stinking sure."

He nodded. "We'll let Caden know. That'll make his search go a little easier on his end." He paused. Glanced at her from the corner of his eye. "You said you're having a hard time holding on to your sanity. You're not having suicidal thoughts, are you?" His voice was low and concerned.

She swallowed. "No, but . . . I can see why people who struggle with PTSD can be pushed over the edge to spiral into that pit." She could feel his eyes on her. "I'm not there, Gavin, just saying I have an understanding of how it could happen." Which made her wonder about Dustin. "I'm a reporter. An *investigative* reporter. I'll do

whatever it takes to find out about Dustin."
Whatever it takes.

He didn't approve of her tactics. And she had to admit, she wasn't real thrilled with them either — which was why she'd tried to backpedal a bit on the phone, but the truth was, she wasn't completely sure she didn't need to talk to someone. "She asked me that too and I hedged my answer. Then felt guilty. I did try to back up and say I wasn't suicidal, but she cut me off." And Sarah had gone with it. Maybe because deep down, she wanted the appointment for more reasons than she wanted to admit to. She glanced out the window, wishing she could turn off her thoughts, while noting the passing scenery for the first time. "Where are we going?"

"Thought we'd take a little drive."

"What for?"

"You look tired, and the last time you fell asleep while I was driving, you didn't have any dreams."

He was right. Interesting. "So, you're treating me like a toddler and driving me around until I fall asleep?"

A laugh slipped from him. "I hadn't thought of it quite like that, but if the description fits . . ."

"Funny." She took another look around.

147

"It's really peaceful out here, though, isn't it?" A two-lane road with green trees lining either side. "Wait a minute, are we in North Carolina?"

"Close."

"Okay, then." She blinked, yawned, and refused to close her eyes. "What do your tats mean?"

He shot her a quick look. "Different things."

"Like?"

"Nosey, aren't you?"

She pursed her lips. "You say that like it's a bad thing. I'll have you know it's considered a strength — an actual requirement — in my profession."

"Hmm."

"Hmm? What does that mean?"

He raised a brow. "Nothing."

"Okay . . . so?"

"So what?"

She was going to hurt him. "Quit avoiding the question. The tattoos. What do they mean?"

"They mean different things. They represent different areas of my life."

"And?"

A sigh slipped from him. "If I tell you my story, are you going to finish telling me yours?"

148

Ouch. "Um . . . touché."

Another glance from him. "Okay, this one." He pointed to the cross on his right bicep. He wore short sleeves even though fall was coming and the days were cooler. "I was in a really tough spot and thought I was dead. It was only by divine intervention that I'm not. When I start to question things like why I'm on this earth, I just look at that reminder and know that I'm here for a purpose."

Chills danced up her arms. "I love that," she whispered.

He smiled. "Thanks."

"What kind of divine intervention?"

His jaw tightened. "My parachute didn't open."

She gasped. "What?"

"Neither did my backup."

"Gavin, that's . . . that's awful."

"Fortunately, a buddy saw I was in trouble and managed to get to me in time. It was a rough landing, but at least we lived."

"Did you ever find out why they didn't open?"

"Yeah. One of the guys saw me talking to his girlfriend and assumed I was hitting on her."

"So he decided to *murder* you?"

He shook his head. "The guy and I had

had our issues in the past. Stupid competitions that I looked at as fun, but he didn't feel the same way about."

"Because you beat him?"

He grimaced. "Sometimes."

"More times than not?"

"Something like that."

"What happened to him?"

Gavin's jaw worked and his eyes narrowed. "When the Military Police went to arrest him for the parachute incident, he grabbed a gun. There was a shootout. In the end, he was killed and two officers wounded."

"That's terrible — and terrifying. How did I not know this?" But there was an inkling somewhere in the back of her mind that she'd heard the story and just hadn't connected it to him. "Is that why you left the Army?"

He chuckled — a forced, raw sound that sent goose bumps pebbling her skin. "It probably played a part in it, yeah. But there wasn't really one specific reason. It was just time. I'd done my tours and I was ready to do something diff—" He stiffened and his eyes locked on the rearview mirror.

"What is it?" she asked.

"That sedan. I saw it in the hospital parking lot and it's closing in pretty fast."

"Maybe it's a different car."

"Maybe."

"Maybe they're just in a hurry and will go around us."

"Maybe."

He took his foot off the gas.

Now Sarah had her eye on the mirrors. The car drew closer. And closer. "Gavin —"

"Or maybe not." He jammed the pedal, and with a roar, the truck leaped forward.

CHAPTER ELEVEN

"Hold on!" Gavin spun the wheel and slammed on the brakes. Tires squealed, the truck slid sideways into the right lane, and the sedan zipped past. The driver hit his brakes. A gun popped out of the back driver's side window and a hail of bullets split the air, pounding down the driver's side of the truck as the sedan spun out off the road onto the shoulder.

"Get down!" Gavin let the truck rotate a full one-eighty while he grabbed Sarah's arm and pulled her head to his right thigh.

Sarah covered her head while Gavin floored it, flying past the other car still trying to get back on the road.

He spared a quick glance at her while the needle climbed to eighty, then eighty-five. Sarah sat up. "You okay?" he asked.

She held her side with one hand, lips clamped, face pinched. Her right hand gripped her seat belt. "Yes."

"You sure?"

She grimaced. "As well as I can be after being shot at and almost run off the road." Her irritation eased. "That was some really good maneuvering back there, Black."

"Just a little defensive driving. Fortunately, it was clear enough to do that, otherwise . . ."

"Yeah." She grabbed her phone. "I'm calling 911."

"Good, give them the description while I figure out where to go from here." Gavin glanced in the rearview mirror while his heart pumped. His brain was already in combat mode, that zone where everything he did was geared for survival — and in protection of the woman sitting beside him.

"They're coming back," she said, breathless, her gaze on the mirror, phone in her right hand.

"I see them."

"Give me a weapon. I know you have a gun in here somewhere."

"Glove box, but it's a peashooter compared to what these guys are using. Leave it and just stay down."

An eighteen-wheeler barreled toward them in the other lane. Gavin passed an exit and a car pulled onto the road behind him, causing the sedan to fall back. "This could work out nicely," he muttered.

"What?"

"Nothing. Just thinking." And praying. He heard her talking to the dispatcher.

"The tunnels are just ahead," she said, breaking off her conversation midsentence. "If they catch up and decide to start shooting in there, it won't be pretty."

"Yeah. And now I've got to worry about the person behind me."

Gavin sped closer to the mouth of the tunnel while the sedan fell behind, trapped by the slower-moving Honda between them and the eighteen-wheeler at his side. Gavin pressed the gas pedal harder.

Sarah glanced at him. "She said they're on the way, but three minutes out."

"Yeah, we don't have that long."

He knew this highway like the back of his hand. If he could get through the tunnel, he could disappear. Maybe. A quick glance behind him showed no sign of the sedan that was still blocked by the truck and the other vehicle. "Keep watching for them," Gavin said. "Let me know as soon as you see them behind us."

He pressed the gas a fraction harder and within seconds was finally in the tunnel. The fluorescent lights zipped by over his head.

"I don't see them," she said. She spoke

154

the words into the phone as well.

"Good, just need a couple more seconds."
He continued around the curve, slowing.
"Be ready, I'm going to slam on the brakes."

"Okay."

"No one's behind me, right?"

"Right — at least not close — and no sign
of the shooter."

He shot out of the tunnel and hit the
brakes while directing his truck onto the
shoulder.

Before he came to a full stop, he threw
the transmission into reverse. The tires spun
as Gavin backed through the gap in the
dismantled guardrail, guiding the bed of the
truck onto the dirt road that led down the
side of the mountain. To anyone exiting the
tunnel, she and Gavin would be invisible.
Hopefully. As long as those behind them
weren't looking in their rearview or side
mirrors.

Gavin could only pray whoever was in the
vehicle would be focused on the lane ahead,
thinking he and Sarah had disappeared
around the curve.

Sarah pressed a hand against her side, lips
pinched, but her attention was on the road.
"There," she said. "They just came out.
He's flying, but I got a partial plate. It had
an H and a 1." She spoke into the phone

for the dispatcher.

"And the sedan is a Buick Regal," Gavin said. "Sportback, I think."

"Good eye." She passed on the information and nodded. "Okay. Thank you."

The Buick was soon out of sight and Gavin waited a good minute before he pressed the gas and roared up the dirt road, maneuvering through the deconstructed guardrail once more and back onto the highway.

"How did you know that was there?" she asked.

"I come this way a lot. One of my unit buddies and his family live in Asheville. Workers have been in this area for months."

"That's fortunate." She rubbed her nose and shook her head. "I can't believe this."

He shot her a tight smile. "Keep your eyes open and let me know if you see that sedan ahead of us. I sure don't want to catch up to it."

"Right."

Gavin drove slowly, hoping the driver was speeding, thinking he was going to catch up with them. Sirens sounded behind them. Sarah gave the dispatcher their information and a cruiser pulled up beside them. "They want us to get off at the next exit," she said.

"Will do."

156

Sarah hung up and Gavin took the off-ramp. He followed one of the small-town back roads to an out-of-the-way service station. Two local police deputies pulled in behind him. He kept his hands on the wheel and noted Sarah made sure hers were on the dash.

When the officer motioned for him to roll the window down, Gavin did so.

"Anybody hurt?"

"No, bullets got the truck, not us. Did dispatch fill you in?"

"She did. Two highway patrolmen are in pursuit of the sedan. We're here to take care of you. Why don't you and the lady step out here and give us a statement?"

For the next thirty minutes, Gavin and Sarah told their story separately and out of earshot of one another until the officers were satisfied. Finally, the officer who'd approached first closed his little black book. "All right, we know where to reach you should we need you. Have a safe trip back home."

Gavin noted Sarah's drooping shoulders and helped her into the passenger seat, then turned back to the officer. "Any word on the sedan?"

"Unfortunately, no one's spotted it. We've got a BOLO out on it, so hopefully we'll

157

hear something soon."

Gavin didn't plan to hold his breath. They'd probably ditch the Buick soon if they hadn't already. "Thanks." He climbed in the driver's seat and shut the door. Sarah let out a long sigh. "You okay?" he asked her.

"I will be. Think I might have bitten off more than I can chew."

"Yeah. Let's get you home."

Home.

Somehow Caden's home had become hers in the short time she'd been there. Sarah lay on Caden's couch with the remote in her right hand and a bottle of water in her left. She was sick of resting. She hadn't been able to face getting back in the bed. And yet, her body demanded it. The couch was a good compromise.

Caden had been all over working to find out who the shooters were, but even Annie — one of the bureau's best technical analysts — with her incredible resources hadn't been able to discover who the sedan belonged to, although she'd concluded that the plates had been stolen from a car similar to the one they'd used.

Great.

Sarah set her water bottle on the coffee

158

table and aimed the remote at the television. "Hungry?" Gavin asked, stepping into the room, hands behind his back.

"Not really."

"Not even for ice cream?"

Her taste buds perked up. "What kind?"

"Mint chocolate chip or strawberry."

"Both."

He smiled and pulled his hand from behind his back. "I thought that might be your answer." He handed her the bowl that held four scoops of ice cream. Two of each flavor.

Her jaw dropped. "How did you know?"

"A good guess."

"Or Caden?"

"Nope, he's not here. The credit is all mine."

"That's a lot of ice cream."

"You can eat it. The calcium is good for you."

"Yeah, but what about the sugar?" She took a bite of the creamy sweetness and closed her eyes to savor it. When she opened them, Gavin had taken a seat in the recliner. He eyed her with amusement. "What?" she asked.

"You *really* like ice cream, don't you?"

Heat crept into her cheeks. She *loved* ice cream. "Shut up." She said the words without rancor and earned herself a grin.

Which faded all too soon. "Someone tried to kill you today," he said. "Or at least do some permanent damage."

She raised a brow. "Me? Why couldn't it be you?"

Gavin hesitated, seemed to think about something, then leaned forward. "Okay, I'm going to tell you something because I think you need to know it."

She stilled. "What?"

"Your father's been receiving threats."

"What kind of threats?"

"He's made some enemies in the Middle East. Most specifically in the Helmand and Kandahar provinces."

"That doesn't really surprise me. He has to make decisions that don't always resonate well with others — especially terrorists."

Gavin rubbed his hands together, causing the tattoos on his arms to ripple. "I talked to your dad quite a bit while you were recovering."

"He's not a dad. He's a general." A pause. "And I didn't realize you two were on such friendly terms." She'd admit to being curious — and wary.

"We weren't. I knew who he was, of course, but hadn't met him until he contacted me to lead your rescue. I also didn't

160

realize he was your father until I helped Asher keep Brooke safe last year when they were caught up in that organ trafficking ring."

She shuddered. "That was truly awful. All that aside, what are you trying to say?"

"He's not sure your kidnapping and subsequent transport to Omar's compound was simply a case of being in the wrong place at the wrong time."

Sarah closed her eyes, not wanting to relive the nightmare, but unable to stop the flashes. Rough hands, terror, gunshots. Her guard's face exploding milliseconds after she pulled the trigger. She sucked in a deep breath and opened her eyes. "I still think about the man I thought I killed. I could have sworn that was my bullet that . . ."

"It wasn't. Ballistics proved it. One of mine hit him and so did the soldier's behind you."

"I'm glad I wasn't responsible, even though he was so . . . evil." A shudder rippled up her spine. "I saw his eyes just before I pulled the trigger and there wasn't anything there. Just black pits of darkness."

"And he'll never hurt anyone again."

She shook her head. "Sorry, I didn't mean to go off on all of that. What were you saying about the kidnapping? It was something

161

more than a random thing?" She was quite proud of her outward composure.

"He said he was worried your kidnapping had something to do with the threats against him. It was one of the reasons he did what he did with getting you discharged." He held up a hand when she started to protest. "I'm not saying what he did was right, I'm just telling you the reasoning behind it."

Sarah snapped her lips shut, keeping a tight rein on the bubbling rage. "You're defending him."

"No. But maybe trying to understand and . . . explain him?"

"*You're* trying to explain him?" Of all the nerve. "That's almost worse. *You* don't know him well enough to be able to do that." She paused. "And if you do, then it's time for you to leave."

The words were cold, frigid even. Not caring one bit, she held his gaze when she said them, feeling betrayed, but mostly angry that he would side with her father.

"Of course," he finally said, "you're absolutely right. I don't know him like you do. All I have are impressions from our conversations."

"Exactly." She paused. "So, what else aren't you telling me?"

It was obvious there was no way he could say anything more about the situation without her kicking him out. And if the bullet holes in his truck were any indication, that could result in some very bad things happening to her.

Like death. He couldn't be responsible for that.

Her eyes never wavered as she waited for his answer. He'd never met anyone who could hold his gaze for very long before looking away. Sarah didn't seem to have that problem. He cleared his throat. "I'm just trying to figure some things out. Like who was gunning for us out on the highway."

"And?"

"And what?"

"What else aren't you telling me?"

He fell silent, unwilling to tell her about his agreement with her father, yet even more unwilling to outright lie to her. "What do you think I'm not telling you?"

"Like why you're sticking around?"

He blinked. "Why shouldn't I?"

"Because the more I think about it, the more it doesn't make sense." Another pause. "Did Caden ask you to watch out for me?"

"No. Caden didn't say a word." At least that was one hundred percent true. Before she could ask another question he didn't want to answer, he leaned forward. "Look, Sarah, I was just minding my own business working a contract job in Kabul with a well-trained team when the general contacted me about your kidnapping. I passed the job off as quickly as I could, and the team and I headed to the compound." Also true. "We got you out of there and back to the States so you could heal. And then Caden asked me to stay for the funeral. You seemed to want me around, and Caden wanted whatever you wanted. After the funeral, you were still really sick and" — he shrugged — "I wanted to know you were going to be okay."

She studied him as though trying to decide. "Don't you have a job?"

"I'm friends with the boss. I can help delegate. Besides, Travis and Asher are sending me regular updates and reassuring me that I'm where I'm supposed to be, so it's all good."

She continued to study him, weighing his words. Finally, a sigh slipped from her. "Why didn't they kill me? Or torture me? Or whatever?"

Her out-of-the-blue change of subject made him pause. "Who?" The fact that he

164

had to ask unnerved him.

"The terrorists. If they knew I was the general's daughter when they took me — and that's the impression you've just given me — why bother to actually *take me?* Why not just shoot me in the school where I was teaching and be done with it? Why keep me alive?"

All very good questions. "I'm not exactly sure." But he had a few ideas.

"Because if, as you say, they were trying to kill me when they cut loose with that hail of bullets on the highway, that means they followed me back here — or hired someone. Again, why? Assuming it's the people who've been threatening the general, why not when they had me in their custody for hours on end?"

Because they wanted to torture her for information they thought her father might have revealed to her — or information they thought the man would be willing to trade in exchange for her life? He bit his tongue on the words. If she hadn't come to that conclusion, he wouldn't put it in her head. "Maybe they were supposed to and decided they'd rather make more money by trafficking you?"

She frowned and gave a slow nod. "Okay, that makes sense."

But he could tell she wasn't completely sold on the idea.

Bad pun not intended.

"It makes sense," she said again, "but it doesn't."

"Why don't you sleep on it?"

"And this whole thing with Brianne doesn't make any sense either," she said as though he hadn't spoken. "Brianne Davis."

"Caden's friend at the FBI, Annie, is looking into her as well, isn't she?"

"Supposed to be. I haven't heard anything." She flicked a glance into the kitchen. "Speaking of Caden, where is he?"

"Working, I would think." He paused. "What was it like growing up with the general?"

She turned the television off and set the remote on the back of the sofa. "Painful."

The soft word barely reached his ears. When he processed what she said, he winced. "How so?"

She shrugged. "It just seems every time I turned around, he was leaving again. Mom never seemed to mind. Or if she did, she simply accepted it."

"She knew what the life was like when she married him, didn't she?"

"Of course, but in my opinion, they shouldn't have brought kids into it."

166

"That's pretty harsh, don't you think?"

She locked her gaze on his. "After one particularly nasty confrontation with the general, I asked him why they had us. You know what his answer was?"

"No."

" 'I agreed to shut your mom up. Kids were her idea. I just went along with it because I was tired of hearing her whine about it.' "

"Okay, *that* was harsh." He paused. "He really said that?"

"A direct quote." She set the half-eaten bowl of ice cream on the coffee table. "Just for the record, my mother never whined about anything — not even when she was dying from stomach cancer."

He stilled. "I didn't know. I'm sorry."

"I am too."

"She was strong."

"So very strong."

"You're like her."

She started, then smiled. "I'd love to think so."

"Regardless of what he said or whether you believe it or not, your father loves you."

Sarah gave a light snort. "No, he doesn't. He's learned he needs to put on the appearance of loving us — such as flying to Afghanistan when he thought I was going to die — but he doesn't."

Gavin thought he was beyond feeling shocked these days, but found himself stunned that she truly believed what she was saying. "He wouldn't do the things he does if love wasn't behind it." Would he? He flashed to the man's devastation when he'd walked into her hospital room to tell her Dustin was dead. That kind of agony couldn't be faked. And the worry on his face when he practically ordered Gavin to be her personal bodyguard? Was that fake? If he didn't care, why bother?

She shot him a look that could only be described as pity. "Are you really that naive?"

"Naive? I don't think I've ever been accused of that before." Was he? He knew it was a sad fact that not everyone loved their children, but he didn't get that from the general. Quite the opposite, actually.

"Just because you have a great relationship with your father," she said, "doesn't mean everyone does."

"What makes you think my relationship is great with him?"

"The tat."

Gavin glanced at his right forearm. A man and young child sat on the end of a dock, fishing lines dipped in the water. They wore matching jerseys with the name Black across the top. "Oh. Okay, yeah, I consider him one of my best friends, but that doesn't mean I have blinders on. Trust me, your father loves you."

She gave a small sigh. "I'm sorry you've fallen for his act. I won't. So, let's just agree to disagree and figure out what the next step in Plan B is."

"Plan B? What's Plan B and what happened to Plan A?"

"Plan A is to figure out what truly was going on with Dustin. Plan B is to find Brianne."

Okay, apparently this time there was going to be a Plan B.

CHAPTER TWELVE

After reassuring Caden that she was fine and asking him one more time to try a little harder to find Brianne, the next few hours consisted of naps, food, movies, and watching Gavin pace to the window, then step outside to walk the perimeter — "just to make sure there aren't any surprises out there."

And waiting for Caden to bring news about Brianne.

Not to mention the nonstop thinking about the fact that her kidnapping may not have been a random terrorist thing due to threats against her father. Truthfully, she wasn't surprised at the threats — only that it hadn't happened before now.

Her brother finally walked in the door and dropped his keys on the foyer table. "I've got Brianne's address. Or I guess I should give Annie the credit. Having the last name helped. She was able to find her, thanks to one of her contacts with the Army's CID."

Sarah blinked. "You're kidding."

"Nope."

She sat up and let her feet drop to the floor. "So, where does she live?"

"Not too far from here, actually. About a thirty-minute drive."

"Do you know anything else about her?"

"I spoke to her dad. He said she was wounded in Afghanistan about a week before you were kidnapped. Like you, she was shipped home for care here at the VA hospital."

"So, she was there."

"He said she was, but turns out that the hospital didn't contact them. Brianne was there for three days before they actually learned she was back from Afghanistan. He said an anonymous caller phoned them, refused to give his name, but told them to get her out of the hospital because it wasn't safe for her."

"What?"

"Annie ran the number he said the call came from, and it was made from inside the hospital."

"Then why would Dr. Kilgore and the nurse deny her presence when it's very obvious her family knows she was there? And what did the caller mean she wasn't safe?"

171

"Her father didn't know but said they went to get her and had her admitted to the VA psychiatric ward because she was suicidal. I asked her father if he could think of a reason she wouldn't be in the system and he had no idea. Said there must be a glitch or something."

"Right. A glitch." Sarah pressed her lips together. "Can they — or we — ask for an investigation into the hospital?"

"We could, but I'm not sure our argument would be taken seriously. I mean, there could be a very valid excuse why she's not there. Or if there's something more sinister behind it, the hospital would just come up with some plausible lie. I'm not saying I want to let them get away with it, should there be something they're getting away with. I'm just saying I think we need more information to back up your belief that the hospital did something wrong."

He was probably right. "So, where's Brianne now?"

"Her father said she took a turn for the worse mentally, even as she was healing physically. She started hallucinating and having paranoia."

"She was in restraints. She thought they were trying to kill her."

Caden nodded. "Her dad said she was in

172

bad shape for the next two days. She was kept sedated, then like I said, was moved to the psych ward. Over the next several days, she got on some different meds, spoke to the psychiatrist twice a day, and seemed to do a complete turnaround. Her outlook was brighter and she was hopeful about going home. In fact, she insisted on it."

She's better off where she is. Maybe that's all they meant. It made sense. "That fast? I thought it would take longer than that for the meds to make a difference."

He shrugged. "Apparently, it's rare, but not completely unheard of."

"Is she still on the psych ward?"

"No. The doctor said it was fine for her to go home as long as someone was with her at all times. She has a small house on a lake outside of town. Her dad said it was her happy place — a place where she could relax and heal. She has a friend staying with her, but he said she'd probably welcome a fellow vet if you wanted to visit."

"I do." She rubbed her eyes. "Do you have her number?"

He handed her a piece of paper. "I figured you'd need it." He glanced at Gavin. "You're going with her?"

"Of course."

"I don't need a babysitter," Sarah protested.

"You just got shot at and you're still recovering," Gavin said. "If you want to do it on your own, fine, but I'd prefer it if you let me tag along."

"Or me," Caden said with a raised brow, "because you still can't drive, remember?"

"No, I keep forgetting that small fact." Sarah shrugged and looked at Gavin. "Fine. I don't mind the company, but don't you have a business you need to be running?"

"I have people I trust helping me out. And remember, those bullets could have killed me too. I have a personal interest in whatever's going on."

She couldn't argue with that. "Okay, then. I'm ready when you are."

"We can take my truck." Gavin stood and pulled his truck keys from his pocket. "She might be scarred, but she still runs like a dream."

Sarah rolled her eyes. "Why are trucks always a 'she'?"

"Because while they respond well to tender loving care, they can still be high maintenance and temperamental."

Caden choked on a snort and Sarah narrowed her eyes. Oh no, he did *not* just say that. He did. He really did. That was going to cost him. As soon as she could think of an appropriate way to extract payment.

On the drive across town, Sarah decided that spending several hours on the couch had been a good thing, because at the moment, she had only a slight twinge in her side and her energy level seemed to be sufficient for the visit. Gavin parked his truck on the row of gravel at the top of the sloping front yard. An older model Honda and a newer Toyota sat in the drive to their left. The ranch-style brick home stretched across the middle of the property, and Sarah knew the backyard would extend down to the edge of the lake.

"Looks like someone's here," Gavin said.

"My mom used to bring us here," she said softly. "My brothers and me."

"Here?"

"Well, to the public access area. We didn't have a boat, but we would spend hours swimming and playing in the sand on the beach area."

"Not your dad?"

She grimaced. "The general was never a *dad*. He didn't have time for such *frivolity*."

"His word, I presume?"

"Sure wasn't mine."

She opened her door and stepped out. A

175

thought hit her and she walked around to look at the driver's side of the truck.

"What are you doing?" he asked.

"Just noticing something."

"What's that?"

"The bullet holes. They're all on your side."

Gavin looked. And frowned. "Yeah. I suppose it is kinda weird," he muttered, shooting another look at the truck. "Maybe because I went into a spin, I took the bullets meant for your side."

"They were shooting before you were spinning." Right? Or, had they been spinning first? She'd have thought the moment would have been etched in her memory, but she honestly couldn't remember.

He shook his head. "One thing at a time."

"Right. Brianne."

He followed her up the short walkway to the front door, stood behind her — close enough for her to feel the warmth of his chest against her back — and waited while she rang the bell.

She shifted, putting a few inches between them, his nearness unsettling. A brief flash of the kiss they'd shared in Kabul zipped across her mind, and heat crept into her cheeks.

Gavin turned sideways, his head on a

swivel. "It's a nice place. Quiet."

"I wouldn't mind having something like this one day." Good idea. Talk about anything that would take her mind off the fact that she severely regretted there couldn't be anything romantic between them.

"Why one day? Why not now?"

She shrugged. "I wouldn't have time to take care of it like I'd want to. At least I wouldn't have when I was deployed." She jabbed the doorbell again and scowled. Now that she'd been discharged, it was a very real possibility that she could have a home like this. One day. After she got herself back in the Army — and separate when it was *her* choice to leave. She glanced at him. "What about you? Where do you live?"

"I have a small house not too far from my parents. My dad's been kind enough to keep the yard up for me. I've gone by a few times while you've slept, and Caden's been around to keep an eye on things."

"You mean me."

"Only in the sense that he's got your back."

She nodded. "He does. I've never had to worry about that."

"I've got your back too, Sarah."

His words washed over her. Warming her. "Thanks." So, not only did his nearness affect her, the look in his eyes was doing odd things to her pulse. "Okay," she said, clearing her throat, "there are two cars in the drive, but no one's answering the doorbell."

"Maybe they went for a walk."

"Or they could be out on the lake."

"It's too cold to swim."

"Maybe, but it's never too cold to boat and fish. Just like it's never too chilly to eat ice cream."

"True."

Sarah stepped off the porch and followed the stone path around to the garage where she looked in the window. "Hey, there's a car in here too."

"Probably Brianne's."

"Then who do the other cars belong to? One to the friend and one to . . ." She shrugged. "Could be another friend or family member visiting, I guess."

"Could be."

She continued around the side of the house to the backyard. Once again, Gavin followed. A large deck extended from the back door, and she walked up the steps to rap on the glass. "Hello? Brianne? Are you here?"

"The boat is tied to the dock," Gavin said, "so they're not on the lake. In that anyway."

Sarah went to the window. The blinds had

been pulled up and she cupped her hands next to her temples to look in. A gasp slipped from her. "Gavin, there's someone on the floor, and I see something that sure looks like blood." She pounded on the window. "Ma'am? Can you hear me?" Nothing.

He peered in. "Call 911."

Sarah grabbed her phone from the back pocket of her jeans and dialed while Gavin rammed a shoulder against the door. Once. Twice. With the third hit, it swung inward, ripping the safety chain from the frame and sending it across the room.

Sarah rattled off the information to the 911 dispatcher while Gavin rushed to the fallen woman's side. Sarah stepped closer. "That's not Brianne."

"She's been shot." Gavin pressed two fingers to her neck. "I have a pulse. Quick, grab a towel from the kitchen but touch as little as possible getting it."

Sarah stuck her phone in her pocket and bolted toward the kitchen, ignoring the squawking from the dispatcher and the pain the quick movement sent through her side. She snagged the hand towel hanging on the oven door. When she turned, her elbow knocked into a pill bottle on the counter. The top popped off and pills rolled out.

She darted back to Gavin, and he folded the cloth, then pressed it to the woman's chest. "Thanks."

"I knocked over a pill bottle."

"Just leave them. We'll tell the officers what happened when they get here. You see any gloves?"

"Not yet. I'll look."

Opening and closing the drawers with the hem of her shirt just in case there were prints left by whoever shot the woman, she finally found a box of rubber gloves. She pulled four out and yanked two over her hands, grabbed another hand towel, then rushed back to Gavin and handed him the gloves. "Might as well use them if you have them."

"Thanks." He pulled them on. "Stay here with her and press on the wound. She's lost a lot of blood, but her pulse is steady, and if we can get her to the hospital, I think she'll be okay. I'm going to check the rest of the house."

"You think whoever did this is still here?"

"Need to figure that out and see if Brianne's back there."

Sarah nodded. "Go, I've got this." She replaced the bloody towel with the clean one and pressed. Prayers whispered from her lips. The sirens in the distance sent relief

180

shooting through her. The woman moaned and her eyelids flickered.

"Hey," Sarah said, "help is almost here. You're going to be okay."

Another soft moan, but the woman's lashes never lifted.

Belatedly, she remembered the dispatcher and lifted her phone to her ear. "Did you hear all of that?"

"I heard. How's she doing?"

"She's still breathing, but I'm not a doctor, so it's hard for me to —"

A sound behind Sarah snagged her attention, and she glanced over her shoulder to see a man step out of the closet next to the back door. For a moment, her throat froze. His dark eyes locked on hers, his gaze startled, surprised. He backed toward the door, then hesitated. Cursed.

Paralysis fled. "Gavin!"

He lunged at her. Sarah lurched sideways. Her heel caught the edge of the rug and she stumbled, sending her phone flying and her hip crashing onto the hardwood floor. Pain arched through her and she gasped even as she tried to roll.

Hard hands stopped her and yanked her to her feet. A gun pressed against her temple and a forearm jammed against her throat, choking off her scream.

Sirens reached her ears over the pounding drum of her heart.

"Put the gun down!" Gavin swept into the room, his own weapon raised, aimed at the man behind her.

"She's coming with me. Back off. Back up!"

"What do you want?" Gavin asked.

"I just want to leave."

"You shot them."

Sarah gasped in spite of the pressure against her throat. Them?

"No! They were dead when I got here."

She flinched. *They.*

"You were stealing her jewelry," Gavin said, "and whatever else you could get your hands on." His gaze flicked to the still-bleeding woman on the floor.

"Yeah, yeah, I was stealing, but I didn't kill them!" Her captor's breathing came in harsh spurts next to her ear as he pulled her toward the door she and Gavin had entered just a bit ago. "But no one's going to believe that. I'm finished now. I gotta get out of here. Gotta get out of here. Gotta get out of here."

Gavin stepped forward from the hallway, eyes narrowed, jaw locked, weapon steady. While Sarah's terror had shot her adrenaline into the stratosphere, something about

Gavin's expression gave her comfort. Hope. If she couldn't think of a way to escape, he'd get her out of this. He was a rescuer. It was what he did.

Right? Oh please be right.

The muzzle pressed harder against her temple and the man behind her shifted. "Back up! Back up!"

She wasn't sure if he was telling her to do that or warning Gavin, but Gavin stilled and her captor moved. She churned her feet to keep from sagging against the already too tight pressure against her throat. Should she try to tell him the woman was still alive? No, if he thought she could identify him, he might decide to finish her off.

Gavin continued to stalk them, his weapon steady.

She looked at Brianne's friend, then back at Gavin. "Help her," she mouthed.

His lips tightened even more, but he didn't look away from the man behind her.

The sound of the sirens grew louder and his arm spasmed. Hard. She gagged, coughed. Pain lanced her side, but she kept her eyes on Gavin while dragging in shallow breaths. Sarah could feel the man's heart pounding against her back. Or was that hers?

"Okay. Here's the plan," he said. "My car

is in the driveway. We're going to get in it, and I'll drive away, then let you go. Yeah, that's what I'll do. That's the plan. Let's go."

He pulled her outside onto the deck and down the three wooden steps to the grass. An officer rounded the side of the house followed by two paramedics. The man holding her froze, his harsh breathing almost sobs. "No, no, no."

The cop spotted the weapon and pulled his. "Gun! Put the gun down!" He waved the paramedics back while he ducked out of sight against the siding. "Put the weapon down! Put it down!"

A chorus of the same words from other out-of-sight officers echoed around her. How many were there? *A lot, please be a lot.*

Gavin hovered in the doorway, watching, his hand gripping his weapon at his side.

"Stop! Stay there!" The man shook, his fear strong. "Nobody come any closer!"

Her eyes caught Gavin's once more. He needed to stay with the wounded woman inside and keep pressure on her wound and he knew it but was torn.

"Go," she mouthed. "Go."

He frowned, looked over his shoulder, then back to her.

"Gotta get out of here," the man behind

her muttered. "Gotta get out of here."

"Calm down," she whispered.

"What? What'd you say?"

"Please. Calm down." If he jerked or twitched or fell, she was dead. *Don't think about that. Just breathe.* "I'll help you." Sarah continued to focus on breathing while dark spots danced in front of her eyes. Her captor kept her between himself and the officers he could see. "What's . . . ," Sarah wheezed, ". . . your name?"

"Shut up. Oh man, this is crazy. This wasn't supposed to happen."

"Please, tell me your name."

"Sam! My name's Sam, now shut it. I need to *think*. Why can't I think?"

His panicked breaths echoed in her ear and his grip slipped a fraction. Just enough to let her drag in a lungful of much-needed air before his hold tightened again.

Escape scenarios zipped through her mind. Unfortunately, all of them ended with her dead.

CHAPTER THIRTEEN

As soon as Gavin saw the officers had their weapons trained on the man called Sam, he put his own weapon away. He didn't need them worried about him and his gun too.

Sarah had told him to go to the woman, make sure she was okay, but he couldn't leave. A glance back told him the wounded woman was still breathing. Barely.

Right now, he was just inside the door, trying to avoid being a target should someone decide to start shooting, but close enough to keep Sarah in his sight. However . . .

He raced to the front door and threw it open. At least the paramedics could come in and take care of the woman. He knelt next to her to check her pulse. Slow and thready. Faint. And the blood flow had slowed. He bolted back to the door onto the deck — and Sarah — and stepped outside onto the wood.

"You!"

Gavin turned. Two officers had entered the doorway Gavin had broken through. Both cops held their weapons steady and trained on Gavin.

"I'm one of the good guys. My ID is in my back pocket."

"Keep your hands where I can see them."

Gavin held his hands in the air, only slightly comforted that the cops had the man holding Sarah surrounded. "There's a woman in here who's been shot but is still alive. She needs help now or she's going to die!" If she hadn't already. "Let the paramedics in."

"Check it out, Pete. I've got this guy covered." Pete slipped behind the cop holding his weapon on Gavin and into the house. "On your knees, now!"

Gavin went to his knees, keeping his hands where the officer could see them. His position allowed him a good view through the deck spindles, and he kept his gaze on the man holding Sarah. *Think, think!*

Gavin noted another officer coming up on Sarah and her captor's flank and taking cover behind a tree. "Give it up, Sam," Gavin called. "Look around. You're surrounded and not going anywhere. Why don't you make this easier on yourself and just let her go?"

"Dude," the officer who had his weapon trained on Gavin said, "shut up and let us work. Stay down and be quiet."

"Of course." Unless it meant rescuing Sarah. Paramedics were already working on Brianne's friend, so that was one worry off his plate. "The guy's name is Sam," he said. "He claims he didn't shoot the two women inside. He was burglarizing the place and panicked."

"Good to know. I'll pass that on to the negotiator. Now stay put."

Sarah's attacker swiveled, pulling her with him, the gun never wavering from her temple. "I don't want to hurt her, but I will. I'm not going to prison! I don't know why I'm doing this. Why am I doing this? Ahh!" He glanced at Gavin, who still knelt on the deck floor. "Tell them to get back! Tell them!" Sweat poured down from the man's temples.

"I'm not a cop," he said. "But things will go a lot easier for you if you just put the gun down and let Sarah go." He used her name hoping it would make her a real person to him. "Her name's Sarah. She has a brother and a dad who want her to come home without another bullet hole."

"Shut up! Shut up! I was just doing a

favor for someone. This wasn't supposed to happen! Why is this happening?"

Gavin noticed the guy's eyes. Thought about the pinpoint pupils he'd noticed earlier in the initial confrontation. Sweating. Agitated. It wasn't withdrawal, he was on something.

From his vantage point of still being sprawled on the deck a mere ten feet away from Sarah and the gunman, Gavin could see two officers to the side of the house communicating with one another once again. He'd give anything to have an earpiece to hear what they were planning.

Something tapped his shoe and he jerked. Looked back to see the officer motioning him inside. He scooted back until he was inside. The cop still held his gun on him.

"My name's Gavin Black. I'm with Black Ops Security. The woman being held hostage is one of my clients because I dropped my guard." *Stupid, stupid.* He should have checked the closet.

"ID?"

Gavin carefully removed his wallet and tossed it to the man, who caught it midair. He gave it a quick once-over. "Military, huh?"

"Yeah. Three tours in the Middle East."

"Special Forces, I'm assuming."

189

"Part of the time, yeah."

The officer hesitated, glanced at his partner, who was supervising the paramedics loading the woman on the gurney. "All right. Let's get you out of here."

Gavin shook his head. "I'll let you guys do your job, but I'm not going anywhere until I know Sarah's safe." Right now, he still had a view of the weapon and Sarah. "Is SWAT here?" he asked.

"Yeah. We actually have a guy with us who's a fill-in sniper on the SWAT team when they need someone. He's the one on the roof."

Gavin let his gaze scan the tops of the nearby houses and finally spotted an officer on top of the house next door, a rifle to his shoulder.

Gavin swung his attention back to Sarah and found her attacker had turned, allowing Sarah to see him. Her gaze locked on Gavin's. The terror in her eyes seared him, but the hint of steel mixed with it encouraged him. She'd be okay. She had to be. *God, don't let him pull that trigger. On purpose or by accident. Please.*

The man shifted once more, trying to see where the officers were. He spotted the nearest one and removed the weapon from

Sarah to point it at the cop. "I said get back!"

Sarah slammed the back of her head against his chin.

Her captor jerked, stumbled away from her, even as he turned his weapon back toward her.

He fired as Sarah dove for the ground.

Gavin let out a harsh cry and shot to his feet and out onto the deck, ignoring the shout of the officer behind him.

The rifle on the roof popped and the gunman went down just as Gavin vaulted over the side toward Sarah — who was scrambling to get out of the way.

He bolted toward her while the officer behind him yelled at him to get down. The others raced for the gunman. Gavin dropped to his knees beside Sarah while two officers cuffed the bleeding man.

"Are you okay?" Gavin demanded, looking for a bullet wound — another one — and finding nothing new. The shot had missed her.

"My ears are ringing," she said, "and my side hurts, but we're both alive, so I'm pretty much okay with that." She shuddered, looked at the officer. "You can stop pointing that at him. He's a good guy."

The officer didn't lower his weapon until

his partner gave the all clear. Gavin pulled Sarah into a loose hug.

"Did you find Brianne?" she asked.

He shuddered. "I did. At least I assume it's her."

"And?"

"She's dead," he murmured. "Gunshot to the head."

"I was afraid of that." Sarah bit her lip and looked away, blinking hard. "I'll take a look and make sure."

"No, you don't want to see that."

"I need to. I can tell you if it's her or not. If it's not, then we need to find her." Sarah pushed away from him, and he followed her into the house and down the hall. She took one look and gasped. "That's her."

Gavin took her back into his arms, relieved that she let him.

"We were too late," she mumbled against his chest. "Too late."

"We tried."

"Did *he* kill them?"

"I don't know. The ME will have to do her job and the cops will do theirs before we'll know that."

"Of course." She swallowed. "Thank you for not leaving me," she said, her voice soft, barely there. "Knowing you were there, behind him, behind *us,* kept me from losing it."

He leaned back and she looked up at him. He brushed strands of hair from her eyes. "Something's going on, Sarah. Something . . . weird."

"I know."

"And somehow we've landed right in the middle of it."

"Yeah, I think I've kind of figured that out."

Caden paced the small area just outside Sam Wilmont's hospital room. The man had come through the ninety-minute surgery to remove the bullet and bone fragments with no complications. Now Caden just needed him to wake up. The SWAT member who'd pulled the trigger had had to aim for the shoulder since he couldn't get a good bead on Wilmont's head. With Sarah's timely headbutt, the risky shot had worked, and that's all that mattered to Caden at the moment.

As much as he would like to get his hands around the man's throat, he wanted to talk to him more. He needed answers and he needed them yesterday. But he'd have to play it cool if he wanted to stay anywhere near this case. Wilmont's actions had connected Sarah to the case, which made things awkward for him and for the other detectives. It had been all he could do to convince his supervisor that he could exercise self-control and be objective. He wouldn't be surprised if they asked him to step away.

Detective Caroline Attwood and her partner Elliott Bancroft were the official lead investigators, but Caden was hoping they'd at least fill him in on whatever they learned. Elliott approached, with Caroline following a few steps behind him.

Caden shook Elliott's proffered hand. "Thanks for letting me be here."

"Your sister is the victim?"

"Along with two other women. One is still in surgery, the other is in the morgue downstairs."

"Sorry to hear that," Caroline said.

"We — as in my family — are hoping Brianne Davis's friend, Michelle Nelson, will be able to tell us what happened in that house."

"You think Wilmont's good for the shootings?"

"He was in the house with a gun. Then he pulled that gun on my sister and held her hostage. Until someone proves differently, he's good for them."

"All right, then. Brianne's family is here.

As is the family of Mrs. Nelson. We've asked them to stay and answer questions. They're desperate for answers, as you can imagine."

"Of course."

"We'll keep you updated."

"I'd appreciate that." He paused. "Do you mind if I talk to Brianne's family? I've already talked to her father once, but I'd like to express my condolences and ask him a few more questions if he's up to it."

"Fine with me," Elliott said. Caroline nodded.

"Thanks." Caden was grateful for two detectives who didn't mind keeping him in the loop. It allowed him to breathe a little easier, knowing he wasn't going to have to fight tooth and nail for information.

Sarah was on the second floor getting checked out, and Gavin had opted to stay with her while Caden waited for Wilmont to wake up. He shook his head, finding it unbelievable that Sarah would once again be involved in a hostage situation. She'd certainly defied all the odds in a very short span of time.

"What's the background on this guy?" Caden asked. He knew the detectives would have done their homework before coming — or on the way.

"Wilmont has a record, but nothing like

this," Elliott said. "Up to now, he's been small time. Shoplifting, car theft, but not carjacking, petty theft, vandalism, et cetera. He's never hurt or *threatened* to hurt anyone." He paused. "And it's interesting. Over the last year, he appeared to clean up his act, got a job at the VA hospital as an orderly. He hasn't missed a day since he started and has gotten good reviews from his supervisors and patients."

"So, this was a big leap."

"Huge."

"Another thing," Caroline said. "They also found pills in his pocket that matched the pills in the house, so he may have been high when all of this went down."

"Sounds like the pills may have been too big of a temptation for a former addict to resist," Caden said.

Elliott raised a brow. "Looks like that might have been the case. How'd he get a job at a hospital, of all places?"

Caden shook his head. "I don't know. It's possible someone did someone a favor and got him hired. Who knows? Have you talked to Sarah yet?"

"No." Caroline glanced at her phone and tapped the screen, sending a caller to voice mail. "The doctor was with her, so we decided to come check on Wilmont."

"I talked to her briefly when they first brought her in. She started going step by step through what happened at the house, so I recorded it with her permission. I can send it to you if you want it."

"Absolutely." Elliott gave Caden his number, and Caden sent the man the file.

"If you need anything more than that," Caden said, tucking his phone back into the clip on his belt, "I know she'll be happy to cooperate."

"Good. We'll have a few more questions after we listen."

"Sounds like my sister has a lot to be thankful for." Caden swallowed the sudden surge of emotion and turned when Wilmont's door opened.

The nurse exited and looked at the three of them. "He's groggy, but awake."

Elliott nodded to Caden. "Let's see what this guy has to say for himself."

They were going to let him listen in? It was more than he'd hoped for. "Thank you." He followed them into the room. Wilmont lay on the bed, looking rough, his pale cheeks discernible from the white pillow only by the freckles that dotted his nose. His red hair spiked in all directions and his eyes were closed.

"Hey, Sam," Caroline said. "Can you

197

wake up a minute?"

"Go 'way," he muttered.

"Wake up. Now!" Caroline gave his foot a hard nudge.

Wilmont grunted, but he blinked and pried his eyes open before they fell shut again.

"Sam, we're not going away," Elliott said. "You might as well wake up and tell us why you shot those two ladies."

The man frowned and shook his head, even though his eyes remained closed. "What are you talking about? I didn't shoot anyone."

"The doors were locked from the inside," Caden said to Elliott. "Gavin had to break in to get to Mrs. Nelson."

Elliott gave a short nod. "Come on, why'd you shoot them?"

A flush crept into Wilmont's cheeks. And finally, his eyes opened a crack. "I'm telling you, I didn't shoot anyone."

"You had a gun. You took a hostage."

"What? I didn't. I . . . I was just . . . I . . . where am I? What's going on?" He licked his lips. "Water? Please?"

Caden took the cup from the tray and held it to Wilmont's lips.

The man took a long draw and sighed. "Thanks."

"Why'd you take the gun?" Caden asked. He shot a look at the two detectives and stepped back. "Sorry. Forgot my place."

Elliott allowed a small smile to curve his lips, then turned his attention back to Wilmont. "Well? Answer the man. Why'd you take the gun?"

"What gun? I didn't take a gun. I was . . . I was . . ." He licked his lips and squinted. "What was I doing again? Why am I here?"

The detectives exchanged a glance.

Caden rubbed a hand down his jaw. "You don't remember what happened?"

"I remember going to the house and then . . ." He shook his head. "I don't know. It's a blank." Fear flashed in his eyes.

Something wasn't right. The guy wasn't faking.

"You took a gun and shot two people," Elliott said.

That pulled him fully out from under the anesthesia. His eyes widened and he gasped. Choked. "Wha— ? No! No way. I wouldn't. I didn't!"

"Let's get a doctor in here," Elliott said. "We may have to question him after the doctor checks him."

Caden stepped into the hall and found the nurse, made the request for the doctor to put in an appearance, and returned to the room.

"He wants to continue," Elliott said.

Caden wasn't sure that was smart, but didn't buck the detectives.

"We had him checked for gunshot residue," Elliott said to Caden. "But I haven't heard the results yet."

"All right," Caroline said, "let's say I believe you and you didn't shoot those two ladies." Her expression said she believed anything but. "Then what were you doing at the house and why were you hiding in the closet?"

Wilmont lifted a hand to his right temple and squinted. "Um. The house. Oh yeah. I remember the house. I was there to deliver some drugs."

"Do tell," Elliott said.

A flush darkened Wilmont's cheeks, and he blinked, his eyes clearing a bit. "Not like that. The lady, Brianne, had left her pain pills at the hospital. Max found them and asked me to bring them to her."

"Max?"

"The old guy at the hospital. He does a lot of cleaning around the place. Her address was right there on the pill bottle, so Max asked me to take them to her."

"What happened when you got there?"

"I . . ." He blinked. "I don't know." His

eyes darted from one detective to the other and finally landed on Caden. "Why can't I remember?" He took a deep breath and his lashes fluttered, but he kept his eyes open.

"Did you take anything before you went?" Caden asked.

"Wha— no."

His eyes shifted and Caden pounced. "I think you did. You were on something. What was it?"

"Nothing. Noth—"

"We found two pills in your pocket," Elliott said. "They match the ones that were in the bottle on the counter. We counted and guess how many are missing?"

Wilmont shifted. "I took them. I saw her on the floor and it messed me up. I was scared. I needed something . . . anything to help me deal with what I was seeing. And I didn't figure she'd miss them."

"Wow. Compassionate guy, aren't you?" Caroline muttered. "So, you took two and kept two for later?"

"Yeah." Wilmont frowned. "I remember taking them, but after that everything kind of goes fuzzy. I know one thing, I didn't shoot anyone."

The door opened and the doctor entered. The stitching on his white coat read DR.

MILES JANSEN, MD. "Everything okay in here?"

"Not really," Caroline said. "The suspect says he doesn't remember shooting our two victims."

"I didn't! I didn't shoot anyone! Why do you keep saying that?"

Dr. Jansen removed the stethoscope from his neck and eyed the monitors showing Wilmont's vitals. "Heart rate's up. He's really agitated."

"Yeah, well, he shot two people, killed one, and got caught," Elliott said. "I'd say he has good reason to be agitated."

"Right." The doctor continued his examination.

"So how'd you get in the house, Sam?" Caroline asked. "All the doors were locked. The guy that found them —"

"Gavin," Caden said.

"Gavin had to break down the door."

Wilmont's breathing increased and he shifted under the sheet. The doctor shot them a warning look. "If this continues, I'll have to ask you to leave."

"No," Wilmont said, "I want to finish this."

The doctor shrugged. "Go ahead."

Wilmont squinted, thinking. "I went around to the back and knocked. No one came to the door, so I tried it and it was unlocked. I walked in and . . . and . . ." He let out a grunt. "I don't know! I don't know!"

His head snapped back, the monitor went wild, and the doctor bolted to Wilmont's side. "He's seizing! You three, get out!" The two detectives and Caden backed out of the room while the doctor shouted for a crash cart.

Caden stood in the hallway with Elliott and Caroline. "What do you guys think?"

Elliott shook his head. "I don't know. He sounded sincere enough. Like he really didn't know what we were talking about, but I've come across some pretty convincing liars in my years on the force. I'm not fully sold that he wasn't yanking our chain so he can get off on some insanity defense or whatnot."

Caroline looked up from her phone. "If the guy was high on something, he might really not remember going into that house and killing one and putting the other in surgery."

Her partner rubbed his eyes. "Yeah."

"Which was probably why he couldn't resist the drugs," Caden said.

Elliott scowled. "Someone's head is going to roll if it's found out they hired an ex–drug addict to work in this hospital. I don't

203

care how clean he was when they hired him."

"He'd have to pass a drug test," Caroline said. "Maybe he really was clean and the scene at the house freaked him out so much, he relapsed."

Elliott grunted. "Didn't freak him out enough to do the right thing and call for help. Instead, he decided to burglarize the place."

"Yeah." Caden couldn't argue with that. He leaned against the wall and crossed his arms. "One thing I don't understand. The door was locked when Gavin and Sarah arrived. Gavin had to break the door down to get in. This guy was inside hiding in the closet. Why was the door locked if it was really *un*locked when he got there?"

Caroline raised a brow. "Maybe he locked it when he heard Gavin and Sarah drive up, thinking it would discourage them and they'd leave."

A reasonable explanation. Caden sighed. "We may never know." He glanced at the room. "I just hope he makes it. And I'm surprised I'm even saying this, but I'll be honest. His story rings true to me."

"That he didn't shoot the ladies or that he just doesn't remember?" Elliott asked.

"That he doesn't remember. But if he

really didn't shoot them, then who did?"

"I don't know." Caroline tucked her phone onto the clip on her belt. "But I'd like to talk to this Max person and get his take on Wilmont. He obviously trusted him enough to send him to deliver the drugs."

"The question is," Caden said, "did he know Wilmont's history when he asked him to run his little errand?"

Caroline shrugged. "Like I said, I want to find him and talk to him."

Elliott nodded. "We'll track him down and see what he has to say." He shook Caden's hand. "We'll keep you posted."

CHAPTER FOURTEEN

"You told her about the threats?" Sitting behind the wheel of his luxury Mercedes E300 sedan, Lewis Denning looked like he might stroke out all over his cream-colored leather seat. He'd texted that he needed to speak to Gavin but didn't want to risk pulling Gavin away from Sarah while Caden wasn't home.

Gavin had slipped out of the house shortly after Sarah drifted off in front of the television.

"You hired me to keep her safe," Gavin said. "Telling her about the threats was the right thing to do — and played a part in helping me keep her safe."

"If she finds out about my role in all of this —"

"I'm aware, sir. She has no idea you hired me, and I plan to keep it that way." For now.

Denning rubbed a hand down his cheek. "She thinks the worst of me. She hates me for what I've done, doesn't she?"

Gavin hesitated, then gave a mental shrug. The man had asked. "Yes, sir, I believe she does."

Denning winced. "Well, at least I don't have to worry about you pulling punches and kowtowing, do I?"

A laugh slipped from him. "No sir, you'll never have to worry about that. I respect you and your position, of course, but I'm no longer in the service, so . . ." He shrugged.

"So you don't have to pucker up anymore?"

"That's one way of putting it."

The general laughed. "I have a feeling you never were the kind to kiss anyone's rear end." A pause. "Good for you."

Gavin shot him an amused look. The man never ceased to amaze him. Honestly, he liked the general — didn't agree with his methods in handling things, but liked him — and wished he and Sarah could find a way to settle their differences, but right now, he didn't see it happening. "Have you thought about apologizing to her?"

"No."

"Then don't expect a reconciliation anytime soon."

"I don't." The man paused. "It's more

complicated than just an apology."

"Maybe so, but it's probably a good place to start."

The general shook his head. "You don't know. You just don't know. She's a rebellious punk. Always has been, always will be apparently."

"I don't believe that. I don't see that at all."

"Then you're blind. I see it and I won't accept it — or deal with it."

Even with the hard-hearted attitude, Gavin could sense the pain beneath it. Interesting. He didn't want to ask the man to explain what he meant. Sarah had already promised to tell him. He owed it to her to let her do it. "Why can't you tell her you love her?"

The general flinched. "She knows I do."

"No sir, she doesn't. And she doesn't think you have any respect for her — as a woman or as someone who chose the Army as a career."

"Respect? No, not much respect, that would be correct."

He bit his tongue on the desire to ask *why*. Again, he had a feeling that was all related to what Sarah promised to tell him. "But you love her."

"She's my child. Of course I do." He

sighed and threw up a hand. "You sound like Caden." Gavin raised a brow and the man's jaw tightened. "I'm just trying to protect her."

"I understand that, but you might want to go about it a little differently."

"You and Caden decided to gang up on me about this, didn't you?"

"No sir. I don't suppose it's really my business, so you can forget I said anything."

The man grunted. "You think she'll ever forgive me?"

"I can't say. But you and I both know forgiveness comes easier when it's asked for, so you might want to rethink that apology." Gavin reached for the door handle. "Then again, I have a feeling Sarah doesn't do things the easy way, so you might be off the hook. Eventually. On that note, I'm going to scope the perimeter and get back inside before she wakes up." He hesitated. "I really think we ought to tell her the truth about what I'm doing."

"No. Not yet. If she kicks you to the curb, she'll be a sitting duck for whoever's after her. I'd rather have her hate me forever than have her get killed because of her stubborn, bullheaded . . . ." He stopped and drew in a breath. "Never mind. Just keep her safe. That's all that matters."

"Yes sir, we can agree on that."

Gavin stepped out of the vehicle and headed back toward the house, his nerves twitching. Before he had a chance to figure out why he was so on edge, Caden drove up and parked in the drive. He climbed out of the vehicle.

When he spotted his father's car, his eyes narrowed and he frowned. "Everything all right?"

"Sarah's sleeping. The general and I were having a little meeting."

"She's going to kill you — both of you — when she finds out about this, you know."

Gavin grimaced. "I know."

The general rolled his window up, shook his head, and drove off.

"I'd take over being the watchdog if I could," Caden said, leaning against his car.

"You don't have the time," Gavin said. "And besides, this is what I do. It's my job."

"But she's *my* sister."

"Which is why it's probably better that I'm the lead on this one."

"The lead, huh?"

"Come on, man, like you said, she's your sister. You want to encase her in bubble wrap and lock her away until it's safe to come out." That actually sounded like a good idea to him too.

Caden smiled. "Yeah, but I don't think that'd go over very well."

"Exactly. Which is why I'm here."

"You care for her, don't you?"

"Sure, the more I get to know her, the more I can see us being friends."

Caden chuckled.

"What?" Gavin asked.

"You might want to be friends, but you want more than that. When I say you care for her, I mean you *care* for her."

Gavin met his eyes. "What makes you say that?"

"Because of the way you look at her when you think no one's watching. And the fact that you were here before my father *asked* you to be here."

"Hmm." He'd have to work on hiding his emotions a little better.

"Hmm," Caden echoed.

"Shut up, man."

Caden laughed, then sobered. "Just so you know, I approve."

"Well, I'm afraid Sarah doesn't." Yet.

"Why not? What'd you do?"

"You want the list?"

"There's a list?"

Gavin grimaced.

"But she's let you stay around since . . . everything. So that's good, right?"

211

"It's very good." Odd, actually. Then again, he hadn't really given her a choice. He'd just . . . stayed.

"She thinks you're too much like our dad, doesn't she?"

Gavin blinked. "So, you're a mind reader?"

"No, a sister reader." His brows drew together over the bridge of his nose. "She had it tough in high school. Made a lot of lousy choices that resulted in consequences she can't shake to this day."

"She said something about that. Said she'd tell me about it soon."

Caden's brow reached record heights. "She did? Well, then you're more special than you think you are." He paused. "She hasn't dated many guys. Really dated. Like longer than one date. There was one guy in college she decided to let her guard down with who was a jerk. Another guy in the Army dumped her when he got promoted — so I guess make that two jerks."

"Dumped *her*? Was he crazy?"

"Greedy. The general had a hand in the promotion. Thought he was helping out his future son-in-law. When the future son-in-law didn't need either of them anymore, he said goodbye."

"Ouch."

"After that, she kind of swore off guys and focused on her career."

Gavin blew out a low breath. "A career she no longer has, thanks to her own father."

"Right. I tried talking to him, but he wouldn't listen."

"I did too. He accused me of collaborating with you and ganging up on him."

This time it was Caden who grimaced. "He's stubborn."

"A family trait apparently."

"I believe we've already established that."

Gavin rubbed a hand over his jaw. "Is Sarah going to be okay with you telling me this stuff?"

"I didn't tell you so you could rat me out." He sighed. "I want Sarah to be happy. I'm just trying to help you understand her a little."

"I'll take all the help I can get in that regard," Gavin said.

"And if you break her heart, I know places to bury a body that no one would find."

Gavin wasn't sure whether to laugh or not. He met the man's eyes — and decided not to laugh. "What happens if she's the one who breaks mine?" She'd almost done it once. While she hadn't *broken* it before, she'd sure left it hurting.

Caden clapped him on the bicep. "Then

we can drown our sorrows together."

"*Our* sorrows? Who broke your heart?"

Caden shook his head. "That's a story for another day." He nodded to the porch. "Looks like Sleeping Beauty has awakened."

Sarah stood on the porch, arms crossed, eyes narrowed. Gavin gulped. How long had she been there?

Sarah sat on Caden's couch and sipped a mug of hot coffee loaded with creamer and three sugars while she only halfway pondered the information her brother had just passed on. She was still curious about whatever it was she'd interrupted when she'd stepped outside. He and Gavin had been immersed in conversation when she opened the door. So deep it had taken Caden a moment to notice her. Whatever they'd been talking about, she had the strangest feeling it had something to do with her.

Unsure what *she* had to do with *them* drowning their sorrows, she'd let it go and demanded every last piece of information Caden had acquired. He'd been forthcoming, and now she had even more questions.

She focused back on Caden. "So, let me get this straight. Wilmont had a seizure and is in a medically induced coma?"

"For now."

"And you believe his whole 'I'm innocent, I didn't do it' routine?"

"Somewhat."

"In case you forgot, he held a gun to my head." She could still feel the press of the weapon against her temple. A shudder rippled through her.

"Trust me, I haven't forgotten," Caden said. "He's guilty of that for sure, but that doesn't mean he shot the ladies."

Her gaze flicked back and forth between the men. They both looked at her with expressions that said they were worried she might snap at any moment. Great. "All right. Let's recap. I was kidnapped in Kabul, discharged from the Army unfairly — and probably illegally — thanks to my father and that spineless psychiatrist. I ran into a woman in restraints who said that she knew too much and they were going to kill her, overheard Dr. Kilgore and another man talking about something that sounded suspicious to me because they used phrases like 'she's better off' and 'the other girl was so drugged up, I doubt she'll remember anything' and —"

"And," Gavin said, "you think they were talking about you."

"Who else?"

215

"Another patient?"

She shook her head. "No. And Brianne kept calling for a guy named Max."

"Max?" Caden asked. "That's the name of the guy Wilmont said asked him to deliver the pills to Brianne."

She frowned. "So, who is he?"

"I don't know. Elliott and Caroline said they'd look into locating him." He tapped a message into his phone, then looked up.

Sarah picked up where she'd left off. "Dr. Kilgore also said that if his phone fell into the wrong hands, he'd be in trouble."

"Sarah —"

"I wasn't drugged up. I'd quit taking the meds and was quite lucid, thank you very much. Except for the fever making me a bit light-headed. And then there was the mention of a package . . ."

"What package?"

"Beats me. They said something about a package and that it would turn up eventually."

Caden frowned. "I don't want to disagree with you, but I feel like I need to play devil's advocate here. All of that could have multiple meanings. I think you're reading more into it than is there."

"I suppose I imagined someone shooting at us and the bullet holes in Gavin's truck

216

are just figments of that imagination," she snapped.

"No, not at all," Caden said, holding up a hand in a gesture of peace, "that's not —"

"And Brianne is now dead," Sarah went on, "her friend fighting for her life, and a guy with a gun tried to use me as leverage to get away from the scene of it all. I suppose I imagined that as well?"

"Sarah, come on. Of course not. That's not what I'm saying."

"Then why don't you say what you're saying so I can understand it?"

Caden raked a hand through his hair and glanced at Gavin. Sarah cleared her throat. Gavin's lips twitched.

"No bro-language going on here," Gavin said. "I happen to agree with Sarah."

She blinked. "Well, thank you."

"Look," Caden said, "the general asked me not to say anything, but I think you need to know a few details that might help make things a little more clear."

Gavin cleared his throat. "I . . . uh . . . told her about the threats, if that's what you're referring to."

Caden frowned. "You did?"

He shrugged. "It was a judgment call at the moment."

"All right." Caden drew the words out

slowly, as though trying to decide whether he was okay with that or not.

"Have they figured out where the threats are coming from? Like narrowed it down to a specific person?" Sarah asked.

"That's what he's trying to determine. It's probably Hibatullah Omar."

"Omar!" She gaped. "I thought he was dead."

"We all did," Gavin muttered.

Caden cleared his throat. "To be honest, I don't care who's making the threats. All I care about is that even though they never directly included us in that threat, we're going to assume it's there. Everything is being investigated very thoroughly."

"By who?" Sarah asked. "The general?"

"Yes. Or rather, CID, but I'm sure he has his finger on the pulse."

She nodded. "Ever since Gavin mentioned the threats, I keep circling back to Dustin's death. If they're coming after me, they could have been after him. Set his death up to look like a suicide. Right?"

Caden grimaced and exchanged another glance with Gavin.

"What?"

"We've already discussed that and decided that wasn't likely."

"*You've* already discussed that? Is there a

reason I wasn't in on the discussion?"

"Come on, Sarah," Gavin said softly. "You were sick, passed out, or high on painkillers. When would we have discussed it with you?"

"I don't know. When we were getting shot at out on the highway?" He raised a brow and she sighed and looked back and forth between the men. "So, all that stuff in the hospital. You really think I've completely misinterpreted it?"

Caden cleared his throat. "I don't know for sure, of course, but even you have to admit, you've been through some major trauma. So, I guess all I'm saying is that it's possible what you heard sounded weird enough to your traumatized brain after everything that had happened, that you put a spin on it that wasn't there."

"And yet, Dustin is dead. And so is Brianne. I want to know why."

"Well, there is that," Gavin said.

The doorbell rang and Sarah flinched. "Who's that?"

Caden shot her the look that he used to flash when they were kids and he had something up his sleeve. "You'll see." He headed for the door.

"See what?" she asked.

"A surprise," Gavin said. "Caden and I

219

thought you could use one."

"What kind of surprise?"

"Us!" came a chorus of voices in the entryway.

"Heather? Brooke?" Sarah blinked. "Ava!" She rose to her feet and crossed the room to greet each woman. "And Asher too?"

He kissed her cheek. "Glad to see you're in one piece."

"Glad to be that way, thanks."

Asher and Gavin shook hands while Heather grasped Sarah's fingers and pulled her to the sofa. "How are you feeling?" she asked, a friend's concern mingled with a doctor's scrutiny.

"I'm better. Sorry I couldn't stay awake long enough to see you when you came by the hospital."

"We understood. Thanks to Gavin and his text with that picture, we were able to chill out a little and leave you alone, but enough is enough. We decided to coordinate our schedules with some time off. We've missed you."

"I've missed you guys too." And she had. So very much. "How much time off?"

"I have to head back tonight. My brother is with Mom," Ava said, reaching around Heather and placing a hand on Sarah's wrist. "We're so very sorry about Dustin."

220

Sarah swallowed and nodded, glanced at her brother, who stood next to the fireplace. "Thanks, it's been tough."

"We were at the funeral, but you were still pretty out of it to note that, I think," Ava said.

"I know. Caden told me. I have flashes of it, so I'll content myself with the fact that I was there."

Ava sighed and bit her lip. "I wanted to stay and visit with you awhile, but I had to leave right after to get home to Mom."

"I understand, Ava. You know I do."

Her friend smiled, crinkling the corners of her dark eyes. Half Mexican and half Caucasian, she was a beautiful combination of her lovely parents. The sadness in her eyes and the faint shadows beneath spoke volumes.

"How's she doing?"

Ava shrugged. "She has good days and bad."

More bad than good would be Sarah's guess.

Brooke still hadn't said anything other than a quick hello and given a tight hug, but now her gaze snagged Sarah's and she raised a brow. Sarah nodded. When Sarah was ready to talk, Brooke was ready to listen. She knew that and appreciated it more than her friend could possibly know. And she might take her up on that at some point, but for now, she had things to do.

"So, tell us what's been going on?" Heather said. "What's this about getting shot at and more?"

"You'll think I'm making the whole thing up."

"Start with the kidnapping," Brooke said, "and go from there."

Sarah shuddered and Brooke's eyes narrowed.

"Fine." She could tell them. They were her friends. She'd stick to the facts and leave the absolute terror of those hours in the locked recesses of her mind.

Gavin, Caden, and Asher gathered around the kitchen island, and Caden passed the bottle opener to Gavin. Cold root beer, a mix of pretzels, nuts, and M&Ms, and three kinds of potato chips weren't exactly on the healthy list, but he'd been shot at, almost run off the road, and had dealt with a hostage situation in the span of less than twenty-four hours. He'd eat the junk and enjoy it.

He hoped Sarah was doing the same in the other room. Caden had delivered the goodies and then hurried back to the kitchen with a frown. "They kicked me out of my own den."

"Want some cheese with that 'whine'?" Asher asked.

"That's so old. It's time to find some new material."

Asher grinned and sipped his drink.

Gavin turned serious. "Heard anything about Wilmont?" he asked Caden.

"Oh, yeah. He made it. The theory is the seizure was brought on by the stress of everything." He shrugged. "He's expected to make a full recovery, even though he claims he doesn't remember anything that happened after he got to the house." Caden's phone rang and he snagged it. "Excuse me, I need to take this." He stepped out onto the patio and shut the kitchen door behind him. Gavin watched through the window, wondering at the man's expression. Intense and focused. Something about Dustin or Sarah?

When Caden returned a few minutes later, his frown spoke volumes. "Anything you can share?" Gavin asked.

Asher pointed to the door. "I can step out if you guys need to discuss something private."

Caden shook his head. "No, nothing like that. Elliott Bancroft is one of the detectives on the Brianne Davis case. The friend, Mrs. Nelson, is out of surgery and holding her own for now, but she hasn't come to yet. Here's the interesting thing, though. The gun was registered to Brianne, and initial findings are showing that she was killed by a self-inflicted gunshot — and while Wilmont had residue on his hands, it was a very small amount and none on his clothing. Which could be accounted for by the fact that he picked the gun up after it was discharged . . ."

"Which means he might be scum, but not necessarily a murderer," Gavin said.

"Exactly. There's no way to prove he fired the weapon, and the evidence pretty much says he didn't."

"So," Gavin said, "all of his protests about not shooting anyone could be true."

"Could be," Caden said. "Here's the other thing. They found traces of some drug in his system."

"Pain meds, right?" Gavin asked. "We know he took two of Brianne's pills."

"No. No traces of any narcotic. This is something else, but he swears all he took were the two pills from Brianne's bottle."

Gavin frowned. "So he's lying."

"Maybe."

"Okay, going on the assumption that he's

not lying, what's the other drug they found?"

"They're trying to figure that out. They've ruled out the usual. Elliott said this one is something the lab says they've never seen before. They're trying to break down the components of it as we speak."

Gavin frowned. "Weird."

"No kidding."

"What about our guy Max at the hospital?" Gavin asked.

"Nothing yet. Which is also weird. Elliott said there's no worker there named Max."

"No Maxwell? Maximillian?"

"Apparently not. I'm tempted to ask Annie to work her magic and find him. I don't think either detective would mind as long as he was located."

"Good idea," Gavin said. "Now, back to Brianne. If she shot herself, who shot the friend? Do we have an attempted murder-suicide here?"

Caden ran a hand over his cheek. "They're not sure. The big hope is that Mrs. Nelson will wake up soon and tell us what really happened."

"Us?" Asher asked.

Caden grimaced. "Okay, *them*. Sorry. Habit. I don't mean to treat it like it's my case, but I can't help it."

225

Gavin shook his head. "If they're keeping you in the loop, then that's a huge plus."

"Tell me about it. They're great and I let them know how much I appreciated it."

Gavin's phone pinged and he let out a slow breath. "Finally," he murmured.

"What is it?"

"I have a friend who's got a friend who got me some hospital security footage of the night Sarah was ill and wandering the halls."

"How'd you do that?"

"Connections." He tapped the screen on his phone and let the video play. The longer it played, the more he frowned.

"What is it?"

"It's not showing anything."

"Nothing?" Caden asked.

"Just a typical quiet hallway with nurses and doctors walking back and forth and going room to room."

Asher set his drink on the counter. "What's the time stamp?"

Caden looked over at Aden's screen. "It's the right day and time."

"Is it the right floor?"

"I can't see the room numbers, but wait. There's Sarah. She looked out of her room, then turned and went back in. So, yeah, it's the right floor."

"Someone messed with the footage then," Gavin said, eyes on the screen. "I was on that floor and I know what should be there." He shook his head. "Something happened that night, and someone is desperate to cover it up. I don't know who's involved, but I suspect that Dr. Kilgore and the nurse, Donna, know what's going on."

"Then maybe someone should have another chat with them."

Gavin shrugged. "Could try, I suppose, but unless you have something official you can bring them in on, I doubt they'll talk. It looks like they simply want to erase any trace of Brianne Davis from their hospital." He shook his head. "My mind is spinning, trying to make sense of everything. There's a reason they're denying Brianne's existence. There's a reason she killed herself. There's a reason Dustin was doing great, then all of a sudden bottomed out and jumped off the roof. There's a reason for all of it and it's related to that VA hospital. The problem is, we're missing too many pieces of the puzzle to connect everything."

"So," Caden said, "we keep looking for those missing pieces."

Gavin nodded. "I think so."

CHAPTER FIFTEEN

Wednesday morning, Lewis sat across from his buddy Marshall again and sipped his coffee. They'd been chatting about not much of anything for the past fifteen minutes, but now, Marshall looked out the window, eyes narrowed, mind obviously not on their meeting.

"Everything all right?" Lewis asked.

Marshall blinked and nodded. "Sure."

"So, what's wrong?"

His friend sighed. "The funding for this project I'm working on is iffy. I'm waiting to hear back from a potential investor, but it's not looking good."

"Ouch. How much do you need?"

Marshall leaned forward. "We're in the home stretch, Lewis. Another five million would help. Seven or more would go a long way, because we're finally seeing some pretty amazing progress. Our test subjects are showing real promise, and I can see getting the product on the market within six months once we have approval. I would say two months after that, we'd recoup every penny invested."

Lewis raised a brow. "That's not just pocket change you're talking about."

"Trust me, I know." He paused and took a sip of his coffee. "You know as well as I do, we're a private company. We don't have the big government backing, but we're almost there. So very close. People believe in this project and have put their money where their mouth is." His fingers flexed around his glass. "I can't fail, Lewis, I *won't* fail."

"I hope not. I've got a lot invested in this myself. Even more so now that Dustin is gone. Just like you can't fail, his death can't be in vain."

"Of course not." Marshall blew out a slow breath and Lewis could feel the man's passion in an almost tangible way. "Enough about that. How's Rochelle? Is she recovering?"

"Physically."

"Mentally?"

Lewis shook his head. "I don't know. She still won't speak to me. I haven't seen her since she was released from the hospital. Caden keeps me updated about once a day."

229

He sipped his coffee. "And if she knew that, she'd probably smash his phone and leave his house."

Marshall frowned. "That's not good."

"She's always been able to hold a grudge, but she'll eventually come around." Maybe. "At least she always has before." But he'd never done anything quite like this to her. "We've never been close, though. She was a mama's girl. And after Tara died, Rochelle just went wild. Did everything she could to destroy her reputation — and mine. She wouldn't listen to a thing I said."

"When you were around to say it?"

Lewis scowled, and his friend held up his hands in a gesture of surrender.

"Don't shoot. You said yourself that you weren't really around."

"Trust me, I know." Lewis cleared his throat and glanced at the two men who sat close by. His security detail. "Gavin said someone tried to run them off the road yesterday. Shot up his truck."

Marshall stilled. "What?"

"Local police were called in, but CID's taking over the investigation since there's the possibility it could be related to the threats against me."

"I see. So, when are you headed back into the fray?"

"My leave is up in another week. I'm using the time to do a little investigating of my own, since Rochelle won't have anything to do with me."

"Investigating what? The shooting?"

The general shook his head. "Dustin's supposed suicide."

"Supposed?"

"It's just a theory. A crazy one probably."

"Want to share?"

Lewis hesitated, then filled him in on Caden's last visit with Dustin. Marshall listened intently. "But he jumped."

"I know."

"Is there the possibility he was pushed?"

"No. The security footage is very clear — and it's not doctored, according to CID."

"Then I'm confused."

"Join the club."

Silence fell between them. "So, what are you going to do?" Marshall finally asked.

Lewis shook his head and let his shoulders slump a fraction. "I don't know, Marshall. For the first time in my life, I don't know what to do."

Sarah walked toward the psychiatric ward with Gavin next to her. Seeing her friends had been a soothing balm to her wounded soul, but not even Brooke's subtle question-

231

ing had been able to break down the wall she had erected in an effort to protect herself from the trauma she'd endured.

The truth was, once she'd finished describing the kidnapping and subsequent rescue, she'd wanted to lighten the atmosphere, not talk about her issues. The others had seemed to understand and let her. They'd shared some funny stories and the laughter had been good. For all of them. Now it was time to get back to business, and she was grateful to have Gavin at her side. She pressed the button on the wall.

"How can I help you?"

"Sarah Denning. I have an appointment with Dr. McCandless."

Three seconds later, the door buzzed and swung open. Sarah took a deep breath and walked through. Gavin took a seat in the waiting area. In front of her, a woman sat at a desk and waved her over. "Good morning, Ms. Denning."

"Good morning." Sarah looked around. This was where Dustin had spent his last days. She found it depressing and enlightening. He'd sought help. He wanted to get better. He wanted to *live.* So, why had he died?

"I'm Elizabeth," the woman said, handing Sarah a clipboard with a stack of papers. "If you'll just fill these out —"

"I . . . um . . . went on the website and filled them all out." Sarah pulled them from her bag and handed them over.

"Oh, great. That'll save some time."

"Right." Because saving time was important. Nerves attacked her. Gavin had insisted on escorting her, and she was grateful for his presence, but now it was time for her to step up and deal with this alone. And she'd have to be careful. So very careful in what she said and how she said it. But the guilt was pounding her. Was she taking an appointment away from someone who truly needed it?

She took a seat next to Gavin.

"You ready for this?" Gavin asked, his voice soft in the muted environment.

"I don't really have a choice."

"If you question her outright, she's not going to be forthcoming with anything."

"I know, Gavin, we've already been over this on the way here, remember?"

"I know."

He was nervous for her. Great.

"I can do this," she said, her voice as low as his. "I have to, but . . ."

"But what?"

"I don't want to."

"Why not?"

233

"It's not right. I shouldn't be taking up her time when —"

"Sarah Denning?"

A nurse with a clipboard stood at the door at the opposite end of the waiting room.

Sarah stood. Gavin reached up and squeezed her hand. "You've got this," he said.

"I can't lie to her, Gavin."

He rubbed his chin. "Look at this like a journalist. You're here to do a job and get the facts on your brother. Period. Who knows? You may write his story one day."

She pulled in her bottom lip. "Right."

"Sarah?"

"I'm coming."

Heart thundering, conscience nagging, she nevertheless followed the woman into the back, then down the carpeted hallway to a door that had Dr. McCandless's name on the nameplate. The woman twisted the knob and pushed the door open. "Have a seat. The doctor will be with you in just a moment."

"Thank you." Sarah walked in and settled herself in one of the comfortable chairs facing the window. Had Dustin sat in this very seat? Had he looked at the same view? Had he felt the same trepidation now pounding through her?

She stood to pace.

Four times to the window and back. Why did doctors always do that? Why make you wait in their office? Why weren't they ever seated in the room to welcome you when you walked in the door?

Maybe it was so the client would be so anxious, they'd just spill everything? Or maybe it was so the client would have time to gather their thoughts before being required to voice them?

Or maybe it was because the doctor simply needed a restroom break between sessions.

Whatever the reason, Sarah just wanted to get this over with.

Gavin's phone rang and he snatched it, his eyes still on the double metal doors Sarah had passed through. "Hello, Son."

"Dad, hey, how are you doing?"

"Doing well. I got your message and thought I'd call to make sure I understood exactly what you needed."

Gavin rubbed a hand over the stubble on his chin. "I have a favor to ask."

"You know I'll do whatever I can to help you out. Lay it on me."

"I have a friend. She was wounded in Afghanistan and is home to recuperate. She's been discharged."

"I see."

"She loves what she does and she's good at it. Google the bombing of the orphanage six months ago in Kabul and you'll see the piece she wrote. She also helped bring down an organ trafficking ring at one of the orphanages in Kabul and received national recognition for it. Anyone who hired her would be getting a prime investigative reporter. Her name is Rochelle Denning, but she goes by Sarah."

"Sounds interesting. I'll look her up."

"So, here's the favor. Once she's recovered, she's going to need a job. She'd be an asset to any paper or television station. I know you have contacts in this area."

"Of course." His dad blew out a sigh. "I take it this young woman is someone you care about?"

The man could always read him easier than a large-print book. "Something like that."

A pause. "I'll see what I can do."

"Thanks, Dad. How's Mom?"

"Busy. Doing her thing. Cooking a lot."

Cooking? *His* mother? "What's up with that?"

"I think it's stress."

"Spill it, Dad. It's not like you to hem and haw around something."

His father cleared his throat. "Right, well, it's your sister."

Gavin refrained from releasing an audible sigh. "I haven't called her. I'm sorry. I've just been caught up in this . . . thing . . ." Trying to keep Sarah alive. ". . . and I just —"

"Stop. I get it."

No doubt about that. If anyone understood, it would be his father.

"But something's going on with her, and your mother and I are at a loss to figure out what. I need you to talk to her, meet with her. Something."

"Okay, I can do that." He paused. "Can I have a few more details?"

"She's . . . I don't know. Being reclusive. She goes to school, then comes home and locks herself in her room. Comes out for dinner occasionally, says three words, eats even less, then heads back to her room for the night. Often she's gone before I'm even up in the morning."

Gavin frowned. "She's always been reserved and an introvert, but that seems a bit extreme even for her."

"This is her senior year of college. I know she's stressed, but this has been going on since the end of August, and I think it's more than just school stress."

"I've only talked to her a handful of times since she started school." Because he'd been working contract after contract, staying so busy he didn't have time to think, much less worry about the baby sister who wasn't interested in hearing from him. Guilt hit. "Have you followed her? Tried to find out what's going on?"

Silence. Then a sigh. "Yeah. I think she's involved with one of her professors."

"Kaylynn? Seriously?"

"She went to his home and was there for several hours before she came out. I tried to get a look in the window, but no luck."

Gavin frowned. "Did you ask her about it?"

"No. I'm still trying to figure out the best way to deal with it. I don't want to say anything and have it make her mad enough to do something stupid."

He could understand that.

"Can you come to dinner tonight?" his dad asked. "You'll see what I'm talking about."

"Tonight?"

"I know Kaylynn will be here for sure tonight."

"I'll see what I can work out."

"Bring your girl . . . friend."

"Dad . . ."

His father chuckled. "I'll work on that job for her. I'm thinking Owen Grant could use another reporter on his team. He's big in competition with Jefferson Wyatt, you know."

The two men Gavin had been thinking of when he'd brought up the idea. "I'm assuming you have your weekly lunch with them today?"

"Of course. I promise I'll take care of it."

"Thank you." Gavin hung up the phone and thought about Kaylynn. She was ten years younger than he was. They'd lived in the same household for eight years before he'd gone off to college, then joined the Army, and during that time, they'd never been particularly close, simply because he'd been into teenage guy stuff and she'd been . . . a girl. He loved her, and hated they didn't have much of a relationship, but that came with the nature of his career path. However, at least they'd spoken to each other regularly. Until a year ago. He'd been home for Christmas break and caught her boyfriend sniffing a line of cocaine in the guest room.

Gavin had thrown him out and threatened him with great bodily harm if he ever came near his sister or family again. Kaylynn had overheard the entire exchange but hadn't said a word to him. Just looked at him with her big expressive eyes and slipped into her room. He hadn't seen her before he'd had to head back to Afghanistan, and they'd barely exchanged two paragraphs' worth of words since. But that was wrong. It was time to make sure she knew he loved her.

And just as soon as he made sure Sarah was safe, he vowed to do just that.

He prayed he wasn't too late.

The door opened. Finally. And the doctor stepped inside.

"Hello, Sarah, I'm so sorry to keep you waiting, but I'd had three cups of coffee and simply couldn't wait a minute longer." She laughed at herself and Sarah instantly liked the woman. And that was one question answered. "So," the woman held out her hand and Sarah shook it. "I'm Dr. Melissa McCandless. You can call me Mel. How are you doing today?"

Mel's bubbly personality went a long way toward putting Sarah at ease — and making her feel even more guilty for lying her way through the door. "I'm doing better today than I was when I called, but thank you for agreeing to see me so quickly."

"Of course. Why don't you have a seat and you can tell me what's going on."

Sarah sat. Crossed her legs. Then uncrossed them. She blew out a breath. "I'm nervous. Sorry."

"I could say, 'Don't be,' but have found that doesn't help much."

A laugh slipped out. "I guess not. Okay, first things first, I have to confess. I'm not suicidal. I only alluded to that so I could get a quick appointment. So, I'm sorry. And if you don't want to talk to me, I understand."

The doctor studied her. "I see."

Sarah shifted under the woman's watchful gaze, then stood and backed toward the door. "That was incredibly low of me. I promise, I try to act with integrity in all situations, but I've really blown it this time." Her fingers touched the doorknob. "I started thinking that maybe I'm taking a spot away from someone else who truly needs it, so I'm sorry. This was a mistake. The guilt is killing me. I shouldn't have gone about seeing you this way."

"Well, at least we know you have a conscience."

A startled laugh slipped from Sarah. "Yes, I still have that." The woman hadn't said anything predictable so far. It was . . . disconcerting and . . . interesting. She reminded her of Brooke in that way.

"Sit down. Please."

Sarah stilled. "Really?"

"Really. I have this half hour blocked out for you. We might as well put it to good use."

"Oh, I see," Sarah said, deflating. "You think I'm just saying that because I'm being a chicken and trying to get out of the session. But that's not the case."

"Sarah, sit. Please."

Great. In trying to right her wrong, she'd just convinced the woman she was lying. About being suicidal anyway.

Sarah sat.

"If, as you say, you're not thinking of harming yourself," Mel said, "why did you want to see me so desperately?"

Sarah wanted to blurt out questions about Dustin but bit her lip and sighed, trying to figure out the best way to approach the subject. "Okay, so here's the deal. I'm having some . . . issues . . . and I don't know how to make them stop."

"All right. Tell me about these issues."

"Nightmares. And . . . other things. My past won't stay buried. It keeps popping up to remind me that I'm not . . . good enough."

"What are the nightmares about?"

Sarah paused. Focused. "Several incidents that happened while I was in Kabul. And . . .

242

about my brother's death. Mostly about him."

"I see. I'm so sorry for your loss."

Sarah swallowed. Dr. McCandless sounded like she meant it. "Thank you. But I just keep . . ."

"Keep what?"

She could do this. It was all part of finding out what happened to Dustin. She was pretending, right? Then why did it feel so real? Because she wasn't lying about the nightmares — or the past. "I keep seeing him. I see him jump off the building and I see him land. And I see what happens when he lands." She choked. Gagged.

The doctor jumped up and grabbed a bottle of water from her refrigerator. Sarah took it and drank half of it, her heart pounding. Why was she doing this?

"Just breathe a moment," Dr. McCandless said. "Take a minute."

"Sorry. Thank you." Sarah met her gaze. "My brother was Dustin Denning."

The doctor flinched and deep sadness filled her eyes. "I noticed the last name and wondered if there was a connection there. I'm so sorry."

"I know he talked to you. He said you helped him."

"Not enough apparently." Dr. McCand-

243

less rose and rubbed her palms down her black slacks. "I was absolutely stunned to hear of his death."

"Yeah, that makes two of us." She paused. "Was he like this? Did he have nightmares and feel helpless to do anything about them?"

"Sarah, I can't —"

"Please. I'm on his HIPAA paperwork. You can tell me about him. I think it would really help settle some things in my mind if I could just understand what he was thinking, feeling . . . please."

The doctor took a deep breath and clasped her hands. "Dustin had a good many problems, as you know, but honestly, I thought he was doing better. That we were making some breakthroughs. That's why his suicide floored me."

Exactly what Caden had seen. "Dr. McCandless?"

"Please, call me Mel."

"All right, Mel, I'm not suicidal, I promise. I admit, I probably have some . . . um . . . PTSD issues" — man, that was hard to say — "but I've no desire to die."

"I'm starting to believe you."

Heat swept into Sarah's cheeks and she looked away. "I've had some pretty down moments over the last few weeks, I'll admit that as well." Her father's betrayal came to mind, and she curled her fingers into tight fists. "And when I tried to get in just to talk to you — to ask you about Dustin — I was shut down faster than I could blink. But, yes, I wanted to ask about Dustin as well."

"As well?"

Shame burned a path up Sarah's neck and into her cheeks. She cleared her throat. Tears gathered and she sniffed. "The nightmares are real," she whispered. "I only fall asleep when I can't stay awake any longer or I'm drugged up." She held up a hand. "Prescription drugs that I haven't taken in a couple of days. The last thing I need is an addiction."

The doctor's hand covered hers. "I'll work you in if you want to be a patient. For real."

Sarah gave a slow nod, then shook her head. "I don't know. I want the nightmares to stop, but I won't take medicine, and I know that's the route you'll probably want to go."

"Meds can be a last resort. Sometimes just talking and me offering some coping skills, strategies for handling the nightmares, can do a lot."

"You can do that?"

"Of course."

Sarah nodded again. "I'll think about it."

She paused. "What did Dustin do? Did he choose to take meds or go the other route?"

The doctor hesitated. "Why?"

"I don't know. I guess I just need to know."

"Everyone is different. Dustin's choices shouldn't reflect yours."

Sarah sighed. "I'm not saying they will. I'm just trying to understand him."

"I know." She tapped her chin. "He chose medication and it seemed to help him." She paused and shook her head, then cleared her throat. "So, what did you do over there in Kabul?"

"I'm an investigative journalist."

"Ah. That explains a lot." Sarah raised a brow and the doctor smiled. "Your inquisitive nature."

"Oh right. Yeah." Other questions surfaced. "Do you know who Dustin was hanging around? Who his friends were? Who he may have confided in?"

"He talked a lot about your brother, Caden, and he mentioned you quite a bit. He was very concerned about you, but when I tried to press for more information, he shut down."

"I see. Anything or anyone else?"

Mel hesitated, then walked behind her desk and picked up a pen and paper. "There was a woman. Her name was Dr. Helen Craft." She wrote on the paper and folded it. "Dustin talked about her quite a bit. He said he met her in Afghanistan and said he was surprised that she lived only an hour away from him. He looked her up when he moved home, and they had some group counseling sessions together."

"She was a good friend of his?"

"I'm not sure of the nature of their relationship, but yes, I know he cared about her. She . . . uh . . . killed herself about three weeks before Dustin did."

"What?" Sarah whispered. She took the paper the doctor held out. Had Dustin mentioned her to Caden?

Mel hesitated. "Look, I'm not supposed to discuss patients, but Helen was different. One thing she made very clear is that she wanted to get better and she wanted to help people. She told her story to anyone who would listen, anyone who she thought needed to hear what she was experiencing in order to make a difference. So, I know she would be completely fine with me sharing this."

"Okay," Sarah said.

"Helen was part of the medical team that was there when an orphanage was bombed. Kids were on the playground at the time, and as you can imagine, it was horrific. She operated on as many as she could, but couldn't save the majority. It was something no one should ever have to see or experience." The doctor shuddered. "She had PTSD and nightmares for months until she finally requested to be sent home to seek help. Helen's sister, Lucy, moved in with Helen when she came home to make sure she wasn't alone at night and got to all of her appointments. I spoke with Lucy and she agreed with me in my assessment that Helen was doing better. Her PTSD was under control and Lucy was getting ready to move back home. So when she walked in the door to see Helen standing in the window of her fourteenth-floor apartment, she was shocked. Lucy called out to her but said Helen didn't even hesitate. She just jumped."

"Oh my. How awful."

Sarah knew just how ghastly the bombing had been. She'd covered that incident, had seen the dead bodies. Had held the weeping mothers. A small terrorist organization had taken credit for the attack, but a rumor had leaked that an American soldier had been the instigator. She'd cleared the soldier's name and passed on intel to the higher-ups. The terrorist cell had been wiped out before it had a chance to expand any farther — or kill any more innocent people.

A pang hit her. She'd done good work over there. She'd been making a difference. Swift, hot rage consumed her, and she vowed once more not to let her father win.

"I don't know what else Lucy can add to that," Mel was saying, pulling Sarah back into the present, "but I believe she met Dustin several times, so I can't help but think she might be able to answer some of your questions."

"All right. I'll talk to Lucy and see what she has to say. Thank you."

Mel cleared her throat. "Normally, I wouldn't say a word about my patients, but Lucy was on Helen's HIPAA list and she specifically told me that if I ever came across anyone who might have answers for Helen's death, to share whatever I needed to. You two have a lot in common because she's desperate for answers and I know she'll want to talk to you. I'll call her and let her know you're going to be in touch. Is that all right?"

"Yes, of course. Thank you again." Sarah stood and walked to the door.

"Sarah?"

She turned.

"Come back if you need to."

Sarah hesitated. Nodded. "Thank you." She stepped to the door of the waiting room and blew out a breath. Tears battered her lids and she refused to let them fall. For several minutes, she simply stood there and battled to get her emotions under control.

Footsteps sounded behind her. "Sarah?"

Sarah pressed her fingers to her eyes and turned. "Yes?"

"I called Mrs. Long," Mel said. "When I explained everything, she said she could meet you right now if you could head to her house."

"We can do that, thank you."

"Of course. And again, I'd love for you to come back."

"We'll see."

Mel nodded, then disappeared back into her office. Sarah took another five minutes to simply breathe and process. Then pushed through the door to fill Gavin in.

And tell him they had a couple of stops to make.

CHAPTER SIXTEEN

When Sarah stepped through the door into the waiting room, Gavin caught her eye and held out a hand. "How'd that go?"

"Not exactly like I'd envisioned." She gripped his fingers and he could feel the tension running through her.

"What do you mean?"

"She's a nice woman. And just as confused as everyone else about Dustin's . . . suicide."

Gavin gave a mental grimace at the way she choked on the word.

"She said the same thing Caden did. That Dustin was up and looking forward to getting on with his life."

"So, that was a bust?"

She sighed and offered him a slight smile. "Not completely. I don't think the doctor had anything to do with Dustin deciding to jump off the roof. And I don't think she missed anything, which is unfortunate, because I doubt she can help us figure out why he did it."

"I'm sorry. I know you were hopeful."

"I was. I still am. She gave me the name of a former patient's sister." She told him about the patient — a doctor who witnessed the bombing of an orphanage.

Gavin shook his head. "I can see how that would be horrific to live with."

"She saved some of them, Gavin. Because of her, some of those kids are alive today."

He sighed. "As much good as she did, she could probably only focus on the ones she lost."

"Yeah. So . . . I need to take care of something."

"Let me guess. Dustin's place?"

She raised a brow. "Yes, eventually, but first, Lucy Long."

"Who's Lucy Long?"

"Helen Craft's sister. It's about an hour drive."

"That's fine. We'll leave now." Gavin pulled his keys from his pocket, and Sarah filled him in on more details of the woman's story as they walked toward his truck.

"Thank you," she said, crawling into the passenger seat. "For the first time, I have some hope that we may learn something new about Dustin and his state of mind in those last few days."

Sarah twisted her fingers together, then released them. Twist, release, twist, release.

He reached over and placed a hand over hers. "It's going to be all right."

"Sure."

She fell silent and he left her alone while she disappeared into her thoughts.

An hour later, Gavin spun the wheel, entering the neighborhood where the Longs lived. He pulled to the curb of the second house on the right and parked. The front door was open and a small dog sat just inside the storm door. When they approached, it barked and ran in circles until a woman hurried to sweep it up into her arms and open the door.

"Hi, I'm Lucy. This is Buster."

Gavin introduced himself and Sarah, and they soon found themselves in the den with the dog happily seated in Gavin's lap.

"Let me know if he bothers you," Lucy said. "I can put him in the backyard."

"He's fine," Gavin said. "I'd like to have a dog one day."

"Then I like you immediately. Dog people are the best." She shook her head. "I'm sorry, I need to remember my manners. Can I get you anything to drink?"

Gavin declined.

"I'm fine, thanks," Sarah said. "I really

appreciate you being willing to talk to us about your sister."

"I like talking about her. It's a way of keeping her alive and close to me." Tears welled in her eyes but didn't fall. "What do you want to know?"

"Let me start with my brother, Dustin Denning," Sarah said. "He committed suicide not too long after your sister did."

"Oh, I'm so very sorry! I only met Dustin a couple of times, but he seemed like such a nice young man."

"Thank you. It's been hard, as you well know. I suppose I'm having a difficult time accepting it because of how he was just prior to his death."

Lucy frowned. "What do you mean?"

"My other brother, Caden, brought Dustin home from the hospital when he was released, and apparently, he was doing well. He was happy and upbeat and looking forward to the future."

Lucy was nodding.

"Helen too?" Sarah asked.

"Yes, that's why I was so stunned to walk in and see what I saw." She shuddered. "She'd been so happy about being released from the hospital and was talking about going back to Kabul so she could get back to work. And now, I can't close my eyes without picturing her standing there in the window. I yelled at her and she didn't even acknowledge me. Or hesitate. She just . . . jumped."

Sarah shivered. "According to my father, security footage shows Dustin doing the same thing. He went to the hospital where he was supposed to be meeting with his therapist. Instead of going to her office, he went to the roof and . . . jumped. Two days ago, another vet, Brianne Davis, shot herself."

"Brianne Davis!" Lucy pressed a hand to her chest. "I know her."

"How?" Gavin asked.

"She and Helen met in the group therapy sessions. They had a lot in common. Brianne had worked in the hospital with Helen in Afghanistan, and she assisted in the surgeries after the bombing." She swiped a stray tear. "Neither she nor Helen were ever the same after that."

"So, Dr. McCandless worked with Brianne as well?"

"Yes."

Sarah frowned. "That's three patients of hers who have committed suicide in the last few weeks? I don't like those odds at all."

Gavin shook his head. "I'm inclined to agree with you."

"So, what does all this mean?" Lucy asked.

"I don't know," Gavin said, "but I think we're getting closer to figuring it out."

"One more question," Sarah said.

"Of course."

"Who was Helen's doctor?"

"Dr. Kilgore."

Gavin tensed and caught her eye. "Okay. Now I have another question. Was Helen on any medication?"

"Several. An antidepressant, something for her blood pressure, and she took something to sleep at night."

"Do you have the names of the meds?"

Lucy bit her lip and shook her head. "I threw everything like that out shortly after Helen died."

"Could you get the names of the meds from the doctor?" Sarah asked.

"I suppose. I'll see what I can do."

"Thank you." She looked at Gavin. "I think the next step is Dustin's house, but we can't go without Caden."

"Of course."

Sarah called Caden while Gavin chatted with Lucy. When Sarah hung up, she nodded. "He's going to meet us there."

Gavin stood. "I'm ready when you are."

Sarah stood outside Dustin's duplex door

and drew in a steadying breath. He'd lived in the place for only three days before he'd jumped off the roof of the hospital. How *moved in* could he have been? Gavin was still on the phone with whoever he'd called to get information about Dr. Helen Craft.

Caden had just driven up. "Not thinking about going in without me, are you?" he asked as he approached.

Sarah snorted. "How do you expect me to do that? You're the one with the key."

He joined her at the bottom of the steps, fingers clenched. He unfurled them to study the little piece of metal. "Dustin gave me this the last time I saw him. Said he wanted me to have access to the place so I could do surprise searches."

"He wanted to be held accountable," she said. "He was planning ahead, Caden. Someone who does that doesn't jump off hospital roofs."

"I know."

Gavin hung up and joined them. "Three people dead of suicide, all treated by the same doctor, all taking medications prescribed by that doctor. I don't know what the puzzle is going to look like once it's finished, but I have a bad feeling about it all."

Caden unlocked the door and pushed it

open. "So, let's see if we can find some more pieces."

Sarah stepped around him and took in the chaos. Upon closer inspection, she could see it was organized chaos. Boxes lined the walls, but they were labeled. To her right was the dining area. A table and four chairs were tucked into the space in front of the bay window overlooking the backyard. Off that was the galley kitchen.

Straight ahead, the hallway led to the back of the duplex. Sarah headed that way, passing a bedroom on the left and a bathroom on the right. She ended at the master bedroom. Dustin had placed a mattress on the floor under the window with an end table next to that, but no other furniture. His clothes were stacked in neat piles against the wall nearest the closet. He'd tossed a pair of jeans onto the impeccably made-up mattress. She picked up the denim and buried her face in the fabric, inhaling.

"They still smell like him," she whispered.

"Don't do this to yourself," Caden said, his voice husky.

"Wish he'd asked for help," she muttered.

"I know."

"Could have at least gotten him a dresser or something."

"Sarah."

She dropped the jeans back onto the bed and glanced at her brother, her emotions roiling near the surface. "What?"

"He wanted to do things his way. He was an adult. Interfering would have only caused him to distance himself."

"Like I've done with the general?"

He shrugged. "If the shoe fits."

Gavin stood in the doorway watching, the compassion in his eyes nearly her undoing.

Sarah headed for the master bathroom, her heart aching. How she missed Dustin. She'd missed him in a different way while they were in Afghanistan together, but at least she had the hope of seeing him at some point in the future. Now, his absence left a hole in her chest, like a piece of her heart was missing. And while the thought of seeing Dustin in heaven gave her comfort, the grief of the temporary earthly separation still hurt.

With a shaking hand, she opened the medicine cabinet.

"Need any help in here?" Gavin asked from the doorway.

"I'm looking for drugs," she said. "I want to know every chemical he put in his body. Maybe he mixed up some medications and it messed up his thinking. Or something."

He studied the contents of the cabinet.

"Maybe."

She pulled down three bottles. "Anti-depressant, decongestant, prescription-strength Motrin, something I don't recognize, and another something I'm not sure about. You know what they are?"

She handed him the two bottles and he pulled his phone from his pocket. "That's what Google is for." A quick search had him frowning. "One is a painkiller. The other a muscle relaxer."

"Well, I sure hope he wasn't taking all three of those at the same time." She paused. "Of course, that's not what killed him, so I guess not."

"I'm not a medical doctor, but those would all just make him sleepy. And if he'd taken them together, he would have fallen asleep and died. None of those are going to make him jump off a building."

"Unless he was depressed and taking *none* of them," Sarah said. But that didn't fit with what Caden or the psychiatrist had described. "And assuming this is all of the medications he'd been prescribed."

"I'll check the kitchen and make sure there's nothing else in there," Caden said. "I looked through his closet. There are some boxes with personal papers in there. I guess we'll need to go through those at some

260

point. He's actually pretty organized. I found his life insurance policy and other stuff." Caden blinked and looked away. Cleared his throat. "I talked to his landlord a couple of days ago, and Dustin's rent is paid through the end of this month. I'll extend that if we need to. Now I'm going to see if there are any more pill bottles in the kitchen." He headed back down the hallway, and Sarah blinked back tears.

Gavin pulled her into a hug, and she leaned her forehead against his chest, taking comfort in his presence even while her brain was telling her to back away. At the same time, another part of her head was rationalizing that it was just a hug. And she desperately needed a hug.

And yet another part of her mind reminded her that Caden was in the other room and would be more than willing to comfort her should she let him know she needed it.

Sarah ignored the snarky voice on top of all of her roller-coaster feelings. Gavin wasn't anything like her father. And he was going a long way in proving that.

"No more pills," Caden said from the hallway.

Sarah pulled away from Gavin and turned to face the doorway. Caden stepped into

261

the bathroom.

"Anything more in here?" Caden's gaze bounced between the two of them, and she thought she saw a flicker of curiosity, but thankfully, he kept his curiosity to himself.

"No," Sarah said, "nothing." She walked back into the bedroom and spied the jeans on the bed one more time. And sighed. She couldn't just leave them like that. She picked them up by the waistband.

"What is it?" Gavin asked.

"I want to fold them." A tear slipped down her cheek. She used the jeans to wipe it away. "I just want to fold them for him."

"Ah, Sarah." She met Caden's gaze. He remembered.

She shot a wobbly smile at Gavin. "I used to fold his pants for him. Mom would make us do our own laundry, and Dustin hated folding his jeans — or anything really. So he'd bribe me into doing it. Later, I did it because I loved him." She put the waist edges together and smoothed the legs, one on top of the other. Then creased them in the middle and let the top half fall over her forearm.

One little pill fell out of a pocket to roll onto the rug. "What's that?" Caden asked.

She picked it up. "His last dose of meds he didn't get to take?" It looked familiar. A little yellow triangular pill. "Hey, wait a minute. I saw this at Brianne's house. She has the same prescription."

Gavin looked over her shoulder. "That's the same kind of pill Wilmont stole and took. He thought they were a narcotic, but they're not."

"The label says they are. This looks like the same ones that were in the pill bottle on Brianne's counter. The one I knocked over."

"Citalopram."

"Nice," Caden said, "give an addict something else to get addicted to."

"Well, I'm not sure Brianne was an addict. And there's no bottle here to match it up to."

"Then what's he doing with it?"

"No idea."

"These are the only bottles in the house as far as I can tell," Caden said. "I don't think he would keep any anywhere else, do you?"

"I don't know, Cade, I feel like I don't even know who Dustin was anymore." She left the bedroom and headed into the den area. Then the kitchen. The guys followed her. "Did you check the fridge?"

"Yeah. It wasn't full, but it was all food he bought the day before he jumped." He held up a small piece of paper. "Found the receipt in one of the bags. He was probably going to file it somewhere."

"Again, not the sign of a person planning not to be around."

She opened the first drawer. Three forks, a couple of knives, two spoons, and a manual can opener. The next drawer held receipts and other small pieces of paper. "Found his filing system."

"I meant to come back to that," Caden said. "I was on a hunt for pill bottles, not papers."

Sarah laid the papers on the counter while Gavin started going through the other drawers. "Receipts for gas, fast-food runs, and . . . what's this?"

"What?" The guys stepped over.

"It's a shipping receipt from the post office near the hospital. It's got my name on it, but it's my neighbor's address. Why would Dustin send something here when he knew I was in Afghanistan?"

"You were approved to come home for Thanksgiving, right?" Caden asked.

"Yes."

"Dustin was too. Maybe he sent you an early Christmas present but didn't want you to get it and open it."

She nodded. "So, he sent it to Mrs. Howard for safekeeping?"

"Possibly."

She squinted at the label. "He mailed it two days before he . . . jumped." She swallowed. "I'll have to go by and get it, along with the rest of the mail I had forwarded to her."

And soon.

Gavin's phone rang and he excused himself to answer it. She heard him say, "Yes sir, I'm fine, thanks." Then he slipped from earshot.

"Who's that?" Sarah asked, a picture album in her hand.

He shrugged and took the book from her. "Not sure. Give him a few minutes. He's still got clients to keep happy."

Clients he'd put on hold so he could be with her.

She bit her lip, unsure how she felt about that — a bit guilty or very glad.

Mostly . . . both.

Gavin hung up with the general and joined Caden and Sarah in the small living area where he found Caden on his phone and Sarah looking through a picture album and swiping tears. He grabbed a tissue from the box on the coffee table and handed it to her.

"Thanks," she whispered and sniffed.

"Sorry. Everything okay with you?"

"Yes. Just a client seeking some reassurance." All true.

She shut the book. "So many good memories with my mom and brothers. I don't look back often because . . ." She shrugged. "I just don't, but we had some good times." He wrapped an arm around her shoulder and she leaned into him. "I can't believe he's gone. I know I keep saying that, but it just hits me over and over. I stop thinking about it for thirty seconds and then it's back like I'm just learning about his death for the first time."

"That'll ease, Sarah. It'll take time."

"I know."

"I know you know."

Caden turned and tucked his phone in the back pocket of his pants. He raised a brow at the two of them and their coziness, but Gavin didn't care.

"That was one of the detectives who's allowing me access to all of the information on the shootings," Caden said. "Wilmont is waking up and so is Mrs. Nelson, Brianne's friend. I'm going to head to the hospital and see what I can find out."

Sarah jumped up with a slight wince. "I want to come too."

"Maybe we should sit this one out," Gavin

said. She turned with a raised brow. He held up a hand. "Or not."

"Thank you."

Caden hesitated, then with a glance at Gavin that swung back to Sarah, he shrugged. "Keep your investigative instincts under control and that's fine, but just know that if you get in the way, they'll remove you."

Sarah shot her brother a dark look. "I'm not an idiot."

"Didn't mean to imply you were." He blew out a breath. "And that's my cue to exit. See y'all there."

He left and Gavin led Sarah to his truck. "When are you going to get Herbie fixed?" she asked.

"Her— what? Who?"

"I've named your truck Herbie."

He blinked. "You can't name my truck Herbie."

"Why not?"

"Because."

"Because . . . why?"

He huffed a laugh. "Because . . . well . . . because it's *my* truck and Sheila isn't a Herbie."

"It's Herbie to me."

He thought he heard her mutter something about *temperamental* and *high mainte-*

nance under her breath and smothered a smile. "Well, at least if you're going to give it a guy name, give it something a little more masculine. Wasn't Herbie something like a . . . a . . . Volkswagen bug? This is a *truck.* I'm sure there's a law somewhere that says trucks can't be Herbies."

"I like Herbie. I don't like Sheila."

"Why not? Because it's a female name?"

"No." She scowled at him. "Because it's too close to Sarah." She slammed the truck's passenger door.

Trying not to laugh, Gavin climbed into the passenger seat and cranked Herbie. No, *Sheila.* He glanced at the woman beside him, arms crossed, jaw jutted, eyes narrowed. His heart thundered at the unexpected rush of feeling . . . affection? . . . that swept through him. She cut him a look from the corner of her eye and her expression softened. He paused for a moment, then slid a hand under her ponytail, pulled her to the middle of the console, and pressed a kiss to her lips. A light one that demanded nothing, but hopefully expressed a fraction of his current emotions. He ended it almost before it began — and definitely before he was ready. She blinked at him, wide-eyed.

He couldn't help the smile that spread. "I

like you, Sarah Denning. A lot."

She swallowed and cleared her throat. "I like you too, Gavin. A lot."

"I'm not like your father, I promise."

"I know."

"And baggage doesn't scare me."

"You don't know mine."

"But I feel like I know *you*. And the truth is, I don't mind temperamental and high maintenance when it comes to you."

"What!" She punched him in the arm and he laughed.

She fought it, but finally gave in and joined him in the mirth. For a few seconds, they shared some much-needed relief from the constant tension that had plagued them for the past few weeks.

"You're something else," she said. "Thank you for helping me find laughter when I sometimes think I won't ever laugh again."

He kissed her forehead. "Time will help."

"I know."

Levity faded as he drove, keeping an eye on the mirrors. He noticed Sarah doing the same thing and knew she was remembering their brush with death on the way to the mountains. He couldn't blame her. He was still considering her observation that the bullets could have been meant for him. He didn't think so, but he wasn't as quick to dismiss the idea as he'd led her to believe. If someone was after Sarah because of her father, then it made sense they'd want Gavin out of the way to gain access to her. Then again, if they'd both been killed, it wouldn't have mattered to the shooters. They would have achieved their goal of getting rid of Sarah.

Ten minutes into the silent drive, he glanced at her. "Hey."

"Yeah?" She looked at him and he focused back at the road.

"So, this is pretty random, but would you be interested in eating dinner with me at my parents' house?" When she didn't answer, he looked out of the corner of his eye. "Sarah?"

"Um . . . that's really nice, but . . . why?"

He laughed. "Because I'd love for them to meet you. And . . . I promised my dad I'd talk to my sister. She's got some issues going on, and I . . . could use a buffer."

"A buffer?"

He wanted to smack himself. "I mean, I'd love for you to come regardless, but yeah . . . I'm being a huge chicken in a sense. I'm literally scared to death to talk to my sister and hope that if you're there, you'll give me courage and keep me from saying something completely stupid."

She gaped. He shrugged.

"Well, when you put it that way," she said, "I'd almost feel guilty if I didn't come."

"Great. I'll let them know you'll be there tonight."

"Tonight!"

"What? Does it matter when we go?"

She huffed a slight laugh. "No, I guess it doesn't."

Gavin spun the wheel to the right into the hospital parking lot. Once parked, he kept an eye on their surroundings, a little worried that things had been quite calm. He wasn't sure about the reason for the attempts on his life and Sarah's unless the general's speculation was correct, but the efforts to get rid of Sarah — or him — had failed, so no doubt another attack was imminent. He just didn't know from where. Or how.

And it made him antsy.

Once out of the truck, he stayed close to Sarah, placing a hand on the small of her back. Her warmth seeped into his palm, and he realized how much he was coming to care about this woman. He'd liked her right off when he'd met her in Kabul. Now that he was actually getting to spend time with her, he knew he'd do anything to protect her.

271

Including keeping his mouth shut about her father's involvement in his presence.

While he knew it was the right thing to do, he still struggled with the guilt. He didn't want to keep anything from her, but he didn't want her to die, either.

Because if the threats were valid — and he had no reason to believe they weren't — it was only a matter of time before someone would strike again.

CHAPTER SEVENTEEN

Sarah studied Gavin out of the corner of her eye. He'd been quiet since entering the hospital. As well as watchful, all at the same time. Once on Michelle Nelson's floor, he pulled his phone from his pocket. "I need to make a quick phone call."

"Sure. I'm just going to head on over to the waiting room."

He hesitated, then nodded. She noted that he followed her to the room but didn't enter as he pressed the phone to his ear. He was sticking awfully close. She supposed she should be grateful since it appeared some-one might be trying to harm — kill? — her, but she found it kind of unnerving, if she was honest.

She shook off the observation, instead focusing on the two detectives and Caden huddled with Mrs. Nelson's family in the corner next to the coffeemaker.

She scooted closer, hoping to be able to

273

eavesdrop. Gavin lifted the phone to his ear, then snagged her gaze. The knowing look there sent heat into her cheeks. But it didn't stop her. She snitched a cup from the stack and filled it, moving slowly, adding cream and sugar. Stirring.

". . . can't believe this happened," the girl to the right of Caden said.

"Is she able to talk?" Detective Attwood asked.

"Yes," an older woman answered, "more so in the last twenty minutes. She keeps asking about Brianne. We don't have the heart to tell her the truth, but I think she suspects she's . . . gone."

Detective Bancroft settled a sympathetic hand on her shoulder. "Do you think she'd be up to talking to us? It would help a lot if she could."

"If she's awake, I'm sure she'd like to try."

Sarah caught Caden's eye and he narrowed his. She sipped her coffee and fell into step behind them as they made their way to Michelle's room.

Caden dropped back. "What are you doing?" He kept his voice low.

"Not investigating — just waiting, like you said I could do."

He scowled, then sighed. "By the way, Annie tracked down the Max we've — they've

— been looking for. She got some security footage off the main door of the VA hospital and ran some of the faces through the recognition software. One came up Mark Anthony Xia."

"Max."

"It's kind of a long shot, but worth checking out. And one other thing. He's not an employee, but in the footage, he was wearing scrubs and an ID badge."

She frowned. "What's that all about?"

"I'm not sure. I'm getting ready to pass on the information to Elliott and Caroline after they finish talking to Mrs. Nelson. I'll let them run with it unless they want my help."

She hugged him. "Thank you, Caden, for keeping me in the loop and trusting me."

He patted her head just like he used to do when she was a teen and slipped into the room. The action used to infuriate her. Now she just smiled.

As the door swung shut, Sarah stuck her foot inside to stop it from closing all the way, hoping she'd be able to hear the conversation.

"Mrs. Nelson?" Detective Bancroft asked. Clear as a bell. "Mrs. Nelson?"

"Mom? Can you wake up?" Probably the teenage girl.

"What?" The weak voice must belong to Michelle.

"Mom?"

"Hey, baby. How are you?"

"So glad you're awake." Sobs erupted just as Gavin joined her at the door.

"Eavesdropping?" he murmured.

"No, of course not." She paused. "Well, yes, technically, I guess," she whispered, "but I don't look at it that way. I'm just saving Caden from having to go to all the trouble to fill us in on what's said."

Gavin smirked. "Move over a little."

A soft giggle slipped from her before the seriousness of the situation sobered her. "You guys go on down to get a snack while I talk to the officers," Michelle said.

"Mom —"

"Please, honey, we'll talk later, I promise."

Footsteps headed for the door and Sarah pulled Gavin to the side. The children and the teen stepped out of the room and headed for the elevator. Sarah and Gavin moved back to hear.

"Ma'am, can you tell us what happened?" Detective Bancroft asked. "How did you get shot?"

"Brianne did it."

Sarah gasped and Gavin squeezed her bicep.

"Um . . . she didn't mean to," Mrs. Nelson said, "it was an accident."

"Can you share the details?" Detective Bancroft's voice again.

"Brianne was agitated, sliding into a depression, and getting worse by the minute," Michelle said, sounding stronger and more awake. "She'd been doing so well that it was incredibly shocking to see her go downhill so quickly. Like within hours."

Sarah frowned at Gavin. "Weird."

"What triggered it? Do you know?" Detective Attwood's voice this time.

"No. She was fine. We'd been talking about taking a trip to Hawaii and making plans. She seemed all in. Even got her laptop and started looking up things she wanted to see while we were there. I ran out to grab some burgers, and when I got back, she was distraught, pacing the floors, crying — almost wailing . . . I don't know, but it was awful."

Sarah drew in a shallow breath.

"I tried to get her to tell me what was wrong and she said she couldn't take it anymore. She was so . . . sad. But that word doesn't really come close to describing it." A pause. "I've never seen sadness like that before," she finally said. "It was incredibly unnerving."

"Couldn't take what anymore?" Detective Bancroft asked.

"She didn't say, just kept going on and on and finally started saying the world would be better off without her. She apologized for hurting her family and said she needed to let them move on from her." Michelle coughed and her voice thickened. "She went into the kitchen, and I thought I had finally talked her down, then I remembered she kept the gun in the cabinet above the sink. When I went in there, she had it and was holding it to her head." A sob sounded and Sarah's eyes teared up in sympathy.

"I'm sorry, Mrs. Nelson, I know this is really hard," Detective Attwood's soothing voice broke in.

"I screamed at her to put it down and she wouldn't. She just kept crying and saying she was tired of all the pain. She was frustrated that she wanted to make a difference in the world and couldn't. She said she was worth nothing and didn't deserve to live." She coughed.

"Here, take a sip of this, ma'am."

After a brief pause, she cleared her throat. "I lunged at her and grabbed the gun. It surprised her so much, she jerked. I remember the gunshot, the pain. Someone holding my hand? Then waking up here." Another pause. "Where's Brianne? Please tell me I stopped her."

Silence.

A sob. "No, oh no."

Wetness on her cheeks startled Sarah and she raised a hand to swipe away the tears. Gavin rubbed her arm and she realized how grateful she was for his presence. He was sticking close because he cared. He'd always cared.

Her phone vibrated and she snatched it from her pocket. Her father? Calling *her*? A quick rage swept through her and she disconnected the call. Hesitated a fraction of a second, then blocked his number.

She tuned back in to hear Michelle say, ". . . she really did it?"

"I'm so sorry," Detective Bancroft said.

"This is so unreal."

"Mrs. Nelson," Detective Attwood said, "do you know a man by the name of Sam Wilmont?"

"No." Sniff. "Why?"

"He was in Brianne's house," Caden said, "when my sister and a friend went to see her. He said he was there to deliver some medicine Brianne had left at the hospital."

"I'm sorry, I've never heard of him and I don't remember him being there before everything happened." She sighed. "I'm sorry . . ."

"Looks like she's dropped off back to sleep." Sarah thought it was the older woman's voice. "I'm sorry."

"It's all right," Detective Attwood said, "we got a lot of what we needed to know."

Like it was highly likely that Wilmont was telling the truth and he didn't shoot the women.

An alarm shattered the muted atmosphere and Sarah jumped away from the door. Gavin's hand gripped hers.

"That's the fire alarm," he shouted in her ear.

She pointed to the vent in the hallway. "And there's the smoke!"

A panicked yell ripped past Sarah's ear over the wail of the alarm, and she turned to see a young woman on the floor and people stepping over her in their rush to get to the exit. A security guard burst onto the scene from the stairwell. He held a cloth to his face and nose. "Everyone calm down! We've got a fire in the air-conditioning and heating room, so some floors are going to get a little smoky," he said. "We need to evacuate this floor, but we'll do it calmly. The last thing we need is more patients. Everyone who can do the stairs, head that way. And walk, please!"

Patients and visitors flooded the hallways as smoke continued to pour from the vents.

Sarah hesitated, checked that someone had helped the fallen woman up, turned back to the room that held Caden.

Gavin gripped her hand and leaned close to her ear. "Caden will get out. He'd want me to make sure you're okay. I'm no firefighter, but I've worked with a lot of them. If the fire is in the heating and air-conditioning room, the whole hospital is going to fill up with smoke and have to be evacuated."

Someone bumped into her with a hurried "Excuse me." She stepped to the side and found herself next to the nurses' station. "Then why say it's just these floors?"

"To keep people from panicking."

"Doesn't look like it's working." People crowded together in a mad rush to get to the exit.

"They're trained for this kind of thing. I want to get you out of here."

Sarah pulled away from Gavin. "Not until I check on Caden."

She headed toward the room when Caden's head popped out and his gaze homed in on her. Gavin waved that he was with her and Caden disappeared back into the room.

"Come on," Gavin said, steering her

281

toward the exit. "Can we go now?"

"We can help people," Sarah said.

"We'll help whoever needs it on the way down." His eyes scanned the chaos.

A security officer stepped closer to her, and she heard something about fire trucks arriving on the scene from his squawking radio.

"My son! I can't find my son! Someone help me find my boy! Jackson! Jackson!"

Sarah stopped and spun, pulling Gavin to a halt. "We can't just leave. We have to help."

She darted toward the distraught father. Gavin gave an exasperated grunt and stayed on her heels. Two others had also stopped to help.

"How old is he and what does he look like?" Sarah asked.

"Six. He's got red hair, green eyes, and freckles. I was holding his hand and someone bumped me. I lost my grip and then he was just gone!" He swiped a hand down his face. "My wife is going to kill me. Jackson! Jackson! Where are you?" He swung back, eyes pleading. "Please help me."

"Fine," Gavin said. The smoke drifted lower and Gavin coughed. "What's your name?"

"Jonathan."

"We want to help too," a young man said,

pointing to himself and a girl who looked to be the same age.

"We need to notify the hospital," Gavin said. "Do you have a picture?"

"Yes, yes. On my phone." Jonathan snagged it from his back pocket and tapped the screen. A redheaded Opie look-alike popped up. His gap-toothed grin tugged at Sarah's heart.

"Okay," Gavin said, "show it to the security guy and let him know what's going on." He turned to the teens. "You guys start going room to room."

They left and Jonathan beelined for the security officer who was at the exit, directing people down the stairs.

"Stay with me, please," Gavin said. "I'm not feeling good about this whole thing."

Gavin wasn't kidding when he said he was antsy about the fire. It was too much of a coincidence that he and Sarah were in the hospital when it broke out, but he couldn't just walk away from helping a father look for his child. He and Sarah followed the man to the security officer, who directed them to the stairs.

Jonathan flashed the phone at the man. "Did you see this kid come this way?"

The officer leaned in to take a look while

283

the father looked straight at Sarah. All of Gavin's alarms clanged warning signals. He'd had that happen way too often in Afghanistan to ignore. He gave Sarah's hand a squeeze and motioned to her to back away. She frowned, but something in his eyes must have signaled her and she nodded.

Two steps back and the man named Jonathan stumbled, went to his knees.

With Sarah behind him, Gavin reached down and grabbed the guy's bicep. The man jerked, throwing Gavin off-balance at the top of the stairs. He shot over the guy and the first step, his shoulder hitting the edge. Pain radiated. A kick to his ribs stole his breath. Someone screamed. Sarah? More cries from those around him. Hands reached to help, but he was rolling bowling-ball style down the stairs, crashing into those unfortunate enough to be in his path.

He finally came to a painful stop at the bottom of the stairs and for a moment lay there, stunned and hurting, mentally yelling at himself to move. He noticed a young woman beside him, bleeding from a gash on her head.

Sarah. Gavin rolled to his feet and glanced at the top of the stairs. She was gone.

And so was the father of the missing child.

CHAPTER EIGHTEEN

The gun pressed into her side, and while fear was very present and real, anger burned a path through her gut. She was very tired of being shot at, kidnapped, held hostage, and threatened.

When Jonathan had given Gavin a kick in the ribs and sent him tumbling down the stairs, Sarah had started after him, only to have the man yank her back by the arm and jam the weapon into her still-healing side.

When he pulled her away from Gavin and she realized he had the weapon, she struggled for a brief moment until he twisted her arm hard enough to make her gasp.

"Try to get away and I won't shoot you, I'll shoot someone else. Understood?"

"Understood," she said through gritted teeth.

They'd slipped away from the security guard and he'd led her back onto the floor, past the nurses' station, down the hall, and to the next stairwell also flooded with people.

Sarah decided it was either a genius move or a brilliant color of stupid she wasn't familiar with. Unwilling to risk him being serious about hurting someone, she didn't try to resist, but one thing she was certain of — she wasn't leaving the hospital with him. "How did you know we'd be here?" she asked, dodging a young mother and her toddler.

"We've been watching you for a while. We know everything about you. It was only a matter of time before you showed up to visit Wilmont in the hospital. Now, keep going."

We? The firm grip on her upper arm didn't hurt, but sure had the potential to do so. She was more worried about the weapon pointed at the base of her spine — and keeping her terror under control so she could think. "So, Wilmont was working for you?"

"No. He was just an idiot in the wrong place at the wrong time."

"But how do you know him?"

"Because of his association with you."

Her association with him? Her only *association* with him was when he held her hostage and put a gun to her head. Who *were* these people?

286

"If you're doing this because of my father's decisions in Afghanistan," she said, "the joke's on you. He couldn't care less about me. He never wanted me, and if you kill me, it will probably be some weird relief for him. In fact, he's already disinherited me, you know. Wrote me right out of the will. Why? Because I joined the Army and he didn't want me to." She really needed to shut up, but chattering seemed to help. Help her anyway.

"I don't need the sad details of your relationship with the man," he said in her ear. "Just shut up and keep going. Down to the parking garage."

Goose bumps pebbled her skin and she shuddered. Paused.

He gave her a harder shove. "Go."

Most of the people who were being evacuated from the hospital were directed out of the stairwell at the street level. It looked like Gavin was right. They were evacuating the entire building. Helicopters thumped overhead, probably waiting to take surgical patients to a nearby hospital to finish the surgery.

If she continued down, no one would even notice. She obeyed and took the next flight of stairs down. "What is this all about?"

"We're going to go to your place and get

287

the package your brother mailed to you."

"The package? What package?"

He hesitated a fraction. "The one your brother mailed to you."

"I never got a package."

"Right."

He didn't believe her. *It will turn up eventually.* Dr. Kilgore knew Dustin had sent her a package. Was he the one behind all the attacks against her? But how would he even know what Dustin had mailed? Unless Dustin had said something to McCandless and she had passed the word on to Kilgore?

The list of people she could trust kept getting shorter and shorter. And the parking garage door loomed closer and closer.

Time was running out and she needed to do something fast. Defense moves flipped through her mind and she picked a series she hoped — prayed — would work.

Sarah pushed through the door and chose the moment the pressure of the weapon disconnected from the base of her spine. Still gripping the bar of the door, she twisted and swung her leg in a round kick. Her heel landed on his forearm and her would-be kidnapper cried out, losing his grip on the weapon. It clattered to the concrete floor.

Sarah spun and palm-heeled the guy's

chin. His head snapped back and he stumbled sideways, landing on the bottom step in the stairwell. He recovered and dove for the weapon at the same time she snagged it and scrambled back. "Stop! Don't move or I'll shoot you!"

He froze. Then laughed. "You? Shoot me?"

Terror raced through her and she said the first thing that came to mind. "I've killed one man, what's another?"

The deadly chill in her voice stilled him and his eyes narrowed. Slowly he raised his hands while he worked his jaw. "So, what now? This stairwell isn't going to stay empty for long."

True enough, but she needed answers. "You tell me what this is all about. Did you set the fire?"

He shrugged.

"I'll take that as a yes."

"It's not so much a fire as a distraction. They won't even shut down the whole hospital, just a couple of floors."

In order to allow him to keep access to the parking garage for his escape. With her in tow. "Did you shoot up the truck? Because if you wanted me alive, that wasn't exactly a brilliant plan."

He scowled. "That didn't exactly go as we'd hoped." He dropped his hands. "You're going to take me to the package, Sarah, and we're going to go now or someone's going to get hurt."

She really didn't like him using her name like he knew her.

Footsteps clattered on the stairs. "And that's my cue," he said. He bolted toward her. Sarah pulled the trigger. He screamed and grabbed his shoulder even while he stumbled for the door.

"Sarah!"

"Gavin!" Gun still gripped in her hand, she spun to go after the man. "He's getting away!"

Gavin raced down the stairs and hit the door, pushed through and into the parking garage. Security was right behind him. If it hadn't been for the guy on his heels and his lightning-fast action with the security cameras, Gavin never would have located Sarah and the imposter who called himself Jonathan.

Sarah's footsteps pounded across the concrete parking garage in pursuit of the man who'd attempted to kidnap her. Heart in his throat, Gavin raced after them, noticed the blood trailing, saw Jonathan stagger, then fall to his knees.

Sirens sounded and cruisers pulled into

the garage. Sarah didn't stop. She slammed into the man's back and knocked him facedown into the concrete. He let out a yell and tried to roll, but Sarah planted a knee into his back, grabbed a handful of hair and jammed the barrel of the gun against his temple.

He froze.

Gavin skidded to a stop just before he reached Sarah.

"Doesn't feel so great, does it?" she asked, her voice low.

"Put the weapon down!" The security officer aimed his gun at her. "Put it down!"

Gavin held up a hand. "Let me deal with this, please?"

"I'm bleeding," her prisoner ground out between clenched teeth.

"That breaks my heart," Sarah said. "Tell me why you're after me. What's in that package you're so desperate to get your hands on?"

"I like breathing, so I think I'll keep that to myself."

Keeping an eye on the man, Gavin inched forward. "Sarah."

She jerked and swung her gaze to meet his.

"Give me the gun. It's okay. You did good."

Her eyes narrowed. "I want answers."

"And we'll get them, but not like this. Come on, give me the gun. Hurry before anyone else gets here. Cops are on the way."

She hesitated, muttered something about letting the guy off easy, and released the gun into his outstretched hand. Gavin passed it to the security guard, who lowered his own weapon.

"I had to shoot him," she whispered.

"I know. We saw the footage."

The guard had been able to access it on his iPad, and they'd simply tracked them through the hospital, to the stairwell, then down to the parking garage. With all of the commotion in the hospital and the partial evacuation, there hadn't been a security guard close enough to get to her, so Gavin had to race against the clock. And he'd almost been too late.

"Everything's been recorded. It won't take long to rule it self-defense. You're okay now."

Officers ran into the garage as the security guard clicked cuffs around the bleeding man. Paramedics joined the scene.

"Didn't we just do this at Brianne's house?"

"Yeah, but at least no one got hurt this time." He glanced at the man being loaded onto the gurney. "Except the person who asked for it."

Sarah watched him while officers took the weapon as evidence, then took her into custody. "They have to cuff you, Sarah, you understand?"

She sighed and put her hands behind her back. "I know how it works."

The officer who'd helped him find her nodded. "We'll take you to the substation office in the ER and get your statement. You'll have to remain in custody until the investigation is finished."

"I know."

He clicked the cuffs around her wrists and gripped her bicep. "The sooner we get this started, the sooner you can go home."

She glanced at Gavin. "Will you call Caden and let him know what's going on?"

"Of course." He'd do that while he followed them to the holding area.

Caden answered on the first ring, and Gavin gave him the condensed version of what had just taken place.

"I'll be right there," Caden said.

By this time, they'd reached the holding area, and the officer — who'd introduced himself as Clint Osborne — directed Sarah to a seat. Officer Osborne uncuffed her hands from behind and recuffed them to a steel loop on the table. Her shoulders slumped and she looked near tears.

When he was ready, Osborne turned on his voice-activated recorder and asked Sarah to give her statement.

Gavin noted the details she included in her recitation of the events that he and Osborne had watched play out on the iPad. No doubt it was the reporter in her.

Caden had joined them and now paced the room while he listened. His jaw clenched tighter with each word she uttered. Finally, Caden stepped out of the room, phone pressed to his ear.

Sarah looked up. "Where's he going?"

"Probably pulling some strings to get you out of here before tomorrow."

Three hours later she was cleared, and Gavin held the door while she climbed into the passenger seat of his truck. "Are you sure you shouldn't see a doctor?"

"I'm sure. I'm sick of doctors."

He could understand that. Wasn't entirely comfortable with it, but understood it.

"I could ask you the same thing, though," she said. "You look like you took a few hits."

"I'm okay. Bumps and bruises that will heal." He shot her a tight smile. "Let's get you back to Caden's."

"No, I need to go to my house."

"Now?"

"Now."

Gavin glanced at the sun getting ready to dip below the horizon. "All right, but we've got reinforcements coming with us."

"Who?"

"Travis Walker and Asher."

"Who's Travis?"

"Another guy who works for the agency. From now on, I think we need to keep you surrounded."

For a moment, he thought she might protest, but she gave a slow nod. "I think you might be right."

As Gavin rounded the truck, he got on the phone and asked the two friends to meet him at the hospital. He climbed into the driver's seat, but he wasn't leaving until he had an escort. Sarah leaned her head against the seat rest, and Gavin thought she might be fighting tears.

"Hey," he said, reaching for her hand and threading his fingers through hers. "It's going to be okay."

She sniffed and nodded. "I don't cry," she whispered. "Why am I crying? I think I've cried more in the last few weeks than I've cried in . . . ever."

"It's okay to cry."

"No, it's not. It shows weakness, and I

feel like I've been weak ever since the Taliban walked in that school and took us."

Gavin huffed in disbelief. He cupped her cheek. "Sarah, you're one of the strongest people I know. Man or woman. You've had experiences no one should have — and you've lived to tell about it. You have a beautiful heart and care about people. Strangers like Brianne who most people would have walked away from. And Dustin. I know he's your brother, but in your gut, you feel something's wrong with his suicide and you're going after answers. That takes a strength that's rare to find. So, don't beat yourself up if you shed a few tears. Because you and I both know you'll brush them away and keep going. And that's what real strength is. Pressing on when it would be much easier to simply give up."

A tear streaked toward her chin and she wiped it away. She nodded. "Thank you."

"I didn't mean to preach, but . . . yeah."

She laughed and palmed the wetness from her eyes. "Sounds like you have some experience with the pressing-on thing."

"A bit."

His eyes locked on hers. The vulnerability was there, but so was the strength he'd just praised her for. His gaze dropped to her lips. He leaned in while gently propelling her toward him, his hand still cupped around her cheek, and settled his lips over hers.

Sarah wasn't sure what to think. Not that she really *could* think. She knew that the first kiss they'd shared in Kabul had been amazing. The second one had been more of a peck than a real kiss, but this one was turning out to be just as good as the first. If not better. His lips were gentle, exploring, curious and slightly demanding. Musk and sweat and smoke mingled to tantalize her nose. She threaded her fingers through his short hair, the strands silky and soft, brushing her palms and adding another layer to the heady moment. She wanted to move closer but the large console in the middle prevented it.

Before she could figure out a way around it, the kiss was over and disappointment flickered. He pulled back, eyes hooded, but still on hers. "I hope that was okay."

"More than," she whispered while her heart pounded in her throat. "I didn't want it to end."

He laughed. "I love your honesty."

She paused, then sat back and fastened the seat belt. "Well, mostly honest," she muttered.

He raised a brow. "What does that mean?"

"I didn't exactly tell the cops everything about that little incident."

"Like what?"

"Jonathan — or whatever his name is — said he was taking me to my place to get a package."

"What package?"

"The one Dustin apparently sent me. I think he sent me more than just a Christmas present. I also think that once I have it, we're going to have a lot more answers to what's going on."

He cranked the engine. "Why didn't you tell the cops about it?"

"Because they'd be all over the place." She shook her head. "No way. Dustin sent it to me for a reason. Possibly even risked his life to do so. I'm going to find it and see what's in it before I tell anyone else about it."

Gavin gave a slow nod. "All right. Then let's go get it."

"The problem is, it may not be at my apartment."

"Why not?"

"Because I had all of my mail forwarded to my neighbor. Then again, if that receipt is any indication, he actually *mailed* it to my neighbor."

"Then we'll check with her."

Sarah dialed her neighbor's number and

waited. And waited.

He glanced at the mirrors. "Our escorts just arrived."

"That's weird. She's not answering."

"It's getting close to dinnertime. Why don't I take you back to Caden's and you can wait for her to call you there?"

She frowned. "What happened to doing dinner at your parents' house?"

"I was going to cancel. After your adventures at the hospital, I didn't figure you'd want to go eat with people you've never met before."

"I thought you needed me to be a buffer," she said.

He gave her a crooked smile. "I'll be a big boy and deal with it. And her."

"Actually, I'd kind of like to go, if you don't mind."

He blinked. "Really?"

"I could use the distraction. If I go back to Caden's, he'll interrogate me and I'll dwell on the whole thing, and I just . . . yeah. I'd rather go eat dinner and forget about everything until Mrs. Howard calls."

"If you're sure."

"I'm sure." She paused. "As long as it's safe. I don't want to endanger your family." She rubbed her eyes. "Maybe it's better if I don't."

"Travis and Asher will be with us all the way. One will be in front and one behind. While we're inside, they'll be on guard."

"Fabulous. I just pray we're not putting them in danger, asking them to do this."

He squeezed her fingers. "This is their job. It's what they do every day. Fortunately, they're very good at it."

Sarah nodded. "I'm sure they are. You have some good friends."

"The best."

She shot him a small smile. "I know the feeling."

The friendships they'd formed while serving their country would last a lifetime, and he had no words for the gratitude that filled him when he thought of it. He just hoped he could keep Sarah alive to grow old with those friends. Because someone seemed determined to make sure that didn't happen.

CHAPTER NINETEEN

When Gavin pulled into the driveway of his parents' home, Sarah eyed the place with an envious stare. "You grew up here?" she asked. The two-story Victorian sat on an acre lot, and while the shutters needed a coat of paint, the yard was immaculate.

"I did. It was actually my grandparents' house until I was eight, then they moved into an assisted living home. My grandmother was forty-seven when my mother was born, so when Mom was thirty-five, her mother was eighty-two. Long story short, Mom loves this home and my parents moved us in because she couldn't bear to part with it." He eyed the exterior. "It needs some work, I know. Mom's been renovating the inside and plans to work her way out."

"Your mother's doing the renovations?"

"Yep. She's a pretty amazing woman."

"Sounds like it. I look forward to meeting her."

301

He made no move to open the door.

"Sometime today? Maybe?"

He choked on a laugh and opened the car door. She followed him up the four steps to the wraparound porch. The double swing in the right-hand corner invited her to sit on it, and the bistro table with two chairs begged for a tray of tea and biscuits.

"It's so lovely."

"Thanks."

A rush of anxiety swept through her and she rubbed her palms down her thighs. Why was she so nervous? It wasn't like this was a "meet the parents, *meet the parents*" kind of dinner. It was just . . . dinner. A gathering together to share food and enjoy company. She was there to be a buffer — whatever that meant.

He gripped her fingers and she prayed he didn't notice they were clammy.

Of course he noticed. "Don't get too far from me, okay?"

She frowned. "Okay. I thought you said this was safe enough. Aren't Travis and Asher somewhere watching the house?"

"Yes, they are, but I wasn't worried about you, I was worried about me."

"So, you were serious about the buffer thing?"

He shot her a surprised look. "Of course.

I haven't been this nervous since I asked you out for the first time."

"You get nervous?" He narrowed his eyes, and she bit her lip on a smile. "Are you going to knock?"

"Knock? No."

"Then should we leave?"

He twisted the knob. "Nope. I guess it's go time. For better or worse."

Interesting choice of words.

He stepped inside and she followed him into the small foyer.

"Gavin? Is that you?" The woman's voice came from the delicious-smelling kitchen.

"Of course it is. You need to lock your door."

"Not when I know you're coming." She stepped into view, drying her hands on a dishtowel. "And you must be Sarah."

"Yes, ma'am."

"I'm Priscilla Black. It's a pleasure to meet you."

The woman held out an elegant hand and Sarah shook it. "You have a lovely home."

"Thank you. Well, come on into the kitchen and grab something to drink. We don't stand on formality around here." The woman disappeared back into the kitchen.

Gavin squeezed her hand and led her into the bright, open breakfast room. A table to

303

seat eight sat under a five-bulb chandelier, and just beyond the table was a bar with four stools. Mrs. Black pulled a dish from the oven and set it on the waiting hot plate. "I hope you like chicken casserole."

"I like just about anything," Sarah said. "Especially if it's cooked by someone else."

"I understand that."

"Smells good in here." The gravelly voice came from the man wearing a faded Army T-shirt and a Bahamas baseball cap.

Gavin settled a hand on her lower back. "Dad, this is Sarah. Sarah, this is my father, Tucker Black."

The man studied her, sizing her up in a way that made her want to squirm. The look wasn't offensive in any way, but she wondered if she passed the inspection. He finally smiled. "Good to meet you, Sarah. I hear you're a good woman to have on the team."

She cocked a brow at Gavin. "Well, thank you, I appreciate that."

"Owen and Jefferson are out on the deck. Pris, you about ready?"

Gavin's mom nodded. "We'll serve from the bar."

"Perfect."

Mr. Black headed out to gather his friends from the deck and she looked at Gavin. "Who are they?" she whispered.

"I'll introduce you when they come in, but be forewarned, they're huge competitors."

"Competitors in what?"

"The reporting world."

She gaped, then snapped her mouth shut as a young woman floated into the kitchen. Sarah couldn't even use the word *walked*. The girl definitely floated. Kaylynn, no doubt. When she saw Gavin, her jaw tightened and she spun to leave.

"Kaylynn," Gavin said, "I want to introduce you to a friend."

Kaylynn turned back with a forced smile. "Hi."

"Hi. I'm Sarah."

Gavin stepped forward. "Can we talk after dinner?"

Kaylynn eyed them and shrugged, snitched a roll from the plate on the bar, and *floated* back out of the kitchen. Sarah thought she heard a smothered sigh from Gavin's mother, but the woman didn't say a word.

". . . can't compete with that," a man said, stepping through the sliding glass doors. "I'm telling you, he's the next Tom Brokaw or Dan Rather. You wait and see."

"You're dreaming. He's got about as much talent as —" The second man caught

305

sight of Sarah and Gavin. "Gavin, it's been a long time."

"It has. I see nothing's changed between you two."

"Aw, it's all fun and games."

Right. Sarah knew the two men by reputation only, but their competition wasn't all fun and games. However, it seemed they were at least making the attempt to get along. "How do you all know each other?"

Mr. Black laughed. "I went to high school with these two jokers."

"They've been friends forever," Mrs. Black said. "I know it seems like they hate each other, but they really don't." She handed Sarah a plate. "Please, go first. If you don't, you might not get to eat."

"Hey now," Gavin protested.

His mother winked. "I made extra. Help yourself."

Sarah filled her plate and settled at the table. Once everyone had served themselves, minus the absent Kaylynn, Sarah took note of her companions. She didn't think it coincidence that she found herself eating with two of the best-known men in the local reporting world, and slid Gavin a glance. He sat to her left and caught her eye. And shrugged.

"So, Sarah, I hear you were kidnapped by

a group of terrorists," Owen said. "You want to write that up and let me run it?"

Sarah choked on the bite of casserole she'd just taken. She swallowed, guzzled half of her glass of water, and stared at the man. "What?"

"I hear you're a reporter. I want the story."

"Investigative journalist, but —"

"So do I," Jefferson said with a glare at his rival. "You have no class. That's how you approach someone?"

"I'll pay you a hefty advance for it," Owen said as though the other man hadn't spoken.

"I'll pay more."

Gavin stood and glared at the men. "You two should be ashamed of yourselves. Sarah's a guest in my parents' home and you're like sharks circling bait. Knock it off."

Sarah's jaw dropped. The two men fell silent.

Gavin sighed. "I'm sorry, Sarah. This is my fault."

"How so?"

"I told my father you might need a job and asked him to use his connections to see if these two might be interested. I didn't think he'd invite them both at the same time."

"You asked him to find me a job?"

"In a sense." He paused. "Actually, no. I

just asked him to introduce you to these *gentlemen.* I didn't realize we would be inciting World War III."

Sarah set her napkin on the table. "So, being a buffer was just a . . . lie . . . to get me to come?"

"No, no, no. That part was definitely true." Gavin met his father's gaze. His mother had gone still at his outburst.

Owen sighed. "Well, at least take everything into consideration. Pris, this casserole is amazing."

Those words seemed to be the signal for everyone to start eating again. Except Sarah. She worked hard to keep her anger from spilling over and ruining the dinner Gavin's mother had prepared. She made it through the apple pie, then stood. "Excuse me, please."

Gavin made as though to follow her, and she shook her head. It wasn't hard to find the bathroom, and she stood at the sink trying to convince herself that Gavin hadn't meant anything by mentioning to his father that she might be in need of a job. And that his father was just trying to help by inviting the two men who obviously clashed on every level.

If anything, she should probably be grateful. Part of her knew he thought he was helping. But another part of her was screaming that it was similar to something her father might do, and all of the trust that she'd managed to build up had just been shattered.

"You're overreacting," she whispered. "Let it go. Just . . . don't read anything more into it other than an attempt to help. That's all it is. He's not like the general, he's not." The pep talk helped somewhat, as she forced herself to remember all the things he'd done that were completely opposite of what the general would have done. "He's different. He is. Don't overreact."

She got herself together and opened the door, only to find Kaylynn on the other side. "Sorry, I didn't mean to take too long."

"You didn't. I was waiting for you. I overheard what happened in the kitchen."

"Overheard it, huh?" More like eavesdropped.

"Gavin likes to be in control."

"Hmm. Yes, I'd say that's an accurate observation."

"But he means well."

Sarah raised a brow. "Really?"

A smile curved her lips. "Yes. He may behave like a bull in a china shop, but . . ." She shrugged.

"So, why won't *you* talk to him?"

Kaylynn's jaw tightened. "You're pretty blunt, aren't you?"

"It's the reporter in me."

Kaylynn went still and her face paled even while her eyes sharpened. "You're a reporter?"

"I am. Well, a journalist, but I've done a lot of investigative reporting for the military. Why?"

"Interesting," the girl almost whispered. "I heard them talking about you having a story, but I didn't realize you were an actual reporter."

She must have missed that part. "A currently unemployed journalist-slash-occasional-reporter, yes."

"Sounds like you could be employed should you decide you want to be."

"I don't think I'd like to work for either one of them."

Kaylynn actually smiled. "They're not so bad. They huff and they puff, but they've never actually blown anything down."

"When are you going to talk to Gavin?"

"When I feel like it. He made me mad, and I know avoiding him is the best way to get back at him."

Brutally honest, wasn't she?

"It's working. He wants a relationship with you."

Kaylynn fell silent, but Sarah could see she was thinking. "I like you, Sarah."

"Well . . . thanks."

"I'll think about what you've said, but I'm not ready to talk to Gavin, yet."

"I see. It'll hurt him." *Like your actions hurt the general?* The quiet whisper drifted across her mind.

Something flashed in Kaylynn's eyes, an indecipherable . . . something that resonated deep within Sarah. "Could I get your phone number?" Kaylynn asked.

"Of course." Sarah dictated it to her while Kaylynn tapped it into her device.

"Thanks." And then the girl was gone, drifting down the hall in her silent wraith-like way.

"I'm sorry, Sarah," Gavin said. He stood to her left at the end of the hallway. "I guess I didn't think that all the way through."

She sighed and shook her head. "No need to be sorry. I'm assuming you were trying to help?"

Relief flickered across his face. "Yes, I promise that's all it was. I'm not trying to be controlling or whatever it is that would make you find similarities between me and your father. I just threw out an idea. A bad one maybe, but that's all it was. An idea. An opportunity if you wanted it."

311

"It's okay." She looked at her phone. "Mrs. Howard still hasn't called me back and now isn't a good time for you to talk to Kaylynn."

"What? Why not?"

"Trust me, just don't. Not yet."

He frowned. "Okay."

"Would you be all right with saying our goodbyes to your parents and the others and heading over to my place?"

"I'd be more than all right with that. Let's go."

"Thanks for meeting me again," Marshall said to Lewis, who once again sat opposite him in the café. "I know it's last minute, so I wasn't sure you could make it."

"I didn't have anything better to do. Sharing two meals in one day is nice. Makes things less lonely."

"I'm sorry. You're taking the full six-week leave?"

Lewis sighed. "They offered it and I decided to accept it. For now. I can always go back early, but I'll be honest. I'm getting older and it takes me a while to bounce back from things."

His friend raised his brow. "I wouldn't exactly call your son's suicide something to *bounce back from*."

312

Lewis waved his hand. "That's not how I meant it." He paused, then pushed the pastry away from him. "Caden read me the riot act about Rochelle."

Marshall laughed. "And you took it?"

"On the chin."

His friend stopped and stared. "Getting soft in your old age?"

Lewis scoffed. "I'd like to think wiser." He looked away and out the window. "Initially, I dismissed everything he said, but some of it resonated — especially when Gavin, a friend of Caden's, basically said the same thing a short time later."

"What was it all about?"

"You know my father was a military man."

"I remember."

"He was hard-nosed, as rigid as they come."

"Sounds like the apple doesn't fall far from the tree — or whatever that analogy is."

His friend shot him a pointed look and Denning shook his head. "I'm not that rigid." He paused. "Okay, maybe I am. Now." He sipped his coffee. "Back then, I had dreams of being a doctor, did I ever tell you that?"

"You might have mentioned it one night while you were raging against your father."

"I hated him and yet . . . I've turned into him, haven't I?"

"Are you going to get all sappy?"

A laugh slipped from him. "When have you ever known me to be sappy?"

"Good point."

"No, I was just thinking. My father had to bribe me to join the military. Literally. He said if I didn't, he'd turn my inheritance over to charity."

"That's pretty harsh."

"It was so much money. Old family money that I'd been waiting a lifetime to get my hands on. I let him buy me and I've hated myself for it ever since." Lewis shook his head. "I did the same thing to Rochelle too."

"Only the opposite. You locked her money down because she joined up."

"She thinks I hate her. The truth is, I respect and admire her. She gave up millions to follow her dreams. And you know what's crazy? She did it without blinking. I honestly don't think she even considered anything but joining the Army."

"Sounds like you have a few regrets about some things."

The general sighed. A heavy, weighted breath. "Maybe I *am* getting old and second-guessing myself. My father made decisions for me that I hated. Decisions that hinged on the money." He shook his head. "That stupid money. I sacrificed my dreams for it and most people would kill for it. But honestly, some days it's just an albatross that I'd like to shake off."

His friend snorted and choked on the sip of iced tea he'd been in the process of taking. "Well, shake it my way. I can always put it into the research and development side for this project."

"I'm afraid I've invested all I can. But enough about that. I'm whining. How are you doing finding the last of your needed funds?"

"I think we've got it covered. Or will have it soon. I'm optimistic and ready to see this thing finished and on the market."

Lewis nodded. "I'm excited for you. You're doing some worthwhile things and should be proud of all you've accomplished."

Marshall grinned. "Thanks. That means a lot." He raised his glass. "Here's to making peace with those we love and helping those who can't help themselves."

Lewis clinked his coffee cup to the tea glass and wondered what it would take to get Rochelle talking to him again. Well, if she wanted her mail, she'd have to talk to him. He had a whole bagful to give her.

■ ■ ■ ■

When Gavin pulled into the parking spot of her apartment complex, Sarah tried to see it through his eyes. Run-down, shabby, slumlord owned and operated. All would be true, but she loved her little place.

The surprise on Gavin's face almost made her laugh.

"I have my reasons."

"Something to do with your dad? I'm sure you living in this area of town just thrilled him."

"How'd you guess?" She looked away from him. Time to be honest. "But it wasn't just him. I let him and — even Caden — believe it was, but the truth is, I had other reasons too."

"And Caden's okay with this?"

She scowled. "Caden didn't have any say in the matter."

"I'm surprised he's not camping out in his car every night."

"Are you serious?"

"Yeah, sorry, but I'm serious."

He totally was.

A rap on the window made her blink. A man in his early thirties, wearing a Stetson over dirty blond hair, stood outside the car.

His green eyes were serious. "I'm going to check the perimeter while you stay with her." He reached across Gavin and held out a hand for her to shake. "I'm Travis Walker. Nice to finally meet you, Sarah."

"You too. Thank you."

He clapped Gavin on the shoulder. "Asher's watching you while I check the place out. Sit tight until I give the all clear."

"Will do."

He left and she watched him go. "He's wearing boots and a cowboy hat."

"He's from Texas. He doesn't feel dressed without them."

"Interesting." She turned her attention from the cowboy and narrowed her eyes at Gavin, picking up where they'd left off. "You think I can't take care of myself? That, in normal circumstances, I need Caden to babysit? Or you think that I need you to set up a job interview? You really think that little of me?"

"It's not that, Sarah. I actually think very highly of you. I've apologized for the whole job thing — and I really meant that I was trying to help. But this is a situation where it's about watching out for someone you love. Someone who's deliberately put themselves in a dangerous circumstance when they didn't have to. You're seriously telling me this is all you could afford?"

"Of course not, but I just said I had reasons to move in here, other than just pushing my dad's buttons. That was just a bonus."

"Other reasons? Like what?"

"My mom used to live here."

His lips snapped together. "Oh. What? When?"

"Before she and the general met. Mom didn't have anything but her beauty and brains and the desire to make something of herself. She rented this crummy apartment — which wasn't quite so crummy at the time but is definitely worse now — so she could afford to pay for classes to get her degree. I'd just turned fourteen when she brought me here and told me her story. I didn't know it at the time, but she'd been diagnosed recently. Later, she said she didn't want me to associate my birthday with her cancer. Nine months ago, when I was on leave, I saw the apartment was available and I signed a lease. It's up in three months and I'm trying to decide what to do. At the time, though, it was an impulse thing. Something that made me feel closer to her."

"I know she died when you were young."

"She had ovarian cancer. Four months

318

after she brought me here, she died."

"I'm so sorry, Sarah."

"I am too. And neither she nor the general said a word about her illness until two weeks before she died. They didn't tell us. Can you believe it? Our mother was dying and they didn't tell us." She cleared her throat to fight the surge of tears. "That's the real reason I chose this apartment. At least that's what I tell myself."

"And the fact that it made your father mad was just gravy."

"Yes." She swallowed and looked at him. "I wanted to make him mad. I've been making him mad since the day my mother died."

"Why?"

"Anger. I was so very angry."

"Didn't you suspect something was wrong when she was so sick?"

Sarah shrugged. "I thought she had the flu for a while, and truthfully, I wasn't home a lot. Caden was four years older and already in his first year of college. Dustin was ten and oblivious. The general was overseas." She shrugged. "And you have to understand, Mom was a master makeup artist and actor. I didn't notice anything was terribly wrong until she passed out and I couldn't wake her up. I had to call 911. That's when she finally told us what was

319

going on. I was devastated."

"And angry."

"Yes." She paused. "I think I'm still angry about that." She nodded at the building. "That helps for some reason."

His fingers squeezed hers. "Your father didn't understand why you wanted to live here?"

"My father doesn't know. Mom never told him about this place. She said she was too embarrassed to show him where she lived before they met, but she wanted me to know. She grew up without a father in the picture, and I think she wanted me to see that I could still grow up and succeed without him — that I didn't have to let his disinterest, or lack of love, cripple me for life. She encouraged me to let God be my Father and my role model." She shook her head. "I don't know. Whatever her motivation, it worked. Eventually."

"Eventually?"

"And that's the rest of the story I promised to tell you."

"Go on."

"After my mother died, I turned into someone I . . . can't really describe. I wanted my father to hurt as bad as I was hurting. Or at least be so angry he couldn't sleep. The only way I knew how to do that was to hit his pride."

"Okay."

"So, I made some decisions that had the whole school talking — and one of the general's closest friends made sure he knew about those decisions."

"Such as?"

She drew in a deep breath and closed her eyes. So hard. She'd done this once and been rejected. She honestly didn't know if she could handle it if Gavin held her past against her. But he'd kissed her. He liked her. He was looking at the future and seeing her in it. If she wanted to be a part of that, he had to know her. All of her. "Such as the fact that I became the school . . ." She couldn't say it. She opened her eyes and looked into his. So concerned, so focused on what she was saying. "I had a lot of nicknames. A couple of them began with the letter S. The least offensive one was Sleep Around Sarah."

He sucked in a breath.

The tension running through her threatened to snap every muscle in her neck.

"Was it effective?" he asked. "With the general?"

"Very. He sent me away to boarding school for the last two years of high school. When I graduated, I came home and moved in here. To this place where my mother used to live. And I decided that I hated myself. I hated my father, but I hated myself more. That day, I remembered our conversation and decided I'd be someone she'd be proud of no matter what. This is where, for the first time in my young life, I found some peace."

He lifted a hand to stroke her cheek. "She'd be proud, Sarah."

Sarah couldn't look at him or she'd break down, but she nodded. "Thanks," she whispered. He hadn't responded to her confession. Was he repulsed? Disgusted? Ready to run as far as possible from her?

"She eventually moved, I take it."

"She did," Sarah said slowly, wondering why he hadn't addressed what she'd just told him. Maybe he needed to process it a bit. "She was a doctor and needed to be closer to the hospital. She'd just finished her residency and was working in the Emergency Department on Christmas Day when the general came in with an appendicitis attack. She diagnosed him and he ordered her not to leave him. So, she didn't. Once he was recovered, he came back to the hospital with flowers and asked her out."

"Sounds romantic."

"I know — and completely unlike the

322

general. I'm not sure I believe that's actually how it all went down, but that was her version. They married four months later and she had Caden a year after that. She quit her job to stay home with us."

He reached across and placed a hand on the back of her neck to gently massage. "If you get any tighter, you're going to snap."

"I always tense up when I talk about her — or my past. Simply because I still miss her terribly." And he had yet to say anything about her revelation. Was he going to ignore it?

He hugged her, an awkward embrace over the console — why was there always that blasted console between them? — but she took comfort in it while she pondered his response to her living in the run-down area and his lack of response about her confession.

Was he right? Was her choice a source of worry for Caden? She sighed. Of course it was, but did that make her selfish? It did if her only reason was to tick off her father.

Gavin nudged her. "Travis is heading back this way, but I want to let you know that I don't think any less of you, Sarah."

He didn't? "Why not?"

"You're not that person anymore. You've risen above it."

"Have I?" she whispered. He frowned and she leaned back to catch the expression on Travis's face. "Why does he look mad?"

"Because he found something, and it doesn't look like it's a good something." Gavin rolled the window down once more. "Well?"

"Someone broke into her place and trashed it. I've called the cops."

CHAPTER TWENTY

Sarah shot out of the truck like a bullet and Gavin scrambled after her. Travis and Asher pulled up the rear, the four of them coming to a halt just outside her apartment door.

Her mangled apartment door. It hung from one hinge.

"They kicked it in," she said.

With fingers curled into fists held at her side, she stepped over the threshold. Gavin rested a hand on her arm. "Hold up." He glanced at Asher. "I'm assuming you cleared the place and there's no one in there?"

"Nah, I fixed the guy a sandwich and told him to make himself at home."

Travis smothered a chuckle and Gavin smirked. "You really gotta find some new material for that stand-up act." The blip of sarcasm faded into seriousness when he looked at Sarah. "You can look, but don't touch anything."

She crossed her arms, fists tucked into her

armpits. "I don't believe this. When did this happen? Surely one of my neighbors would have seen it and called it in? I'll check with Mrs. Howard."

Sarah did a one-eighty and walked back through the door and across the hall to knock on the door opposite hers. "Mrs. Howard? Mrs. Howard? Are you in there?"

Nothing.

Footsteps from above sent Gavin into protective mode. He slipped in front of Sarah and palmed his weapon. No time to head back into her apartment. Another footfall and a young man in his late teens appeared. Tattoos covered the right side of his face, and his eyes locked on Gavin's. For a moment, he looked ready to bolt until Sarah lunged toward him. "Jimmy!"

"Sarah." The young man's face lit up and he grabbed her into a tight hug. "I thought that was you. You're back from Kabul."

While Gavin's jaw tightened, he slipped his weapon out of sight behind his back.

Sarah stepped back and Jimmy released her. "Did you see my apartment?"

Jimmy's eyes narrowed. "I saw it. Me and the guys have been keeping an eye on it ever since we noticed it."

"Did you call the cops?"

He shoved his hands into the front pockets

of his baggy jeans and shuffled his feet. "Aw, Sarah . . ."

"I know, I know. Dumb question. I don't guess you saw who did it?"

The young man dropped his head. "Naw, sorry."

Gavin couldn't help but wonder if he had an idea who could have done it, though. Then again, maybe not. He obviously looked up to Sarah, maybe even cared about her.

Jimmy jutted his chin at Gavin. "Who's the bodyguard?"

Sarah rolled her eyes. "He's not a body-guard —"

Gavin hoped she didn't notice his involuntary flinch.

"— he's a friend. He's been helping me out since I . . . got back from Afghanistan."

Gavin held out a hand. Anyone who treated Sarah well was okay in his book. "Gavin Black."

Jimmy hesitated a fraction, sizing him up, then thrust his hand into Gavin's. "Jimmy Lee."

"Nice to meet you."

"I guess my tats don't scare you." He eyed Gavin's arms.

"Should they?"

Jimmy laughed. "Naw, man. Didn't scare

327

the chica here either. Dat's when I knew we'd be friends."

"Um . . . Jimmy," Sarah said, "I kinda need to find Mrs. Howard. Have you seen her?"

"She's not here. Took off on some spur-of-the-moment European trip thing with her granddaughter."

"The granddaughter from the daughter who married that wealthy politician." She shook her head and pursed her lips. "They'll take her on a trip to Europe to babysit their brood, but they won't spend their precious money to move her into a safer neighborhood." Sarah scowled. "Lousy —" She broke off and drew in a breath. "She's collecting my mail."

"And I'm watering her plants and feeding her cat." He held up a key. "That's what I was coming down to do when I heard your racket. We can see if your mail is in there."

"I'll let you check. I guess I need to take care of the apartment."

He shrugged. "I'll bring it over if I see it."

"Thanks."

Gavin led her back into her trashed apartment, and the officers arrived two minutes later. The first officer introduced himself as Carlos Gonzales and his partner as Kristin Gerard.

"When did this happen?" Officer Gonzales asked.

"I'm not sure," Sarah said. She raked a hand over her hair. "Probably sometime last week. I haven't been here, and we don't exactly have a neighborhood watch."

"Right." He wrote in his little black notebook and looked up. "Is anything missing?"

"I was getting ready to figure that out."

He nodded.

"I'll just go knock on some doors and see if anyone's willing to tell us anything," Officer Gerard said.

"Don't count on it," Gonzales muttered.

"Hey now," Sarah said, "don't discount my neighbors. They may not have a lot of money, but they're mostly good people."

"One of them probably did this," the man said.

Sarah planted her hands on her hips. "No, one of them probably didn't. I have a feeling this had nothing to do with anyone who lives in this building." She headed toward her bedroom before she was tempted to say more. She understood his instant leap to judgment. He was a cop. He saw his fair share of human depravity on a daily basis, but she wasn't kidding. She'd gotten to know her neighbors and thought highly of several.

And not so highly of others.

However, she wasn't lying when she said she couldn't think of one who would do this. She walked into her bedroom and sighed. Every drawer had been pulled out and dumped and the built-in bookshelf in the far corner swept clean. Books littered the floor. The en suite bath had suffered the same type of damage. The question was, had they found what they'd been looking for?

Probably not, if it was the package Dustin had sent to her.

Gavin stepped next to her. "I just heard from Caden. He said the detectives tracked down Max's home. Only he's not there and apparently hasn't been for a while. There aren't any airline, train, or bus tickets in his name, so no one is sure where he is."

She frowned. "Odd."

"They're still looking for him. Hopefully, he'll turn up soon."

Once the officers left, she looked around. "I don't guess there's anything else to do here other than clean up — and find Jimmy to see if there was a package in my mail from Dustin."

"There wasn't." She turned at Jimmy's

voice. He stood in the doorway. "I did find this, though. Thought it was weird because it has your last name on it. Who's Lewis Denning?" He handed her a sticky note.

"My father." She glanced at the note and gaped. "Why does Mrs. Howard have my father's address and phone number?"

"Not gonna say how, but I know that address and that's a pretty swanky crib," Jimmy said. He swept a hand out to indicate her place. "What you doing living in this — uh — ghetto?"

Jimmy always cleaned up his language for her. She found it funny and endearing. He knew she was in the military, but the sign of respect touched her. "For various reasons, Jimmy. The main one being I don't get along with my father."

"I get that. You don't gotta say nothing else." He swiped a hand across his mouth. "I gotta split. You got my number if you need anything else."

"Thanks, Jimmy."

" 'Course." He backed from the room and disappeared into the hallway.

Sarah pulled her phone from her pocket and called her father. He answered on the second ring with an abrupt hello.

"It's Sarah."

A pause.

"So, you're talking to me now?"

"Why does my neighbor, Mrs. Howard, have your address and phone number on a sticky note?"

Silence.

"General?" she pushed.

"She . . . uh . . . got in touch with me and said she needed to forward your mail to me. I came by and picked up the bag she had, and then we forwarded the rest to my address."

"*You* have it?"

"I believe I just said that."

Sarah's brain spun. "Wait a minute. How did she even know you were my father? I've never told her." She never talked about him to anyone.

He cleared his throat and the evidence of his nerves unsettled her even more than she already was. "General?"

"I dropped by one day shortly after you moved in and told her to call me if she thought you needed anything."

Sarah fell silent, unable to wrap her mind around it. "Why?" she finally managed to sputter.

"Because I needed someone to keep an eye on you."

Mrs. Howard was her father's spy? "I'm coming to get my mail. Just put it on the

332

front porch. Please." She forced the word out in as pleasant a tone as she could muster. "Or, better yet, have Mrs. Lawson do it. Thank you." She hung up and realized she was shaking. She curled her fingers into fists.

Gavin eyed her with . . . what? She raised a brow.

"He cares about you," he said.

"He's using my neighbors to spy on me."

"He's worried about you. If my sister or daughter was living here, you'd better believe I'd have some kind of spy network in place."

"You . . . you . . . ahhh . . . never mind." Unable to figure out how to make him understand that the man didn't worry about anything but his precious career, she let it go. For now.

Gavin's phone rang and he snapped it to his ear. "Caden? What's up?" He listened for a few seconds, nodded, and caught her eye. "Thanks for the update."

He hung up.

"What?" she asked.

"They found Max."

"And?"

"He's dead. He was killed in a car wreck a few weeks ago."

■ ■ ■ ■

Gavin stayed next to Sarah as she walked up the front steps of her father's home. When they'd arrived, she had to have him buzz them in.

Now she rang the bell and Gavin marveled at the differences between them. When he visited his parents, he simply walked in and hollered that he was home. Granted, those visits had been few and far between lately, but that was one constant that would never change. He'd always be welcome in his parents' home and he'd never feel like he had to knock to gain entrance.

"They have the wrong Max," she said staring at the front door. "Wilmont said Max told him to deliver the pills. That Max has to be very much alive, because that was yesterday."

"I know, but it doesn't make sense that that's the only Max they were able to find at the hospital. And he wasn't even an employee."

"But he was there on a regular basis. Dressed in scrubs and wearing an ID badge."

"I agree. It's not adding up."

The door opened and an older woman

with gray hair slicked back into a neat bun smiled at Sarah. "Sorry it took me so long to get the door. Come in, come in. Your father's in his study."

"I don't need to see him. I just need to get whatever mail he has."

"It's in a box in the kitchen."

She raised her brows at Gavin, and Sarah sputtered. "Oh, Mrs. Lawson, this is my friend, Gavin Black."

Mrs. Lawson inclined her head at Gavin. "So nice to meet you."

"Likewise," Gavin said.

"Why don't you follow me?" She turned on her heel to lead them through the foyer and into the small hallway that led to a kitchen any cook would be proud of.

A white box sat in the middle of the ten-person table. Sarah made a beeline for it and pulled out a thick manila envelope. "This is the only thing that could pass as a package," she said. She glanced at the front. "And it's got my name but Mrs. Howard's address on it. From Dustin." Tears welled and she swallowed hard while still looking at the piece. Her fingers trailed her brother's name in the left-hand corner.

Gavin stayed put, giving her the moment.

Footsteps in the hallway caught his attention, and Sarah stilled when her father stepped into the room. Gavin noticed her instant defensive stance. If she'd been a porcupine, every quill would be in the man's throat.

Sarah ignored him and slid a finger into a small hole at the flap and pulled. She reached inside and removed a stack of papers, a notebook, and what looked like a white envelope. "It has my name on it." She opened the seal and pulled out a handwritten letter.

" 'Dear Sarah,' " she read, her voice low and gravelly. " 'I miss you, baby sis.' " She looked at Gavin. "I was older, but he called me that because I was smaller than him." Her eyes dropped back to the letter. " 'I'm sending this to Mrs. Howard because I know she's getting your mail. I'd give this to you in person, but something happened the other day that's got me a little paranoid. I think someone tried to kill me.' " She winced and Gavin held still, knowing she needed to do this. " 'I'll tell you about that later after I find out if I'm right or not. If Caden hasn't already told you, I'm doing an inpatient program at the VA hospital here in Greenville. I told myself it was to find out what happened to a friend of mine, but the truth is, I probably was hoping it would help me in my own struggle. Things are tough, Sarah, and I'm tired. Don't tell the general, he'll think I'm weak, but here's the thing. I've got PTSD. You don't know how much it pains me to admit that, but I'm telling you so you understand where I'm coming from. I'm involved in a trial drug program. I signed up for it willingly because I suspect that it's not all on the up-and-up, but I can't figure out why. So, you might say I've signed up to be a guinea pig to get some answers. Although, I'll admit my surprise that the drug is an amazing thing. The nightmares have stopped, the constant anxiety and jumpiness is gone. I haven't had a flashback in weeks. I can sleep again. I honestly don't know how to describe the relief.' "

A choking sound came from the man still standing just inside the door, and Sarah paused but didn't look up. She drew in a shaky breath and blew it out slowly. The general scrubbed a hand down his cheek, and Gavin couldn't decipher the look on his face.

" 'And yet,' " Sarah continued, " 'something's going on. People are dying by suicide. I've done some research into those involved and some things aren't adding up. There's a psychiatrist in Kabul who's working with several doctors in the States. Her

337

name is Emily Winslow. Any patients who exhibit PTSD symptoms are sent to her hospital. She makes the diagnoses and prescribes the medication. She then writes the discharge order and sends the patients home to be treated at their local VA hospital.' "

The general gasped and Sarah finally looked at him. "Did you know?"

"No."

"But you were the one who asked her to discharge me with the diagnosis."

"I did, but not because I knew anything about this trial."

"Was Dustin officially discharged?"

Her father shook his head. "I found out he got out the day he . . . died, but I never asked whether his tour was up or if he was discharged. I'm guessing since he was in the VA psychiatric ward for close to three months, Winslow discharged him like she did you."

"Might want to find that out."

He nodded. "Keep reading, please."

" 'Anyway, I saw the piece you did on the bombing of the orphanage in Kabul. That was truly great work. I could feel the pain. Your article wept with those suffering and I was so proud —' "

Her voice cracked and she swiped a stray

tear. Gavin wanted to gather her in a hug and take away her pain but didn't think it was the right moment. Another shuddering breath and she read on.

" '— so proud to tell everyone you were my sister. You've got a real gift for words and I hope you'll continue to use that gift to keep impacting lives.' " She paused. " 'I don't think I've ever told you anything like that before and I just felt like I should. Okay, back to the issue at hand.' " Sarah focused on Dustin's final words. " 'I've included a list of all of the vets who were a part of the program. I had to get a friend to help me hack into Winslow's computer, but I found what I was looking for. I don't know that she's actually hurting people, but not sure she isn't either, because people are dying. It took me a little bit to figure out the names on the list are people who were a part of the program. When I came across my name, the drug they're testing, and the dosage amount, it was pretty easy to deduce the rest of it. But then there was a second list. Twenty-six names, also with the name of the drug and the dosage. I tried to get ahold of a few of them to ask if they were part of the trial and I couldn't get one person on the phone. I found obituaries for six of them. They're from different parts of the country, but that can't be a coincidence. Since I'm not sure someone isn't trying to kill me, I figured with your bloodhound nose and bulldog tenacity, I'd send this to you and you'd figure it out. Please be careful. Ask Caden for help if you need it, but don't let anyone else know I sent you this stuff. The journal is just for you to put in my safe-deposit box. You know where the key is. Don't read it. It's not your business. I just want it someplace safe in case the worst happens. And now that I've said that, you're the only one I trust to do the right thing and actually not read it. A journalist with ethics. That's a new concept, isn't it? Seriously, thanks, Sarah. I'm looking forward to seeing you at Thanksgiving. Tell the general . . . well, I don't know what to tell him. Tell him I hope we can all do Thanksgiving together and I'll call him soon. I'm talking to Caden so you don't have to tell him anything. Ha. I love you, baby sis. I can't wait to see what you do with this story. This might just be the one to catapult you into that dream job you used to talk about. Anyway, I'll keep sending information as I come across it. Bye for now. Dustin.' "

Tears slipped unchecked down her cheeks, and the general backed out of the kitchen, palms pressed to his eyes.

Gavin stepped next to Sarah. "Can I do anything?"

She shook her head and sniffed, grabbed a paper towel from the roll near the sink. "No, there's nothing anyone can do." She nodded to the package. "What do you think about this?"

"I think Dustin thought he was on to something. And that note doesn't sound like a man who was thinking about killing himself."

"No, it doesn't. So what changed?"

Gavin leaned against the counter and crossed his arms. "I don't know, but I think if we follow the trail that Dustin's left us, we might find out why. Someone wanted that package bad enough to trash your place looking for it — and then stage a hospital fire in order to snatch you in a moment of chaos. That says a lot right there." He paused and frowned. "Sarah?"

"What?"

"Why did he send the package here? Why not to your address in Kabul? Or even the school where you were known to be teaching each week?"

"I sent him a text that I had some leave coming up. I was going to fly home to see Ava for a couple of weeks, hang out with Caden for a few days, then head back to

Kabul — as long as I wasn't in the middle of a story. Dustin knew I'd eventually stop by my apartment." She paused. "He also knew my neighbor would be collecting my mail. And . . . he knew he'd be here." She rubbed a hand down her cheek and switched gears. "I wonder if Lucy's sister was involved in this drug trial."

Gavin picked up the papers from Dustin and flipped through them. "Quite a stack here." He pulled out a map of the United States. "Check this out. What do you think those little red dots mean?"

"I don't know, but they stretch from coast to coast."

He spread the papers out on the island. "There are two sets of data with names and meds and dosages just like Dustin said." He pointed. "There's his name."

"So, this is the list of those who volunteered for the trial."

"Looks like it."

Gavin pulled out another list. "So, who are these people?"

She scanned the paper and gasped.

Gavin stilled. "What?"

Sarah tapped a finger on a name they both recognized. "Brianne Davis," they said in unison.

"And look whose name is just above hers,"

Sarah said.

Gavin's eyes met hers. "Helen Craft."

"I guess that answers that question." She nodded. "And the last name on the list."

"Terry Xia?" He straightened. "I think we need to have a talk with the detectives."

"I'll call Elliott when we get on the road. Right now, I'm going to tell your father goodbye," Gavin told her.

"Help yourself. I, for one, am itching to get out of here." She walked out the front door after giving Mrs. Lawson a hug.

If Travis and Asher hadn't been stationed outside the gates, Gavin would have stopped her. Instead, he let the men know she was headed for his truck while he hunted the general down. He found him in his office and offered his condolences once more. With a wave of his hand, the general dismissed him. Gavin didn't take it personally. He could tell the package and Sarah's attitude hung on him like an albatross.

"I'll be in touch," Gavin said. "Let me know if there's anything else I can do."

"Just keep her safe."

His distracted order almost made Gavin pause and spur him to ask if there was something else going on, but the man didn't invite that kind of relationship, so Gavin kept his questions to himself. He hurried to the kitchen and grabbed the rest of the mail Sarah had left, then rushed down the front steps to his truck. She was sitting in the passenger seat, the contents of Dustin's envelope spread over her lap and the dashboard.

"I wish you would've waited for me."

"This place is a fortress." She turned a page. "No one's coming through those gates unless the general opens them."

"Or someone forces him to."

She shot him a pained look and went back to Dustin's materials. Gavin decided to shut up and not even mention the possibility of a drone strike. It sounded far-fetched, but so did Iraqi terrorists on American soil looking to take Sarah out because of her father.

Far-fetched, but not impossible. Nothing was impossible.

However, while Sarah had an impulsive side, she wasn't stupid and could think for herself. Every moment he spent with her just reinforced that. And yet, the desire to protect her — even from herself — wasn't something he could just ignore. So, he'd do his best and pray that was enough.

Sarah rubbed her forehead.

"Headache?"

"Yes."

He opened the glove box and handed her

a bottle of ibuprofen. She took two and replaced the bottle. "I need to call the detectives," Gavin said, "or call Caden so he can meet us and we can show him what we found and *he* can call the detectives."

"Sure." She leaned her head back once again and closed her eyes, her fingers clutched around the manila envelope. "Sounds good." A slight pause. "Let's go to Caden's house so we can study this stuff some more."

"I like that plan."

He let Travis and Asher know what they were doing, then drove in silence for a few minutes. Sarah still had her eyes closed, and her frown pulled her brows together over the bridge of her nose.

"What are you thinking about?"

"Dustin." She glanced at him. "I just can't get past my confusion about his actions. I know I sound like a broken record, but if there wasn't concrete proof that he jumped, I'd swear he was murdered. I feel even stronger about it now that I've read this letter."

Gavin nodded. "I have to agree with that."

"Tomorrow, I want to go by the VA hospital."

He shot her a frown. "Why? What do you have in mind?"

345

"It's just an idea. Maybe a stupid one, but Dr. Kilgore is involved in all of this somehow — and probably that nurse, Donna." She paused. "I have a feeling they're closer to the bottom of the food chain, though, and someone else is calling the shots with whatever is going on at the hospital."

"Then we'll see what we can find first thing in the morning."

CHAPTER TWENTY-ONE

Lewis dropped his head into his hands and studied the photos in front of him. He'd taken a huge chance in opening the package Dustin had sent Rochelle . . . Sarah. As soon as Mrs. Lawson had told him she was coming to the house and that she'd asked about her mail, he'd known something was up. Only something of dire importance would bring her into the same air he breathed, and he'd gone looking.

Fortunately, he'd been extremely careful and she hadn't noticed the small slit or the extra tape. He'd read Dustin's letter and hadn't seen anything terribly incriminating in it. He'd simply placed it in a new envelope and written her name on the front, copying Dustin's writing as close as he could. He'd had to wait two hours for his hands to quit shaking in order to write her name — a clear sign of just how rattled he'd been by the pictures and other information

Dustin had sent.

He didn't want to believe it, but the proof was right there.

Now, he had to quit stalling and decide exactly how to handle everything.

For the second time in his life, he simply didn't know what to do. After several more minutes of deliberation, he picked up his cell phone and punched in a number. When the person answered with a gruff hello, Lewis said, "We need to talk."

Caden met the two detectives at the hospital, along with a CID detective named Patty Boyer. He had just walked through the door when his phone buzzed. He glanced at the screen. A text from Sarah.

Need to see you ASAP. I'd planned to talk to you this morning, but you left too early.

Caden frowned and typed.

At the hospital getting ready to question Wilmont about this guy Max. We just got approval from the doctor to talk to him so I bolted.

When you finish, we'll be waiting at your house.

Caden texted a thumbs-up, then returned to the picture of the clean-shaven man who had been reported killed in a car accident — and yet facial recognition software said he was very much alive in spite of the beard, mustache, and wire-rimmed glasses shown in the security footage.

According to the official report, Mr. Xia had been driving late at night in heavy rain and hit a deer, which had sent him careening over an embankment and into a gas station tank. A spark had set off an explosion, and by the time rescue workers arrived, there was nothing left of the car or Mr. Xia. And yet, a man named Max — aka Mr. Xia — had sent Wilmont with medication to Brianne Davis's house and was masquerading as an employee at the hospital.

When they stepped onto Wilmont's floor, Caden's gaze landed on Heather Fontaine, standing at the nurses' station pointing to something on her laptop. She looked and waved. He nodded and trailed behind Elliott and Caroline, stopping in front of Wilmont's room.

Elliott knocked and pushed the door open. "Mr. Wilmont," the detective said, "glad to see you're awake and feeling better."

"Yeah. Me too."

349

"Everything okay?" Heather's soft voice came from behind Caden.

He turned. "Yeah, we just have a few questions for this guy."

"He's the one who attacked Sarah?"

"He is." He patted her shoulder. "I'll be back shortly."

Caden slipped inside the room and stood to the left of the door. Heather stayed behind him close enough to hear.

"I trust you've had no ill effects from the evacuation?" Caroline asked.

"No," Wilmont said. "I'm fine. Turns out it was mostly smoke. They got everything contained pretty fast."

"We heard," Caroline said.

"So, why are you back? I don't remember anything more than I've already told you."

Elliott raked a hand over his hair. "We wanted to ask you about Max."

Wilmont shifted under the sheets and sniffed. "What do you want to know about him?"

"How long have you known him?"

"Just a few weeks."

"So, he was new?"

"Yeah." He frowned. "He just showed up one day and said he was the new guy and his name was Max."

"What's his last name?"

"I dunno. I never asked."

"It would have been on his badge."

The man in the bed rubbed his eyes. "Ah man, it's weird. I never can remember it. I just call him Max."

"Was it Xia?"

"Yeah, maybe. Yeah, I think that was it." He pursed his lips. "If you knew, why ask me?"

"Tell us everything you can about the guy."

"There's not that much." He paused. "I like him. He treats me like I'm human, like he saw me. Most of the time, I feel invisible, but Max is . . . nice."

"Did he ever say anything about a car wreck?"

"No. Why?"

"Did you ever go to his house?"

"No! I told you I only knew the guy a few weeks. And besides, I think he's living at the hospital."

Caden straightened. "Why do you say that?"

"Because, one time about two weeks ago, there was a particularly nasty job to clean up in the ER. Max wasn't supposed to be working that day. He'd told me the day before that he had something to take care of. I went looking for some cleaner and

351

caught him coming out of one of the storage closets. He didn't see me and I didn't make it a point to let him know I saw him." Wilmont rubbed his nose and shrugged. "Anyway, after I finished for the day, I snooped around in the closet and found several blankets and a pillow piled in the corner. Underneath the pile, there were a couple changes of clothes and a backpack full of toiletries. Not many people go in that closet, just janitorial staff, so there's a good chance he wouldn't be caught."

"Did you report it?" Patty asked.

"No way. I liked Max. And like I said, he was nice to me. Not many people even notice the cleaning crew."

Elliott glanced at Caden, then handed Wilmont a pad of paper and a pen. "Write down exactly where this closet is."

Sarah shot another glance at Gavin. He'd accepted her disclosure with so much sympathy and understanding that it unsettled her. Her nerves were shot. Before she could recover her composure, her phone buzzed. "That's Caden." She set her coffee aside and tapped the screen. "Hello?"

"I can't talk long, just letting you know I'm still at the hospital."

"I figured."

"It's probably going to be a while."

She hesitated. "Okay, we'll come by the hospital and wait. What did Wilmont say?"

"That Max might be living here at the hospital. We're heading to check out the closet he's possibly been calling home. Look, I have to go. I'll let you know if we find him."

"Okay. Thanks, Caden."

"Sure. Gotta go. Let me know when you're here and I'll tell you where to meet."

She hung up and Gavin raised a brow. "What was that about?"

"Caden said Max might be living at the hospital and they're going looking for him. And . . . we're heading to the hospital to meet Caden to fill him in, because he's going to be a while. But I really think he needs to see this stuff from Dustin."

"I agree."

Sarah studied the paper with the red dots one more time. "Look," she said. "Those dots match up with the states these people are from."

"The people not on the list for the trial?"

"Yeah, they're on the second list."

Gavin pulled his laptop toward him and soon the sound of clicking keys filled the room while she pondered what it could all mean.

■ ■ ■ ■

Heather had been so quiet, Caden had almost forgotten she was there, but when they headed out of Wilmont's room, following the detectives and one of the members of hospital security down the hall, she stayed with him. "Can I see that?" she asked.

Elliott raised a brow but handed her the directions.

"I know where this is," she said. "It's actually a room used as storage."

"You want to lead? It'll be easier than trying to read that chicken scratch."

"Sure."

The CID agent brought up the rear.

When they arrived at the storage closet, the security officer swiped his key card, opened the door, and flipped on the light.

Caroline took the lead, weaving her way toward the back of the room. Metal shelves lined the walls, and more were placed in the center of the room, effectively creating a hidden area in the back, not visible from the door. Caden walked toward a bathroom while Elliott headed toward a pile of blankets against the back wall.

"Found the backpack," Elliott called.

"And I found Mr. Xia," Caden said.

■ ■ ■ ■

After ten minutes of research, Gavin leaned back into the sofa cushion. "They're all vets, obviously. A lot of them are dead. Suicides. Several survived suicide attempts."

She frowned. "It's the drug," she said. She shivered and grabbed a sweatshirt from the back of the sofa and pulled it over her head. "Whatever that drug is, it's not working and they're covering it up." She paused. "I wonder how close it is to being approved by the FDA?"

"That's a good theory," he said, "but Dustin said it *was* working, remember?"

She sighed. "Right. That doesn't make sense. Then again, if you think about it, everyone we talked to said their relatives' mood changed almost lightning quick. Brianne's friend even said she was gone for less than an hour. When she left, Brianne was fine and planning a trip to Hawaii. When she got back, she was in the pit of despair." She stilled as part of a conversation floated to the forefront of her mind. "Wait a minute."

"What?"

"Dr. Kilgore and the other man I heard in the hallway of the hospital were talking

355

about a drug. One asked if Brianne was on it, and when Dr. Kilgore said yes, the other guy told him to take her off of it."

Gavin blinked. "Okay. What if it's not the drug itself that causes suicidal thoughts . . . er . . . actions, but the withdrawal from it?"

She nodded. Then frowned and shook her head. "But Wilmont took the drug too, remember? Has he displayed any suicidal symptoms?"

Gavin pursed his lips. "No, but maybe two pills simply weren't enough. He wouldn't have withdrawals from that, would he?"

"I wouldn't think so."

"Then why was Max sending those pills to Brianne? To keep her from having withdrawals?"

"Has to be. Hopefully, Caden will have some answers by the time we get there." She gathered the papers from the table and stuffed them into the manila envelope. She'd set the journal aside, convinced there was nothing in there but Dustin's private thoughts. One day, she might read them — and share them with Caden — but for now, she knew there was no way she could read Dustin's words and be privy to his most intimate thoughts without losing control of her emotions. Later, once the violent sting of his sudden passing had eased, she might be able to handle it.

Gavin took her plate to the sink, rinsed it, and stuck it in the dishwasher. Her jaw dropped. "Where'd you learn how to do that?"

He turned and frowned. "Do what?"

"Load a dishwasher."

He laughed. "It's not rocket science."

"Might as well be. Neither Dustin nor Caden ever learned how to do that."

A knowing smile slid across his lips. "I guarantee you Caden knows how to load one. And I'm sure Dustin did too. It's just if they played the helpless male, you'd take pity on them and do it for them."

She shook her head. "I've always suspected that. What brats."

"Don't tell Caden I broke the 'bro code' and revealed one of our secrets."

Sarah laughed. Then sobered. "I won't say a word, but he might suspect when I tell him it's his turn to load the dishwasher."

"Who's been loading it since you've been here?" Mirth danced in his eyes.

"Well, duh. The dishwasher fairies, of course. The same ones who load yours, I suspect."

His laughter rang through the kitchen and the sound pierced her heart. He was a good man. An honest one. He had a serious side but didn't take himself too seriously. He could be deadly in a situation that required it — and yet gentle as a warm breeze on a sunny day. He was a mass of contradictions and he fascinated her. And scared her. He could break her heart without even trying at this point. She'd laid it out there for him and felt like she'd been left in limbo.

He called Asher and Travis and filled them in on their upcoming trip to the hospital, then watched the area while she climbed into the passenger seat. Once they were on the way, she let out a low sigh.

"I'm a very selfish person, aren't I?" The words slipped from her lips before she could stop them.

He blinked, glanced at her, then back at the road. "What makes you say that?"

"You were right about the apartment, for one thing. I was only thinking of myself when I moved in. I had no thought or worry that Caden would lose sleep over it. I didn't care about my father's opinion. Still don't, really, but I should have considered Caden's."

Gavin shook his head. "Hindsight is twenty-twenty, Sarah. When we're hurting, sometimes we do things and it's almost impossible to see past that hurt."

Like sleep with anyone who asked? Was

that a reference to her past? Even if it wasn't, it still fit. "You say some very wise things sometimes, you know that?"

A chuckle rumbled from him. "Well, thank you. I try." He paused. "What did your father do to make you so angry? I know he wasn't here a lot, but surely there's more to it than just that."

"He let my mother die without him." Sarah said the words aloud for the first time. "He didn't come home in time to be with her before she died."

"Oh. Maybe he couldn't."

She shrugged. "I don't know. He said he simply couldn't leave when we needed him to and refused to explain further." She settled her elbow on the armrest and looked out the window. "Mom was in the hospital after passing out and she was quickly moved to hospice. I called my dad and left message after message on the emergency number we had for him." She shook her head. "Days passed. By the time he called me back, she'd taken a turn for the worse and slipped into a coma." A shuddering sigh escaped her. He threaded his fingers through hers, enfolding her in his warmth. For a moment, she simply let herself embrace the comfort his touch offered. "When he called, I told him the news and he said he would be on

359

the next flight home. She died the next day and I found out he hadn't even left Afghanistan."

"You were with her. She wasn't alone."

"But she wanted *him*. She had things she wanted to say to *him* and he never gave her that chance. He *stole* that from her, and I, for some reason, can't get past it. I've gotten past a lot of stuff, but not that."

"Don't hate me for asking, but have you tried?"

Sarah flinched, bit her tongue on the first thought that whipped across her mind, and forced herself to really consider the question. Sometimes she hated her inability to be anything but honest. "No," she said, "I haven't. I've been too busy being angry with him."

Gavin shot her a smile and a sympathetic look. "At least you admit it."

She frowned. "Now quit asking me deep questions like that until I'm ready to deal with them."

"Yes, ma'am." He glanced in the rearview mirror.

"Travis and Asher are there."

Gavin shook his head. "Not much gets past you, does it?"

She huffed a laugh. "More than I would like, I suspect. Don't they need to sleep?"

"They're staying together and sleeping in shifts. Just in case."

"Got it."

"Nothing's going to happen to you, Sarah, not while I'm still breathing. And that's a promise."

CHAPTER TWENTY-TWO

Max stepped out of the bathroom, wiping his freshly shaved jaw with a white towel. Another towel circled his waist, the corner tucked in near his navel. "I knew this was too good to last," he said. "What gave me away?"

"A little birdie named Wilmont," Caden said.

"Sam?"

"The one and only." Elliott tossed him a shirt, boxers, and a pair of jeans. "Get dressed, we've got some questions for you. You can use the bathroom to change, but leave the door open."

Max didn't seem inclined to argue or attempt a disappearing act, but Caden wasn't taking any chances. He stood in the doorway, his foot blocking the door from fully closing.

Max changed and Caden handed him his

shoes. "What's all this about?" the man asked.

Caroline gave a short laugh. "We'd like to know how a dead man is working . . ."

". . . and living . . . ," Elliott said.

". . . at a hospital without getting caught," Patty said.

"But you did catch me."

"Not very quickly," Elliott muttered, then scrubbed a hand down his cheek. "Let's find a conference room."

The security officer led the way out of the closet and down the hall to stop in front of a closed door. He swiped the key card and held the door while they all filed in, with Max in the middle and Caden bringing up the rear.

Elliott turned and pointed to Heather. "You don't need to be in here."

Caden cleared his throat. "I think it might be helpful to have a physician's ears on this. I know her and I trust her one hundred percent."

Elliott and Caroline exchanged glances and frowned. Then Caroline gave a slight nod. Elliott shrugged.

"I'll be right out here if you need anything," the guard said.

"Thanks."

The door shut and Caden took a seat at

the end of the table. Mr. Xia sat opposite him, with Caroline and Elliott bookending him, one on each side of the table. Patty Boyer leaned against the wall and crossed her arms. Heather perched on the edge of her seat next to Elliott.

"That was you in the wreck, right?" Caroline asked.

Max nodded. "I managed to get out of the car shortly before it exploded."

"Why play dead?"

"Because the accident wasn't an accident. Someone tried to kill me."

Caden raised a brow. "By planting a deer in the road?"

"There wasn't a deer. There was another car. It cut across in front of me and I went down the embankment."

Elliott leaned forward. "Who?"

Max shifted and rubbed his chin. "Someone from the company I used to work for."

"Marshbanks Pharmaceuticals," Caden said.

Max nodded. "You've done your homework."

"It wasn't hard. I remember the wreck from the news. What about your family?"

"They know I'm alive but in danger. I sent them to London to stay with my sister-in-law until I could figure out how to bring down the company."

The detectives exchanged a look. "Why do you want to bring it down?" Elliott asked.

"Because it killed my son."

Silence fell, then Elliott cleared his throat. "Can you give us some details?"

"Terry, my son, was in Kabul. He was Army. A little over a year ago, insurgents bombed an orphanage and he was part of the rescue crew." Tears pooled in his eyes and he blinked them away. "It nearly destroyed him. Fortunately for him, the psychiatrist there recognized his pain, put him on some medication, and sent him home." He cleared his throat. "By the time he got home, he was doing so much better. It was wonderful and amazing. My wife and I decided it was safe to take a weekend vacation, and when we came home, we found Terry hanging by the neck in the garage."

Caden closed his eyes. Then opened them. "My brother committed suicide when he jumped off the roof of the hospital where he was a psych patient. Brianne Davis, another psych patient who served in Kabul, shot herself. Helen Craft, a doctor in Kabul, jumped from her apartment window. What in the name of all that's sacred is going on?"

"It's the drug," Max said. "And I helped create it."

Heather let out a low gasp and Caden shot her a warning look. She bit her lip and sat back in her chair.

Max pressed his lips together, then said, "The company is marketing it as a PTSD drug, and they're working the numbers so that the FDA will approve it."

"Then why would you send Wilmont to Brianne's house with more of it?" Caden asked.

"Because it's a tricky drug — and it's not fully developed. I saw them bring Brianne in. She was wounded in action and wound up here at the VA hospital. She was Terry's best friend — and probably more. I think he loved her." He sniffed and looked away for a moment. "I'd never met her in person before, but we'd FaceTimed several times a week. She was always with Terry before he was discharged and sent home."

"I'm so sorry," Caden murmured.

"When I saw Brianne, I slipped in to visit her when she was finally alone. She was in a really bad place emotionally. Two days later, she was doing well. I knew they were giving her the drug. I told her not to stop taking it, no matter what happened."

"Why?" Elliott asked.

"Because it's highly addictive. I won't bore you with the details of the ingredients, but even one pill will hook you, and if you stop taking it, the suicidal tendencies go up exponentially."

Caden rubbed his chin and glanced at Elliott, who nodded for Caden to continue. "One pill?"

"Just one."

Elliott shot a look at Heather. "Is that possible?"

She nodded. "Very."

The detective grunted and turned back to Max. "What happens if you take more than one pill?"

"At the same time? Paranoia, uncontrollable impulses like violence mixed with massive confusion about why you're doing what you're doing. And yet you're unable to help yourself." He shuddered. "It's horrible. It's absolutely beyond anything I've ever seen. It's why I sent the pills to Brianne. I wanted her to continue taking them for now until I could figure out a way to get to her and help her get off of them. I would have taken them to her myself, but I was afraid someone would recognize me, so I asked Sam to do it for me."

"Is there a way to get off of them without suffering the suicidal ideations?"

"No." Max's shoulders slumped. "No, there's not. At least not in all of the studies that have been done. I know they were asking for volunteers for the study and they would give the vets the medication and then, in a secure environment, stop the meds and see what happened. Each and every time, the participants went downhill within hours of missing the next dose."

Caden nodded. "One more thing, please."

Max sighed and rubbed his eyes. "Sure."

"Sam Wilmont took two of those pills you meant for Brianne."

Max's eyes widened. "What?"

"He was a drug addict. Granted, a recovering one, but I guess the pills were too much temptation for him. He thought they were painkillers and popped two of them, thinking Brianne would never notice."

"Oh no." The man raked a hand over his head. "Oh no. Is he okay?"

Caden explained the incident with Sarah, and Max gulped. "That sounds about right."

"He says he doesn't remember any of it."

"No, he probably doesn't."

"A sniper and quick-acting officers managed to save the day, but here's the thing. Wilmont took two of those pills, wigged out like you say he would, but then woke up from surgery fine — albeit missing a few hours of memory. However, he has no suicidal inclinations. Just a lot of remorse for his actions — that he doesn't remember."

Max paced in the cramped area. "I don't understand. That doesn't make sense. How could that be? Withdrawing from one pill would be bad enough, but two? No, he would have done anything to end whatever was going on in his head. He definitely would have tried to find a way to kill himself."

"Do you have proof of any of this?" Elliott asked. "That there are people manufacturing this drug, giving it to unsuspecting vets, then falsifying the results?"

"No." Max pulled to a stop and met each agent's eyes one by one. "And that's why I'm a dead man living in a hospital, who was praying I wouldn't get caught before I could find that proof."

Trailed by Asher and Travis, Gavin and Sarah strode down the now familiar hallway while Sarah texted Caden that they were there. She looked up from her phone. "He said to meet him in front of the second-floor conference room."

Five minutes later, Caden stepped out of the room, pulling the door shut behind him. "The detectives are just finishing up questioning Max and will escort him to a safe house while they investigate his story further. What did you have?"

Sarah shook her head and pulled the sleeves of her sweatshirt over her hands. "This is going to take longer than a step-out-of-the-room conversation. We need a place to sit down so I can show you some stuff." She gestured to the manila envelope.

Caden raised a brow. "All right. Hang tight for a few minutes and let me see what I can arrange." He disappeared back into the room, only to reemerge thirty seconds later. "Looks like they've got what they need and will be leaving shortly. Can you give us five minutes?"

"Of course," Sarah said.

Gavin's phone rang. He glanced at the screen and frowned. And hung up on the caller.

"You need to get that?" Sarah asked.

"I'll call him back in a few minutes."

His phone buzzed again. Again, he disconnected the call.

"All of your workers are hanging out around us. How in the world can a business survive that?"

He smiled and glanced at Travis. "I'm just following orders."

Travis nodded. "Don't worry. It's all under control. I promise."

She studied him for a moment. "If you say so."

Gavin's phone vibrated for the third time. This time, a text. He glanced at the screen.

Call me ASAP.

From the general.

The door opened. "I'm just going to stay here and return the call while you talk to Caden," Gavin said. "You don't need me for that."

Sarah nodded and slipped into the room, followed by Asher.

Travis held back. "Anything you need me to do?"

"Just keep an eye on her. No one gets close to her, got it?"

"Got it."

Gavin pressed the button that would return the general's call. Halfway through the first ring, the man answered. "Don't —"

A scuffle? Something in the background.

"General Denning?"

"I should have known you wouldn't cooperate."

Gavin straightened, his heart picking up speed. "Hello?"

"Put it on FaceTime." Gavin didn't recognize the voice but obeyed.

The screen popped up and Gavin blew out a low breath. "Oh boy."

The general sat tied to a wooden chair in front of a black tarp. The concrete floor looked new — or immaculately maintained — with no cracks. And that was it. No windows, no doors, no signs, no glass or mirrors to catch a reflection, nothing. "What do you want?"

"You."

He blinked, expecting to hear Sarah's name. Which, of course, he'd laugh in the man's face. Or ear. "I'm sorry. What?"

"You. And you know the drill. You come alone. Any cops, yadda yadda, Lewis dies."

"Where?"

He gave him an address.

"What do I need to bring?"

"Just you. Stay on the line. Keep the camera on your face until you're in your car."

"Gavin?"

He stilled at the sound of his name, then turned. Asher stood in the door of the conference room.

"Yeah?"

"Everything all right?"

"I might be a few minutes. I've got a client on the line who I need to deal with."

"Anything I can help you with?"

"No, Mr. Hahn and I have it covered."

Asher paused. "All right, if you're sure. Holler if I can help."

"Will do."

Asher stepped back into the room and shut the door.

"You handled that well," the voice said. "Now go. The general's life depends on your cooperation."

"I'm going." Gavin made his way back to the elevator, knowing the man on the phone was watching his every move. He walked outside the hospital and headed for his truck. Asher and Travis would be with Sarah, and that's all that mattered at the moment. He'd find a way to leave some kind of trail.

He clicked the remote unlock. "Get in the passenger side." Gavin paused and walked around the front of the truck, scanning the area, seeing nothing. He reached for the door just as the door of the car next to him opened. A spritz of liquid in his face sent him stumbling backward. A curse from a man in a ski mask.

Darkness closing in.

His thoughts went to Sarah. *God, protect her.*

And the lights winked out.

CHAPTER TWENTY-THREE

Sarah let Caden examine the contents of the envelope in silence. He cleared his throat several times during the process, and her own had gone tight as she watched him. "What do you think?" she asked when he finally looked up.

He pressed thumb and forefinger to his eyes, then dropped his hand. "I think Dustin was onto something. We need to find every person named on this list and get them into protective custody immediately. I can start working on that." He tapped a text to someone and then set his phone back on the table. "I also want to bring in Richard Kilgore and start questioning him. Find out who the other man was in the hallway that night." Caden paused and sighed, reached out to cover Sarah's hand with his. "I'm sorry I didn't do more when you were asking. I'm sorry I didn't put more effort into finding Brianne when you asked. If I had, she might still be alive."

The deep remorse and regret in his words singed her. "You didn't know. Neither of us did."

"You knew something was wrong. I should have trusted you, trusted those uncanny instincts of yours." He squeezed her fingers. "I won't make that mistake again."

"Thank you," she said, her voice husky with emotion.

"We can't help the ones who've already paid with their lives, but we can stop this drug trial and bring down the ones killing them."

"And get justice for Dustin."

"And the others. Yeah." He stood. "I've got some phone calls to make. I want Kilgore —"

"And that nurse, Donna — I don't know her last name —"

"— and Nurse Donna, in an interrogation room ASAP."

"They're here in the hospital," Sarah said.

"We'll get them."

Asher had been listening, his gaze snapping back and forth between them. He slapped a hand to the table and Sarah jumped. Caden's brow rose and Travis flinched. "Dude, what's that about?"

"Something's wrong," Asher said.

She exchanged a look with Caden, who'd narrowed his eyes. "What are you talking about?" he asked.

"Gavin. He was on the phone when I asked him if everything was all right. He said it was a client, a Mr. Hahn. The name rang a bell but has been bugging me. Mr. Hahn died about six months ago." He pulled his phone from his pocket and punched the screen, held it to his ear a few seconds, then lowered it and tried again. He finally met Sarah's gaze, then moved to Caden's. "His number is going straight to voice mail."

"He'd never turn his phone off or let the battery die," Sarah said. "Not with everything going on."

"You guys locate Gavin," Caden said. "I'm going to work on things from this end." He paused. "If you need help with Gavin, let me know."

Caden made arrangements for hospital security to pick up the doctor and the nurse and bring them to the conference room for questioning. "They're going to kick us out of here and lock the doors behind us, thanks to all the problems we bring every time we enter the place."

With a heart that beat too fast, Sarah crossed her arms. Was Gavin really in

376

trouble or had his phone simply died? She supposed it was possible. Then again why would he give Asher the name of a dead client? It had to be a signal that all wasn't right.

When the security officer arrived, he came empty-handed. "I can't find the doctor or the nurse," he said. "Dr. Kilgore never showed up for work, and the nurse, Donna Hayden, left about an hour ago, saying she had some kind of family emergency."

Caden's jaw hardened. "Great. All right. Can you stay here while I make a call? I'm going to need one more thing."

"Sure."

Caden called Elliott and brought him up-to-date — and told him he would be searching for Gavin. When he hung up, he turned to the officer. "I need security footage from the hallway." The man opened the cover on his iPad and tapped the screen. Sarah watched over his shoulder. "There," she pointed, "that's him talking to someone on the phone."

"Now, he's walking," Asher said. "Can we follow him?"

"Of course." More tapping. Then Gavin paused, turned slightly and his phone came into clear view on the iPad.

"Smart," Caden grunted. "He's using the

cameras in the hallway, trying to clue us in." He pointed. "Can you zoom in on the picture on his phone? He's FaceTiming someone."

The guard zoomed. Sarah gasped and Caden stilled.

"That's the general," Sarah said. She looked up. "That's our father tied up to a chair." Her heart pounded. She stared back at the screen. He looked so . . . helpless. Powerless. In any other situation, she might have taken pleasure in seeing him like that. But not this. Out of anger, she might have secretly wished for him to die, but now faced with the real possibility of it happening, she went weak with regret. Fear for him covered her. Along with the deep desire to make things right with him.

"And, if I'm not mistaken," Travis said, "whoever's on the other end of that call is using the general to lure Gavin to wherever he is."

The security guard tapped the screen and the outside cameras came on. "It looked like he went out the east wing of the hospital. If that's the case . . . there." He zoomed in to see Gavin walking toward his red truck in the distance. He glanced around, then his gaze went back to his phone. At the truck, he stopped, then walked around to the passenger side.

Sarah squinted. "What's he doing? Wait, did someone just come up behind him?"

"Yeah." She continued to watch. Then the truck drove off.

"Whoever's driving that truck knew the angle of the camera," Caden said. "He told him to go around to the passenger side. And that's all I can see before he drove away."

"But —" Sarah sputtered, "what does he want with Gavin? I thought they were after me."

"That was the assumption," Travis said.

"I'm confused, but it doesn't matter. All that matters is finding Gavin and the general."

"We can do that," Asher said.

Travis nodded. "If he's in his truck, we can track him."

"How?" Sarah asked.

"We have GPS trackers in all of our vehicles." Asher pulled his phone from his pocket and tapped the screen. "Give me a minute." In less than that, he looked up at Travis. "You stay with Sarah. I'll go find Gavin."

"Alone?" Sarah asked.

"No," Caden said, "definitely not alone. I've got some friends I can call on for help. Give me the GPS data. I can follow him as he's traveling."

Asher did and Caden got back on his phone. Sarah's pulse pounded. What was going on? Fear chugged through her. *Oh, please, God, don't let them die.*

Gavin stirred and groaned. His head pounded and nausea swirled. He hoped the cops got the truck that hit him.

Oh wait.

No truck.

Someone had spritzed him with a face full of chloroform.

Awareness returned slowly, but with each passing second, his brain cleared and he knew he was in trouble as pain in every part of his body made its presence known. Taking inventory, he noted his hands tied together behind his back.

And his feet.

And his hands tied to the rope around his ankles. His muscles screamed and his heart thudded.

Think. Think. There was a way out of this. There had to be, because Sarah needed him. And he needed her.

A groan to his left compelled him to roll. The general was still tied to the chair . . . waking from unconsciousness? Had he been drugged as well? Ignoring the pain of his cramped muscles, Gavin scooted on knees and shoulders, pushing his way like an arthritic inchworm over to the general's side.

"Sir?" he whispered.

Another groan.

Gavin bumped the chair with his shoulder. Hard, but not hard enough to knock it over. "Come on, man, wake up." The general blinked once, twice. "That's it. Wake up and tell me who did this."

Nothing.

Footsteps sounded outside the door and he propelled himself away from the chair, back into his original spot, just as the door opened. A man wearing a ski mask stepped inside, checked on the general, then looked at Gavin. "Well, two out of three of you are here. Now, we wait for Sarah."

"What do you want with Sarah?" Gavin scowled. "Who are you anyway?"

"Doesn't matter. The less you know the better."

Which meant he didn't intend to kill them? Possibly. Doubtful. The voice was familiar, though. *Think!*

He walked over to Gavin and Gavin recognized the cell phone in his hand as his own. The man shook it at him. "Sit tight, Sarah will be joining us shortly."

"You're not the one who snatched me from the parking lot."

"I had a little help."

"What's this all about?"

"I needed the general to get you here."

Gavin narrowed his eyes, doing his best to ignore the fact that his hands were going numb. "I'm here. Now what?"

"Now, you get Sarah here."

"Not a chance."

"Definitely a chance." His jaw tightened and his eyes flashed. "I had it all set up in Afghanistan and you ruined it. None of this would have happened if you'd just stayed away."

Realization was a painful thing. "You set up her kidnapping."

"And lost a ton of money on that because of you. I'd paid for it with money I didn't have, but it was supposed to be fine, because once Sarah signed the papers, I would have made that back and more. So, this is all on you."

"And you plan to get her here how?"

"Easy peasy." He waved the phone again. "All it took was a text from you."

Gavin laughed, the sound more pained than he would have liked. "She has 24/7 bodyguards. Good luck." This man had been behind Sarah's kidnapping. That had been no small feat to set up. That had taken power — and lots of it.

"She'll find a way to slip away from them," his captor was saying, "if she doesn't want to see you die."

"Me? What about her father? You don't think she'd be concerned about him?"

"Not really. That's why I needed you."

Sarah's phone buzzed and she glanced at the screen. "Gavin."

"What?" Asher looked up.

She ignored him and read silently.

Hey, I'm following up on a lead at 11 Harrison Street. I'm almost finished. You want to meet me here and we'll go grab something to eat?

Meet him there? Really? She almost typed yes, but then shook her head. He wouldn't ask her to do that. Her fingers hovered over the keyboard. Then she typed,

Who is this?

Um . . . Gavin? You forget me already?

You're not Gavin.

A pause. Three little dots to indicate

someone typing a response. The dots disappeared. Then reappeared.

All right, then come alone to that address or the general and Gavin both die. How's that?

A picture popped up and she gasped.
Gavin lay on the floor, tied up like a Thanksgiving turkey. Her father was still bound to the chair. They both looked unconscious.

What do you want?

You, Sarah. It's always been you. Be here within fifteen minutes or one of them dies. If I see a cop, they both die. And don't be stupid and leave your phone behind. You'd better have it on you when you get here.

Who are you?

A stupid text, but she had to try.
No answer.
Of course not.
In all caps, she typed,

I DON'T HAVE A CAR!

There's one waiting for you in the handicapped spot just outside the emergency room. A black sedan. Keys are in it. I'm going to call and you keep your phone on so I can listen. Answer on the first ring or they die.

"Everything okay?" Asher asked.

She glanced up. "Yes." She started to say something, then glanced at the camera on the wall. Could she chance warning Asher with a visual cue somehow?

Her brain clicked. She had to think through the fear that wanted to consume her. Not so much for herself, but for Gavin. And, if she was honest, her father. Maybe she didn't hate him as much as she said she did. Or as much as she wanted to. Her phone buzzed. She stood. Asher did too.

"I'm going to the restroom," she said and tapped the screen before it could ring again.

"I'll check it out for you."

Exactly what she thought he'd say. "Fine. I'll just take this call while you do that." She lifted the device to her ear. "Hold on one second."

"I'm waiting."

"I know."

In the hallway, he followed her to the women's restroom and knocked on the door. "Anyone in here?" No answer. He

385

pulled the door open, then looked back at her. "Step just inside and keep your back to the wall while I take a look."

With a glance at her watch, Sarah slipped inside the restroom. Asher started at the end and pushed open the first stall. Then the second. When he reached the fifth one, Sarah backed through the door and out into the hallway. With a grimace of regret, she turned and raced for the stairwell.

Just as she pushed the exit door open, she heard Asher's frantic shout. Gritting her teeth, she refused to turn back. Maybe she was being incredibly stupid, but the one thing that kept her going was the fact that they were tracking Gavin's truck. Whoever had taken him had taken his truck. But the person on the other end of the line didn't know about the tracker. At the bottom of the stairs, she ran for the emergency department, dodging patients and other hospital staff while ignoring the dirty looks and yells to slow down.

She hit the door and pushed out onto the sidewalk. To the left were three cars in handicapped spaces. To the right were four. But only one black sedan. She raced to it and threw herself into the driver's seat.

Sure enough, the keys were in the ignition, the engine running. She glanced at the dash clock. Time was ticking too fast. She took a fraction of a moment to jab the speakerphone button, then set the device in the cup holder. She put the car in reverse, backed out, and sped for the parking lot exit. "I'm on the way," she said.

"Good. We're waiting for you."

"Can I hang up now?"

A laugh. "No."

"Are they all right?"

"They're still breathing, if that's what you mean by all right."

"You're the man from the hospital. I recognize your voice."

A pause.

"Kilgore's an idiot," the voice said. "He said you were too drugged up to remember anything."

"Like you said, he's an idiot. But that didn't stop you from trying to kill me."

"Not kill you, my dear. I very much need you alive."

Sarah frowned, even as her heart beat in triple time and her blood surged through her veins. "Why?" Was there any way she could signal someone from her phone? Or —

She glanced in the rearview mirror and gasped, jerked the wheel to the right, then corrected. A woman sat in the backseat, her

387

weapon aimed at Sarah's head.

"What are you doing?" Sarah screeched.

"No speeding," she said. "Slow down."

Sarah released her foot from the gas. The car slowed in direct opposition to her racing pulse. "Nurse Donna. I knew you were mixed up in this. He said he wants me alive."

"He does, but he wants you alive and *alone.*"

"Right."

"Hand me your phone."

Sarah complied.

Donna spoke into it. "We'll be there in ten minutes." A pause. "No, we haven't been followed. By all appearances, she did exactly as instructed." She fell silent, listening. "Yes, I understand." She hung up. "Turn right at the next light, then left."

"But the address he gave me is left."

Donna snorted. "You don't think he'd take a chance that you'd somehow get word to someone with that, do you?"

"Right." Sarah followed the directions, wishing she had a weapon on her. Finally, she asked, "How'd you get mixed up in all of this?"

"I needed money and Dr. Kilgore knew it. When he asked me to help him with the patients, I agreed."

"Even though it was hurting those patients?"

"There was always the possibility that it would help them. It was worth the risk. A lot of people are going to be helped because of this drug once the testing is done."

"The FDA has to approve it. You were falsifying information."

"It would be fine in the end. We were making progress. The drug was working, it just needed to be refined. Tweaked."

"Tweaked?" Sarah clamped her lips on the scream that wanted to erupt, even as her fingers flexed around the wheel. "What about the people who've been hurt or died?"

"Nothing great comes without a price. Every drug trial is a risk. The participants knew that going in and they found it acceptable."

"And they've all paid the price for it. With their lives. Like Brianne."

No response.

"You remember Brianne now, right?"

"I remember her."

"Why say she wasn't there at the hospital? Why deny her existence?"

"Because she wasn't supposed to be there. Or have the drug in her system. She never volunteered, but we gave her the drug anyway. It would have been fine, except someone let her family know she was there, and when they showed up, Dr. Kilgore had to do something. He said to act like she was never there. So we did."

"He told Dr. Kilgore to take her off of it." Sarah swallowed. "He knew she would kill herself if they quit giving it to her."

Sarah shot her captor a quick look in the rearview mirror and the woman's jaw went tight. "That was unfortunate."

"That was murder — and you're a part of it."

Donna let out a low breath. "I'm not a part of it. I just follow orders."

Sarah didn't bother to laugh. If she truly believed that, then she was just plain stupid. "And my brother Dustin? How did he fit into this whole thing?" She shoved aside the wave of sorrow and focused on the road.

"He volunteered for the study."

"He knew something hinky was going on and offered himself up as a lab rat in order to find out what it was." Sarah couldn't help the snap.

Once again, Donna fell silent until she had to give the next set of directions. Sarah followed them until she was finally instructed to turn into the parking lot of a facility she should know. Why did the name set off all kinds of alarm bells?

CHAPTER TWENTY-FOUR

Once their captor left, Gavin groaned and lay still, trying to catch his breath and work his hands. He needed to get out of the restraints — and fast.

Which meant he needed the general to wake up. Gavin rocked the chair once more and the man lifted his head.

"Is he gone?"

"You were faking?"

"Somewhat." He grimaced. "Feel like I have a two-ton truck using my head as a shortcut to somewhere."

"I know the feeling. He get you with chloroform to the face?"

"Yeah."

"Who is it?"

"A man I thought I could trust." His eyes flashed. "His name is Marshall McClain. He's a former unit member and fraternity brother. And part owner in the company Marshbanks Labs. I'm one of the investors.

391

A heavy investor. I knew he was working on something rather controversial, but I didn't realize he was killing people."

"The suicides."

"I opened that package Dustin sent Sarah."

"Yeah? Why doesn't that surprise me?" Gavin scooted closer, jaw clenched against the bursts of pain. "If I can get behind you, can you feel your way around the knots and untie my hands?"

"They're kind of numb, but I can try."

While the man fumbled with the knots from his awkward position, Gavin closed his eyes and ducked his head against his chest. His muscles burned and his blood pounded.

Hurry, hurry.

The ropes tugged, loosened?

The general stopped. Grunted.

"Keep going, sir."

"My blasted fingers won't cooperate with me."

"Make 'em."

He huffed a soft laugh. "Right."

"What does he want with Sarah?"

"Her money."

Gavin frowned, trying to focus beyond his abused body's protestation of the contorted position. "What money? You disinherited her."

"Yeah, but I can re-inherit her. I've got control of the funds. Sort of."

"Sort of?"

One knot slipped free and they both sucked in relieved breaths. The general went back to work, pulling almost frantically.

"Slow down, sir, feel your way."

The man stopped. Took another gulp of air and resumed his tugging. "Yeah. Sort of. I have to sign off to relinquish the funds and she has to sign that she accepts them."

"How much are we talking here?"

"A little over ten million."

Gavin gasped.

And his hands fell free.

Pain pounded through them, into his fingers, palms, upper arms, everywhere. He shook them and glanced at the door. "Good job, sir."

"Get your legs free before you work on me. At least we'll have a chance if one of us can fight back."

Gavin went to work on his legs, when the sound of a door slamming reached him. He hurried, pulling the ropes and digging into the first knot with his fingernails. "He did these better than my hands. Ten million?"

"Compliments of her mother's mother

from Texas, who liquidated her oil field, then invested the money very wisely."

"I'd say."

"She split the money evenly between the three kids. Dustin's share will be divided between Sarah and Caden."

"Do they know this?"

He hesitated. "No. Well, not the amount, just that they have some money coming to them."

"And she gave you power over it?"

"My wife had power. Until her death. Then it went to me."

"When were they supposed to get the money?"

"When they turned thirty — or when I deemed them mature enough to handle it."

"I take it you haven't deemed it yet." Gavin gave a growl of frustration. "I can't get this knot undone."

Footsteps sounded outside the room and Gavin grabbed the rope and pulled it behind his back, hoping it would fool the man into believing he was still tied up.

"There's one thing you need to know, Gavin."

Uh-oh. "What's that?"

"I've already signed the papers. All he needs is Sarah's signature."

■ ■ ■

Caden paced the hospital floor while waiting for news about Sarah. "Why did she run?"

Asher raked a hand over his head. "I don't know. Someone got to her. Can you access her phone?"

Caden pursed his lips and willed his heart to stop threatening to rupture in his chest. If anything happened to Sarah . . . "I'd need a warrant for her — no I don't. Hold on, hold on. I know her Apple ID and password."

Asher frowned. "How do you know that?"

"I watched her type it in her phone one time. As long as she hasn't changed it, we should be good."

"You watched her one time. And you remember it?"

"I remember a lot of things. I need a computer." The door opened and Heather walked in with her laptop. "Perfect timing."

She raised a brow. "How's that?"

He told her and she handed him the computer. "Fine, but I have something I need to discuss with you."

"Feel free to talk while I see if I can get into Sarah's text messages." He logged

Heather off and said a quick prayer that Sarah hadn't changed her login. Then started typing.

"So, here's the deal," Heather said. "I researched all of those little red dots on the map Dustin provided. Each place has a VA hospital and each one had at least one patient who has committed suicide in the last six months. While that may not seem like a lot overall, considering the number of vet suicides in the country, the thing that stood out with these is they all came from the same area of Afghanistan and from the same base as Sarah, Dustin, Helen, and Brianne."

"All of them?" Caden looked up with a frown.

"Every last one of them."

"Most of them died, but several actually survived their attempts. Not in great shape, but . . ." She shrugged.

"But they survived."

"They did."

"How?"

"Someone interrupted them or got them to a hospital ASAP to have their stomach pumped. One survived a car wreck but is a paraplegic, one is in a coma on a ventilator, a couple have gone back to their lives without any lasting visible trauma once the doctors were able to repair the damage."

"No, Max said they wouldn't be able to fight that until the drug was completely out of their system. So, how did they do that?"

"I have a theory about that, but I need to do some more investigating before I'll know if I'm right or not."

"What kind of theory?" He clicked. "Never mind. I'm in. Just got to wait for the messages to load." Within seconds, they were on the screen in front of him. He scanned through them, then gave a sigh of disgust. "Well, we know why she snuck away and took off like she did." He got on the phone and made a call to get someone to the address in the text, then hung up and leaned back.

Heather frowned. "Why aren't you going?"

"She won't be there."

"Why not?"

"There's no way they'd text the address they wanted her to go to." He shook his head. "It was just a way to get her out of the building."

But the security footage had shown her heading out of the building and getting into the dark sedan. He called Annie. "Hey," he said when she answered. "What do you have on the sedan?"

"Using the traffic cameras, it looks like they went east, but then they fell off the grid. Same with her phone. I was able to track it to a tower in the area about the same time they disappeared from traffic. They turned off on a side road, unfortunately."

"Right." He closed his eyes a moment while he thought. "Get agents out there where they disappeared and just start searching. This is a kidnapping and we've got a good lead in the direction they went. Let's go give this everything we've got and see if we can find her. Oh, and contact the field office's SWAT and have them on standby to take the lead if we wind up needing them to do so."

"On it." Annie hung up and Caden turned back to Heather. He handed her the laptop and she snapped it shut and tucked it under her arm.

"I'm going to make a few more calls and I should have your answer about the drug and how to quickly dilute the effects of it. Stay tuned, but please find Sarah and Gavin."

Caden nodded, noting the worry in her blue eyes and the pinched mouth. She was scared for her friends. He understood. He was terrified.

Sarah climbed out of the driver's side and stood for a moment to gather her nerves. While well aware of the woman behind her with the weapon, Sarah was also painfully aware of one other thing.

"Where's Gavin's truck?"

"In a parking garage about thirty minutes from here."

Sarah drew in a shuddering breath. So, there would be no tracking Gavin via his truck. And now she'd handed herself over to the monsters responsible for Dustin's death — and who knew how many others.

For the first time since leaving the hospital, real fear swept in and nearly paralyzed her.

The gun at the base of her spine pushed her forward. Help wasn't on the way. She'd truly thought they'd beat her and her captor to the location. She was thrown, mentally and emotionally. With her mind processing her new predicament and recalculating the plan, she decided she had two goals.

Find Gavin and her father and stay alive while doing so.

"Go. Inside."

399

"I know this place," she murmured. "Why do I know this place? Marshbanks Labs."

"You can think later. Get inside."

Sarah figured she could get the gun away from the woman with a few well-placed self-defense moves she'd learned in the service — and from two well-meaning brothers who wanted her to be able to take care of herself — but if she managed to do that without getting shot, how would she go about finding Gavin and the general?

Tamping down the desperate need to get away from her captor and the desire to find the men, she bit her lip and let Donna direct her to the glass doors. The woman punched in the code and the doors slid open.

Sarah stepped inside the air-conditioned lobby and stood still, listening, watching — and praying that Donna knew how to use the weapon and wouldn't accidentally pull the trigger. "What now?"

"Walk."

"Where are my father and Gavin?"

"You'll see them soon enough."

Sarah allowed the woman to maneuver her down the stairs. She shoved open the heavy metal door at the bottom and stepped into a long hallway. The basement of the building. "To the end."

"Why am I here? What do you want with me?"

"I don't want anything to do with you. My part ends here." She stopped in front of the first door on the left. "Open it."

Sarah twisted the knob and threw it open. The plush office inside was a direct contrast to the stark exterior. A man sat in a leather chair behind the oversized executive desk, his back facing her. He paused. Drew in a deep breath and turned. "Hello, Sarah."

Sarah blinked. She should know this man. He looked so familiar. Why couldn't she place him? "Who are you?"

He raised a brow. "Marshall McClain."

Everything rushed in. Her father's friend from college. The fraternity brother who owned a private pharmaceutical company. "It's your drug that's killing people."

"I need to get back to the hospital," Donna said from behind her.

"We're almost done here."

"What about Richard?"

"I've taken care of him. Just get back to doing what you do best and then leave the rest to me."

"They're closing in, Marshall. We need to shut this down and get out of the country before everything blows up in our faces."

The man's eyes hardened. "You have no

clue what you're suggesting. As soon as Sarah signs a few papers, all will be fine once again." He opened the top drawer of his desk and set a small stack on the flat surface in front of him.

Sarah frowned. "Sign what papers?"

"The ones your father has already signed. I promised him that I'd let you live as long as he signed them."

"Wow, that was almost convincing. You're a really good liar."

He leaped to his feet, fists clenched at his sides. "Listen to me, little girl, I didn't grow up with every privilege handed to me. I worked hard and clawed my way to the top. I will not let a few million dollars keep me from finally achieving what I've slaved and sacrificed *everything* for!"

Sarah swallowed.

Donna cleared her throat and pushed Sarah farther into the room, then handed Marshall the gun. "I'll be back to help wrap things up. Just let me know what else you need me to do."

"Thank you, Donna." He held the gun on Sarah. "You've done a good job today."

"I'm sure that gratitude will be reflected in my bank account by tomorrow?"

"Of course."

She turned on her heel and slipped out

the door without a backward glance.

Sarah turned her attention back to McClain. "I'm not signing any papers."

"Then your father and Black will die. It's really that simple. Because the only reason they're still alive is so I can use them as incentive to get you to sign."

"Which means as soon as I sign, we're all dead anyway." She paused. "And I thought those signatures had to be witnessed by a lawyer."

"They do."

She drew in a breath. "I see. You have one of those on your payroll as well."

"Of course." He almost looked amused. "You have no idea how big this operation is." He studied her a few minutes. "I'll give you an hour to think about it."

"I don't need to think about it. If I'm dying anyway, you're not getting the payoff that comes with it." However, the longer she dragged this out, the longer she had to think of a way to escape and find the men.

His jaw tightened and he opened a side drawer. "Dr. Kilgore was nice enough to make up this solution for me." He withdrew a bottle with a spray top. "It's very effective."

Her gut churned and the fear she'd been holding at a controllable level just notched up into a new area. "And?"

"And if you don't cooperate —"

A chime sounded and he glanced at his laptop. His eyes went wide and a string of curses slipped from him. He darted to her, pulling the trigger on the spray bottle. Sarah had no time to duck, just turn her face at the last second. The liquid hit her in the cheek. She gasped, then realized that was the worst thing she could have done. Dizziness hit her and her legs gave out. Hands from behind caught her and lowered her to the floor.

"We don't have long, Marshall." Donna had come back. "The pilot's waiting."

Sarah tried to break loose from the hard grip that held her, but she was so weak and the darkness was demanding.

"I can't leave without her," he said. "And I need that guy she's so crazy about. She'll sign the papers eventually."

"What about her father?"

"We don't need him anymore. Kill him."

Noooooo . . .

Sarah lost the fight and let the blackness claim her.

CHAPTER TWENTY-FIVE

Gavin jumped when the door flew open. He'd untied the general, but left the ropes arranged in such a way as to disguise their looseness. He kept his own hands behind him.

A man entered, carrying Sarah draped over his shoulder like a sack of potatoes. Marshall McClain, the man who'd betrayed the general. McClain set Sarah on the floor, then motioned to the woman hovering behind him. "Do it."

"Sarah!" The general stood, the untied ropes falling around his feet.

A woman stepped forward — Nurse Donna? — syringe in hand and aimed at Sarah's arm. Gavin came off the floor and tackled the nurse. She screamed and buckled beneath his weight.

"I'm going to kill you!" The general went after McClain.

A gunshot sounded and Gavin spun to see

the general slump midstep to the floor.

"Don't move!" McClain's yell froze him.

Donna scurried from underneath him, panting and clutching her side. He'd hit her hard enough to break something, but the pain didn't hold her back and she darted to Sarah's side searching for the syringe. Gavin went after her one more time, only to halt when the man aimed his weapon at Sarah.

"Move and she dies, right here, right now," the man said.

Gavin stayed put, but his gaze darted to Donna, who'd found the syringe, needle once again aimed at Sarah's arm.

"Get away from her," the general said. "Don't do it. Please." His eyes closed and Gavin prayed he'd only passed out and wasn't dead.

Donna glanced at McClain, who nodded.

"The shot won't kill her," McClain said, "but it will encourage her to see things my way. It's simple. When she signs the papers, she gets the second dose which counteracts the first." Sarah stirred and McClain raised a brow. "I need her signature and I need it ASAP, but we're going to have to take care of that in the plane."

Sarah groaned and Donna jabbed her with the needle. Gavin hollered, ignored the weapon aimed at Sarah and lunged, catching the man in the stomach. The gun tumbled from his fingers and hit the concrete.

They stumbled backward while Donna screeched at them to stop. Gavin drew his fist back, pausing when the weapon fired again. The bullet whizzed past his face so close to his nose, he could almost smell it. He jerked back.

"Stop! I'll kill her! Do you understand? I'll kill her and you and everyone in here! Stop! Stop now!" Donna's hysterical screams registered, and he stilled, his eyes going to Sarah. Awake, she met his gaze, confusion and fear mingled with sheer fury. She tried to roll to her feet and staggered. Fell on her backside.

McClain scooted backward, breathing hard and shooting black looks at him. He scrambled to his feet and snagged the gun from Donna. "Get up." He gestured to Sarah, who simply looked at him. Her gaze shifted to Gavin, then finally landed on her father and her eyes flickered. She shook her head and narrowed her eyes. "General," she whispered. She reached out a hand and moved, trying to get to her father.

"Pick her up," McClain said. "We need to get out of here now."

"What about the general?" Gavin asked, glancing at the wounded man. He lay still, eyes closed, but his chest rose and fell.

"Regrettable, but he'll be staying here. Go. Out the door. And just in case you're tempted to try something like that again, keep in mind that I'm the only one who can reverse the drug. Neutralize it, so to speak."

Gavin lifted Sarah into his arms. She gave a whimper of protest and wiggled, her gaze fixed on her father.

He'd said something about a "cure" a few moments ago. "What are you talking about?" Gavin tightened his grip. "Hold on, Sarah, please."

"T-64. The drug she was just injected with. I'm the only one who can offer an antidote."

It had a name. T-64. The drug that had killed Sarah's brother and so many others.

Gavin's heart thudded, not with the effort of holding Sarah, but with the knowledge that she was going to soon suffer the effects of the drug. "There's a cure?"

"Of course. Now go!"

Gavin could no longer stall. He stepped out of the room, sparing a backward glance at the general. The man lay still, bleeding, but still breathing.

Nurse Donna consulted her phone and groaned. "They're surrounding the building."

"Shut up," McClain ordered. He shoved the weapon in Gavin's back. "Donna, you go first." To Gavin, "Follow her. Out the door and up the stairs. All the way to the roof."

Help was on the way. Gavin's heart leapt even as he desperately searched for a way to buy some more time. But even if he had to leave with Sarah, law enforcement would search the building and find the general. With that worry off his mind, Gavin could focus on Sarah. He followed Donna with Sarah in his arms.

"General," she said again. "Gavin, my father . . ."

She stiffened and he tightened his grip. "Stay still, please. Trust me."

Sarah went limp and his heart did all kinds of funny things at the instant response that said she fully believed he'd take care of her — and her father.

At the top of the stairs, Donna led them through a maze of corridors and up one last flight of steps. She pushed through the metal door, and Gavin found himself on an airstrip that ran the length of the massive building. A small plane was ready and waiting, the propellers beating the air. He thought he could hear sirens above the whir of the blades.

"Get on the plane, Donna."

"I'm not going!"

McClain turned the weapon on her and pulled the trigger. She screamed. Then clutched her bleeding chest and stumbled backward, fighting to stay on her feet. And failing.

Before Gavin could act, the weapon was once more trained on him and Sarah. "I'm not playing around. Get on!"

Gavin couldn't do much to protest with Sarah in his arms — which was something McClain had no doubt thought of. Regret that he couldn't help Donna or the general overwhelmed him. But there was nothing he could do — except whatever he had to do to keep Sarah safe. Killing was second nature to this man and Gavin would have to tread carefully.

He climbed the portable steps and ducked into the six-seater plane. Sarah slid from his arms and into the nearest seat. He discreetly felt under her seat. A parachute. Good. And bad. He broke out in a sweat at the plan forming in his mind, but he had a feeling it was the only way. Using his body to shield his actions from the man behind him, Gavin pulled the chute from its nook and placed it behind Sarah. "Wiggle your arms through the straps when you can," he whispered.

Her eyes went wide, and she grabbed his hand and squeezed, her grip stronger than he would have thought.

"Hurry up. Get her strapped in," McClain ordered.

He did as instructed, wondering if she was as groggy as she was leading him and McClain to believe. Regardless, Gavin finished and turned to face yet another weapon held by the pilot. Apparently, McClain had an entire army on his payroll. Gavin took the seat next to Sarah while McClain stepped in and shut the door.

"Get this thing in the air," McClain yelled to the pilot. He turned back to Gavin. "No funny stuff or you're dead and I'll figure out what to do about her after that. As soon as we're at cruising altitude and out of danger of being detected, she's going to sign the papers. You hear me, Sarah?"

She ignored the man, keeping her eyes shut.

Gavin raised his hands as though in surrender.

McClain took the passenger seat in the front but stayed facing them, with the weapon trained on them. "Wrap the seatbelt around your arm and tie yourself to the armrest."

After a brief hesitation, Gavin grabbed the

411

lap belt and did as ordered. McClain reached over and grabbed the end, yanking it tight. The strap cut into his forearm, but Gavin kept his expression blank. He wouldn't give the man the satisfaction of seeing him wince.

Sarah's head lolled over onto Gavin's shoulder, and he slipped his free arm around her to pull her closer.

"We have to get out of this," she said, her voice low enough not to be heard by the two men up front.

"We will," he said. "I'm working on a plan. Keep your eyes closed and act like you're still drugged."

"Not hard. I am. A little. Fortunately, I managed to dodge some of it."

The plane accelerated down the rooftop runway and swooped into the air. He looked out the window and saw the authorities below, entering the building. Some pointed up to the plane and Gavin figured they'd have a police chopper on the way, if they didn't already.

"They injected you with that drug, Sarah. You have to tell me if you start feeling . . . it."

She gave a short nod. "Right now, I feel pretty good. Like I could conquer the world. Other than being a little sleepy, that is."

"Good, we're going to have to use that 'conquer the world' feeling as soon as we're in the air."

"How so?"

"Sarah," McClain said, "glad to see you're awake and feeling better. For now."

Gavin wanted to smash the smirk off the man's face. Instead, he narrowed his eyes and waited.

The plane banked left and the pilot said something to McClain, who jerked his attention to the window.

A police helicopter closing in. Thank God. Gavin leaned closer to Sarah. "The bird's here. Please tell me you've parachuted out of a plane before."

She hesitated. "Twice. For a story I was doing on a special forces team. Both times I was strapped to someone who knew what they were doing."

"Twice?"

"I enjoyed it so much the first time, I wanted to do it again. They humored me."

"Okay, good to know."

"What about you?"

"I've got one under my seat, but I'm going to be the distraction that gets you out the door."

She gulped and her eyes went wide. "So . . . you're saying . . . ?"

"Yeah. I'm just saying, if it comes down to it, you're going to have to do a solo jump."

Sarah shook her head and noted the pilot and McClain were still in heated conversation about the helicopter. McClain had a headset on and every so often would tell the pilot what to say, then turn and check on them.

After his last check, Sarah worked quickly. She unbuckled the lap belt Gavin had fastened and stripped off her oversized sweatshirt. She slipped her arms through the straps of the parachute he'd stuffed behind her. She wouldn't be able to get her legs in the harness but fastened the buckle that went across her chest, then yanked the sweatshirt back over her.

She really wasn't planning on jumping out of the plane, but it didn't hurt to be prepared. She'd have to get the sweatshirt off before she pulled the cord, but for now, at least she had a parachute.

Her heart pounded as she kept an eye on the men still arguing in the front. She pulled the shoulder straps from the seat belt back into place. "Your turn," she whispered to Gavin.

McClain spun in his seat, the weapon

414

passing over her and Gavin.

"You need to land," Gavin said. "There's no way out of this."

"We're not landing."

"They'll just wait until you have to land due to low fuel. Or crash."

The man shot him the weirdest smile Gavin had ever seen. "I'll be done by then."

"What?"

McClain got out of his seat and turned to Sarah. The gun never wavered in his right hand. In his left, he held four pages and a pen. He thrust the items at Sarah. "Sign it or die."

"We've already been over this."

"Which is why I brought him." He turned the weapon on Gavin's knee. "We can do this the hard way or the easy way, but one way or another you're going to sign those papers."

"Why not just forge my name?" she cried. "You didn't have to go through all of this! Just sign my name yourself."

"I can't. One of the terms for releasing the money is that a handwriting expert verify the signatures. Now sign or I'll shoot him!"

The look in his eyes said he was close to pulling the trigger. He'd do it. He'd strategically place bullets so they wouldn't kill him quickly, but the pain would be excruciating. Sarah grabbed the papers and the pen.

"No, Sarah," Gavin said, "don't do it."

"What does it matter at this point?" She scribbled her name on each page and shoved them back at him. "There! Now what?"

McClain shrugged out of the overcoat he wore, tucked the papers into his front pocket, and pulled the flap over them. "*Now*, the money will be transferred to my offshore account. *Now*, it's time for me to disappear."

He turned and pulled the trigger. The pilot's blood and brain matter coated the windshield. Sarah gaped, but before she could make a sound, he turned the weapon back on Gavin. "Right now, the plane is on autopilot. Give me the parachute under your seat."

Gavin complied. McClain pulled the emergency lever and the door of the plane flew off. Cold wind whipped around them. He then turned and fired the weapon at the instrument panel of the plane. Once, twice, three times. Sparks flared and the instruments went haywire.

Sarah ducked her head. "What are you doing?"

McClain tossed the parachute out the door. "Give me the other one," he shouted.

"From under her seat."

Gavin met her gaze, then went to his knees to look under her seat. He turned. "It's not there."

Keeping his eyes on Gavin, McClain's scowl deepened. "Back in your seat. If I look and it's there, I'll shoot her."

"I'm telling you, it's not there!"

The man bent, then straightened and moved to the other two seats opposite Sarah and Gavin. He grabbed the parachutes from underneath and tossed them out the door. Then removed the pilot's and sent it after the others.

Once the parachutes were free-falling from the plane, McClain turned the weapon back on Gavin. Sarah screamed.

Gavin kicked out and caught the man in the knee. Sarah heard the crunch over the whistle of the wind. McClain fell to the floor of the plane, screaming a litany of curses while his weapon slid toward the open door. Gavin worked the belt holding him to the seat as the plane listed to the side, the right wing dipping toward the earth. The gun slid farther from McClain.

Sarah's gaze went to the instrument panel. "Hurry, Gavin! The autopilot's disengaged. We're going down!"

Four more tugs and he was loose.

McClain had managed to get to his feet, favoring his injured right leg. When he saw Gavin was free, he dove for the gun, grabbed it, and rolled to aim at Gavin. The plane shifted again, throwing McClain off-balance. Still gripping the weapon, he slid out the door.

The plane tilted once more. Gavin scrambled to his knees, but like McClain, slid toward the opening.

Sarah screamed and unbuckled her seat belt and shoulder harness with frantic fingers. "Gavin! Hold on!"

Finally, she was free just as he managed to wrap his fingers around the leg of one of the seats. She darted toward him and grabbed his wrist. He placed a foot against the edge of the door and Sarah slammed against the side of the plane.

"What do I do?" she screamed.

"Put your legs through the straps and pull them tight."

Working quickly, she yanked her sweatshirt off, then with her back still against the wall of the plane, she loosened the material around her upper body to enable her to maneuver her legs into the proper place. She pulled the straps tight as instructed. The plane lurched and she lost her balance, tumbling to her hip and sliding toward the open door. "Gavin!"

His hand clamped onto the right shoulder strap and yanked her back. Prayers whispered from her lips, even as she struggled to regain her balance. "He had a parachute on," she said. "He's getting away."

"I'm more worried about us right now." Gavin's fingers slipped and his leg dangled outside the open door. The ground rose rapidly and the police chopper hovered close by.

She pointed. "We have to jump!"

Sweat dripped from his brow. "I can't!"

"Of course you can," she shouted above the roar of the wind. "You've done it a thousand times."

"Not since the incident." He shook his head. "I freeze every time I try. Go! Jump!"

"Not without you!"

"I'm going to land the plane."

"Not a chance, my friend. This one is going down and fast."

"Innocent people are going to die if I don't —"

"The helicopter is right there. They're tracking the plane and evacuating anyone in the area where it might crash. Now, let's go!"

"Sarah, I'm sorry, but I . . . can't."

"You promised me!"

He shut his eyes, agony dripping from every square inch of him.

"You promised me that as long as you had breath left in you, you'd make sure I was safe. I'm not safe yet and I'm not going alone!"

"Sarah —"

She looked around. Spotted the pilot's gun sliding toward her and snagged it. She gathered her strength and her feet and moved to the seat belt. She fired the weapon once, twice, three times, effectively slicing a long strip of material from the seat.

Quickly, she stuck one end through the parachute strap buckled on her chest and then inched forward toward the door and Gavin. "Tie this around you! We're running out of time."

"Sarah —"

"Do it!" She screamed the two words. "You have to keep your promise or I'll die with you!"

For a moment, a brief moment they didn't have, he stared at her before his jaw hardened and determination flooded his eyes. Sarah almost wept her relief. He was back. With effort, he hauled himself into the plane and rolled to his side. "Lie down next to me and press against my back."

She did so and slid the end of the seatbelt

under his armpit. He pulled the rest of it around him and tied the ends together. "We don't have time to switch and give me the chute, so wrap your legs around my waist and lock your ankles. Don't let go of me when it deploys."

"I won't."

"Then here we go. Let gravity work for us. I'll tell you when to pull the cord."

Sarah quit trying to resist and let gravity work.

CHAPTER TWENTY-SIX

While the wind rushed past his ears, Gavin held onto control of his mind-numbing fear by a fingernail, reminding himself they had a parachute and they weren't going to die. He glanced at the ground, then up at the plane. "Pull the cord, Sarah!" For a moment her hands stayed locked around his upper body and he was terrified she wouldn't be able to do it. "Sarah!"

"Got it," she said in his ear. "I can do this." One hand closed around the cloth of his shirt, the other released him. He heard the rip of the chute as it deployed, felt the yank that jerked him back and upward. Sarah's grip tightened and the seatbelt strap held strong.

Fear left him. Memories swarmed him. He loved this. Always had. Always would. As long as he got Sarah to safety. He prayed the cops were tracking McClain and would have him in custody by the time he and

Sarah landed. "Good job!"

"Are you okay?"

"As long as you're safe, I'm just fine."

"I'm worried about my father. I don't want him to die, Gavin."

"Let's worry about getting on the ground and then we'll find out about your father." He paused. "He hired me."

"What?"

"To be your bodyguard. He hired me and told me not to tell you." She went silent and Gavin prayed she wouldn't untie the seatbelt. "He was afraid for your life with all of the threats against him."

"So, that's why you stuck around."

"Yes. And no. I would have stuck around even if he hadn't asked me to. Please don't hate me, Sarah." He didn't know why he'd picked this moment to confess the very thing that might cause her to send him away, but he didn't want to keep the secret one second longer. "I'm sorry."

"You should have told me."

"I wanted to, but I was afraid you'd make me leave, and then I'd be arrested for stalking because I couldn't leave you alone. I'd have followed you everywhere."

She choked. Or laughed. He wasn't sure what the sound was. "Why?"

"Because I'm in love with you. I have been

since our first date. Now pass me the steering lines and let me land this thing."

"Where?" She handed him the lines.

"Do you know where we are?"

She went silent for a few seconds. "Over a high school. Not sure which one. We can land in the football field."

"Exactly."

"We're coming back to this conversation if we live."

"We'll live. We have too much to live for."

Gavin worked with the wind to drift as far as he wanted, then used the lines to pull left, then right, then over the field.

The occupied field.

"Gym class?" Sarah asked.

"Football practice. They'll move." Hopefully.

Two men dressed in black shirts looked up, watchful. Pointing. As Gavin and Sarah got closer, it seemed to finally dawn on them that they were aiming for the field.

The kids and adults scattered, giving Gavin plenty of room to land.

His feet touched the ground first and he ran a few steps with Sarah attached to his back, stopped, and went to his knees. Her grip never loosened. "Sarah?"

"Yeah?"

"You can let go now."

424

"Right." Her fingers released.

Gavin looked up to find the entire football team and coaches surrounding them.

"Y'all okay?" the nearest teen asked.

"I think so." There was no way Gavin would be able to get the knot out of the seatbelt strapping Sarah to him. "Sarah? Can you undo the buckle?"

"Um . . . yeah."

He felt her hands working between them and then the buckle released. Gavin pulled away from Sarah. His legs weakened and he wilted to the grass and rolled on his back.

"Gavin?" Sarah asked.

"Yeah?"

"We're alive, right?"

"Feels like it."

"You're alive," a gruff voice said. "Wanna tell me why you had to land on my field in the middle of my practice? You couldn't land on the empty baseball field like your friend?"

"Friend?" Gavin rolled to his feet and pulled Sarah up with him.

"Yeah, he came down not five minutes ago."

"The plane," Sarah said. "Where did it go down?"

"Not sure. We heard the plane crash and then you landed." Chills danced over his skin and Gavin gripped Sarah's hand. "Did you see which way the other guy went?"

"No. Now, if you two don't need medical help, could you please vacate the field so we can finish our practice?"

"Glad to as soon as you let me use your phone."

The man sighed and held his finger to the screen, then tapped it. He passed the phone to Gavin.

"What's Caden's number?" he asked Sarah. She gave it to him. Gavin paused. The fact that McClain had landed so close made him twitchy. "The baseball field, you say?"

The coach narrowed his eyes. "Yeah, why?"

Sirens sounded in the distance and Gavin turned to the coach. "You need to lock down the school."

The man blinked. "What?"

"The school. Lock it down. The man who landed on the baseball field is a killer. Cops are on the way. If he feels trapped, he could be unpredictable. Is anyone else in the school?"

"It's after hours so not many, but yeah, a few people."

"Tell them to stay put and lock their doors."

The coach pulled his radio from his pocket and gave the code to the front office. He turned to his fellow coach. "Get the guys into the locker room and lock it down. Call the cops on the way and let them know where you are."

The team took off and one of the coaches followed.

The other eyed them. "You guys are really okay?"

"We will be as soon as help arrives." He turned his attention back to the phone. "Caden?"

"Are you all right?" Caden demanded. "Where's Sarah?"

"She's right here. We're fine. McClain got away."

"We're on his trail. The chopper tracked him to the ground but lost him in some trees. You and Sarah jumped?"

"We did. We need a ride." He told Caden their location.

"It's on the way, but it's going to take me some time to get there. Local cops are on the way."

"McClain is here," Gavin said, his eyes scanning the area between the baseball and football fields. "He's close to the school. Valley High. I told a coach to lock it down and call 911."

"Good. Find a place to lay low and wait for us."

Gavin narrowed his eyes, searching. McClain was out there somewhere. "Did you find your father?"

"He's in surgery right now but is expected to make a full recovery."

He met Sarah's gaze. "Excellent." He passed the news on to Sarah and the relief on her face encouraged him. "We'll be waiting for you." He hung up and handed the phone back to the coach. "Now, go join your team."

The coach took off, and Gavin stilled, seeing movement. "There he is."

"Where?"

"He's coming this way."

Sarah shivered. "He waited for us, didn't he?"

Gavin pulled her toward the parking lot next to the football field. "Yeah. We should have seen his parachute in the baseball field on our way down. He must have hidden it."

"Really? Out of all of the places to land, we choose the same one he did?"

"Not surprising. It's the only place around with a large enough space — other than the highway — and he's not done with us." He headed for the concession stand. There might not be guns in there, but maybe a knife? Probably not. But if he could keep Sarah behind a locked door until Caden and help arrived, they'd manage to survive it.

"But everyone knows what he's done," Sarah said, hurrying along beside him. She glanced over her shoulder. "He could have disappeared by now. Why continue to come after us?"

"Revenge. He's angry that we're doing out best to derail his plans and he's not thinking straight."

"He had the gun when he went out of the plane."

"Yeah." Gavin tried the door of the concession stand.

Locked.

Of course.

"Head for the restrooms at the edge of the parking lot," Sarah said.

"No windows in there. I won't be able to watch him."

"Maybe not, but he won't be able to see us either. And the door locks. Add in the fact that if he has to shoot the lock off, he can't have that many more bullets left in the gun. It will buy us some time."

"Unless he had a magazine in his pocket."

She grimaced. "Okay." She shot another glance back. "He's getting closer."

"He's spotted the parachute," Gavin said.

"He knows we're here somewhere."

"And now he's heading for the school," Sarah said.

"It's on lockdown by now. He can't get in."

A car turned into the parking lot.

Sirens screamed in the distance.

"But he can take that driver hostage," Sarah said. "Or hijack her car."

The teen stepped out of her vehicle and McClain made a beeline for her, limping on his injured knee, but still moving fast.

"Stay here," Gavin ordered. He raced from behind the concession stand toward the parking lot, aiming to intercept McClain before he could reach the girl. "Get back in the car!"

His shout froze both McClain and the teen. Then McClain put on a burst of speed, heading toward the car.

"Get back in the car and lock the door!"

For a moment, she hesitated. McClain closed in. She dove into the driver's seat and slammed the door just as McClain reached her. He yanked on the door handle, then smashed a fist on the glass.

Gavin never slowed his stride as he slammed into the man. They both crashed to the asphalt, and the impact knocked the breath from Gavin, stunning him into stillness. But at least he landed on top.

McClain dragged in a wheezing breath and swung out with his right hand, catching Gavin in the chin. The blow knocked him to the side.

Police vehicles swarmed into the parking lot.

McClain had pulled his weapon and turned it on Gavin.

Cops' orders blended into a haze of discordant sounds as time slowed. The muzzle stopped moving and centered on his head.

Sarah gave a terrified cry and kicked out. Her shoe connected with McClain's forearm and the weapon lifted, fired, then fell to the ground.

She drew back a fist and landed it square in the man's nose. He cried out, blood spurted, and then he was facedown on the ground, officers cuffing his wrists behind him. Hands pulled her away. The next few moments were a blur, but Sarah soon found herself sitting in the back of an ambulance wrapped in a blanket with Gavin next to her. As soon as the paramedic turned his attention to McClain, Gavin said, "I'm glad you don't follow orders well or I'd be dead."

"You're welcome."

"So, you don't hate me?"

"What for? Not telling me my father hired you to babysit me?"

He grimaced. "It wasn't babysitting, I assure you."

"No, I don't hate you. I'm not happy he did it, but I think I'm coming to understand him a bit. And honestly, when we were falling through the sky, it was the least of my worries. So . . . I'm not going to worry about it now."

He dropped his chin to his chest. "Thank God. I can't tell you how that's weighed on me."

"I realized something else."

"What?"

"I've been angry and rebellious for a very long time and I'm tired of it." She shrugged. "It's not very productive and has caused me to give up the peace God's promised me."

"Sounds like you can be wise when you want to."

She laughed. "Wise might be stretching it, but I'm learning. And growing."

He wrapped an arm around her. "I think you're pretty amazing."

"You said something while we were hovering above the earth."

"I meant it too. I love you, Sarah. I've loved you for a long —"

Tears filled her eyes and spilled over onto

her cheeks. "Oh no," she whispered.

"What?" He frowned. "Sarah? What is it?"

"It's happening." There was no joy at Gavin's proclamation of love. Only anguish filled her. Scenes blipped through her mind. Dustin's loss, her past, the kidnapping, her father's betrayal. She tried to shove it away, but it pressed in on her. Suffocating her. The pain of it all wanted to cripple her. She pressed her hands against her head. Then her chest. How could this be? Everything she'd ever done wrong was played out on a 3-D screen in her head. The anger at her mother for not telling her about her illness, followed by the hate of her father for his role in it and simply never being the father she longed for. The rebellion that led to the guys in high school. The shame of it all. The shame! She didn't deserve love. Gavin's or God's. She wept and bolted from the ambulance.

"Sarah!"

She ran toward the traffic. *Stop it. Stop it. Stop it. End it.* The shame and the pain had to end.

Hard hands caught her. Held her so she couldn't escape. "Oh, Sarah." The anguish in those two words reached her. "Fight it," he whispered.

Gavin.

He'd never want to be with someone like her. Never. She was too messed up. Worthless. She shook her head. "No. No, I'm not. I'm not worthless." A sob ripped from her. "Gavin? Why do I feel so worthless? I . . . I can't do this . . . It has to stop. It all needs . . . to stop." She jerked against his hold.

He turned and grabbed the paramedic's attention. "We need to get to the hospital now."

Chapter Twenty-Seven

Gavin paced outside Sarah's hospital room, phone pressed to his ear. "She can't talk right now, I'm sorry."

"She gave me her number, you know. I have her permission to call her."

"Kaylynn, I'm not keeping you from talking to her out of any kind of spite. The truth is, she had an accident and is in the hospital. I promise as soon as she wakes up and feels like talking, I'll have her call you."

A pause. "An accident? Really? Is she going to be okay?"

"Yes. Yes, she is."

"You sound like you're trying to convince yourself."

He sighed. "I just have to pray she will be okay."

"Then I will too."

"Thank you." He was still reeling that Kaylynn had reached out to him. She must really want to talk to Sarah.

"Okay, then I guess I'll go," she said.

But she didn't sound like she wanted to hang up. "Kaylynn, I'll help you if you need help."

For a moment, silence. "Thanks, Gavin. I'm not sure that I need help exactly. But maybe some advice. From Sarah."

"Got it." Must be some kind of girl thing.

"I called for one other reason."

"What's that?"

"I kind of owe you an apology."

Could the day hold any more surprises? "Uh. No, I think I'm the one who owes you the apology."

"He was a jerk."

The druggie boyfriend. "At least we agree on that."

"So . . . I couldn't say it back then, but thanks."

"Of course."

She let out a little puff of sound that could have been a sigh or laughter. He couldn't tell which. "Okay, I'll be waiting for her call."

"Bye, Kay." The nickname she hated slipped out. "Sorry. Kay*lynn.*"

"You can call me Kay. Bye." She hung up.

Still off-kilter from the conversation with his sister, Gavin watched Caden on his phone, pacing the small area in front of

436

Sarah's room. When Caden finally hung up, he sighed.

Gavin narrowed his eyes. "What is it?"

"Kilgore's dead."

"How?"

"He hung himself in his basement."

Gavin flinched. So much pain, so much death. "It's hard to feel sorry for him."

"Yeah. I wanted him to pay for what he'd done, but I didn't wish death on him. Donna will live to stand trial."

"Good." They fell silent for a moment, eyes on Sarah's room. "Did you see her? In the parking lot?" Gavin asked.

"I saw her." Caden shook his head and wiped eyes that had teared at the memory. "I've never seen anything like that. Is that what Dustin felt in his last moments?" His voice roughened with his effort to control his emotions.

Gavin understood the feeling. "I don't know. I don't want to think so."

"Yeah."

"It was like someone flipped a switch," Caden said. "She was fine one minute — well, safe and happy to be that way — but then it was like a terrible sadness came over her and there was nothing she could do to stop it."

"But absolutely *had* to stop it."

437

"Any way she could." A pause. "She would have run straight out into the road if you hadn't caught her. It was blocked off, thanks to all of the law enforcement vehicles, but I have no doubt she would have kept going and . . . found a way to kill herself if you hadn't grabbed her."

Gavin drew in a deep breath. "Well, it's over now. We just have to pray Heather's right about the treatment."

As though she heard him speak her name, Heather slipped out of Sarah's room and let the door shut behind her. He caught her gaze and simply waited.

"She's going to be all right," Heather said.

"How do you know?"

"Because she has to be."

"That's not helpful."

"I'm sorry. It's all I can offer right now. But she's very peaceful. Calm. No nightmares or restlessness. I'm very hopeful."

Caden crossed his arms, then rubbed his chin. "I hope you're right."

"I'm not going to deny it was a long shot, but without the antidote, I thought it worth taking. All the people who survived the drug with no more effects had undergone anesthesia for surgical procedures. One who slashed her wrists, one who tried to run through a sliding glass door, one who needed his stomach pumped . . . and more. I'm just praying that's the case with Sarah."

"But that was after they actually attempted suicide," Caden said.

"Wilmont didn't." Gavin shifted, his worry meter set at high. "When he came out from under, he was fine." He paused. "But his dose was an overdose — which caused him to go crazy in a very criminal sense. Maybe once the drug started to wear off, he would have tried to find a way to . . . you know."

"I know," Heather said. "Trust me, I know. But the anesthesia is the only connection I could find with the ones who survived and are recovering with no suicidal ideations. We have to pray it's right."

Brooke and Ava came into sight from the long hallway and hurried toward them. "Is she awake?" Brooke asked.

"Not yet."

"What's taking so long? Can't you bring her out of it?"

Heather shook her head. "I want to let the anesthesia wear off naturally — just like with the others."

Ava pressed her fingers to her lips, her eyes wet. "I can't believe this." She looked at Caden. "Thank you for the quick phone call to fill us in, but I still can't wrap my head around it. You're saying her kidnapping was all a ruse to get the money from her father?"

He nodded. "Yeah. That was why they held her in the cell at the compound. They were waiting for McClain to get there with the papers. Once Sarah signed them, he'd only have to convince" — he used air quotes — "the general to do it. McClain would have Sarah and if the general didn't sign, he'd just threaten to kill her."

"Which he would have done anyway once he had the signature," Gavin said. "The plan was probably to kidnap Sarah, get her signature, keep her alive long enough to get the general's signature, then kill them both."

"Only Sarah managed to get a call out on her sat phone," Heather murmured.

Footsteps sounded behind him. Slow, measured steps. He turned to see General Denning coming toward them with the help of a walker.

Caden stepped forward. "General."

"I want to see Sarah," the man growled. His pale face and shaky hands gave away the fact that he shouldn't be out of bed.

"She's still sleeping, General," Heather said.

"Well, wake her up. I need to talk to her."

"I can't do that." The steel in Heather's

words said she *wouldn't* do it.

The general paused. His shoulders wilted. "I helped fund that drug, you know. I thought they were doing good things. I had no idea they were falsifying the data."

"I know, Dad," Caden said. He pulled a chair from the nurses' station. "Why don't you sit down?"

Once he was seated, he took a moment to catch his breath. Gavin eyed him, feeling slightly relieved when the man's face pinked up a bit. "Tell me what that traitor McClain's told you."

Caden shrugged. "Basically everything. He's hoping for something other than the death penalty. He's gone into great detail about everything from Sarah's kidnapping in Kabul — which we messed up for him — to him coming up with a new plan that involved getting to her here in the States. Kilgore and Nurse Donna were as greedy as he was."

"And Max?" Heather asked.

"Max got too close, started asking too many questions, and scared them that he was going to ruin everything by exposing them and the drug. Thanks to him and Dustin's evidence, we have all we need to put away those involved."

"What about the other people around the

441

country?" Ava asked.

"Law enforcement has already taken those involved into custody. It'll take a long time to get it all sorted out, but at least there won't be any more T-64 distributed."

A nurse stuck her head out of the room. "She's waking up."

Sarah opened her eyes and blinked. Blinked again. And groaned. Another hospital? Great. She frowned. What had she done this time?

"Hey, sleepyhead, can you wake up and talk to us?"

Gavin. Warmth enveloped her. She'd never tire of hearing his voice. Her eyes finally focused, and she let her gaze drift around the room. Anxious faces stared down at her.

"Who shot me this time?"

Stilted laughter came from her visitors.

"How do you feel?" Heather asked.

"Sleepy."

"Anything else?"

Was she supposed to feel something else? "Um . . . no, I don't think so. What happened? Why am I here?"

"What's the last thing you remember before landing here?" Brooke asked.

"Uh . . ." She struggled to formulate an answer. "I'm not sure. Everything is kind of

442

fuzzy." She gasped. "McClain. He sprayed me with something then . . . Nurse Donna was there. I think I remember being carried down a hallway and dumped in a room." Her eyes locked on Gavin. Then her father. She struggled to sit up. Heather raised the bed. Gavin never let go of her hand. "You were there."

He nodded. "What else do you remember?"

She shrugged. "That's it."

"Just like Wilmont," Caden murmured.

Heather stepped next to her and looked into her eyes with a light. "You don't feel sad or depressed?"

"What? No. I feel . . . refreshed. Like I had a really good night's sleep with no nightmares."

Tears sprang into Gavin's eyes and he closed them. When he opened them, Sarah caught her breath at the emotion there.

"All right, then, everyone," Caden said, "I think we can get out of here." One by one her visitors left. Except Gavin, who didn't move.

He leaned over and kissed her forehead.

At the door, Caden pulled Heather into a tight hug. "Thank you." His whisper drifted to Sarah.

"What's that all about?" she asked.

443

Heather smiled through her tears. "I'll let Gavin bring you up to speed while I go fill out your discharge papers. Just press the button if you need anything."

She left and Sarah lifted a brow.

Gavin's phone buzzed and he glanced at the screen. "Well, seems you've made an impression on my sister."

"Really? How?"

"I don't know, but maybe you can give me some pointers. Come in!"

Sarah jumped. The door opened. Kaylynn stepped inside and shut it behind her. "I hope I'm not imposing."

"Not at all," Sarah said. "Have a seat wherever you can find a spot."

Kaylynn chose the seat under the window. "I know this is kind of weird, but you offered to help."

"Of course."

Gavin nodded.

"So, it's kind of a long story, but I'll give you the condensed version. And I'll probably be blunt."

"Just say it," Gavin said.

"A professor at my school has been soliciting sex for As."

Gavin lost his laid-back posture and his feet hit the floor. "I'm sorry, did you just say —"

"Yes, I did. Please don't make me say it again."

"Go on."

She fished into her pocket and pulled out a flash drive. "A friend of mine complied and got her A, but she was devastated. She dropped out and went home. I can't tell you how angry I was. I didn't know what to do or how to do it, I just knew I was going to find a way to get the evidence I needed." She rubbed the flash drive between her thumb and index finger while staring at it. "So, I did." She lifted her eyes to meet Sarah's. "When you said you were an investigative journalist, it gave me the idea. I set myself up as bait and he took it."

Gavin's gasp nearly sucked all of the oxygen from the room. "You did *what*?"

"I went to his place and recorded our . . . interaction."

"You have him on video or audio?" Gavin said.

"Both."

"Give it to me. I'll take care of it." He paused. Looked at Sarah. "I mean, I'll take care of it if you want me to. I won't butt in if it's something you'd rather handle yourself."

His sister gaped and Sarah had to smother a giggle in spite of the seriousness of the situation.

Kaylynn raised a brow. "Where'd that come from?"

"I've been taking lessons on how not to be a dictator. Now do you want me to take care of it or not?"

"Sure. I wanted to do it myself, but he scared me the last time I was there."

"Did he touch you?" Gavin's tone had turned lethal.

"No, not at all. But I wasn't sure he wouldn't. I left his home, and when I turned around, he was watching me." She paused and bit her lip, then sighed. "I'm sorry, Gavin. I've been so stupid." She cleared her throat. "I've been angry with you."

"No kidding."

"But it was more than you, I was mad at myself too. Mostly I was angry with you because you took the choice to handle Mitchell away from me." She sighed. "I knew he was into some drugs, but I thought it was just occasionally and he *never* did them around me. I thought he was in love with me and would change. For me. When you caught him with the drugs at Mom and Dad's, it was a punch in the gut. I hated you for finding them and him for having them and I hated myself for thinking I could convince him to quit. But he obviously wasn't going to — and I couldn't make him. It made me sad and angry and spiteful. That night in the professor's house when I wasn't sure what he was going to do, I realized that I was wrong. Sometimes you need someone to step in and save you from yourself." She stood and hugged him. "So . . . thanks."

Sarah swiped a tear. Kaylynn was wise beyond her years. *Sometimes you need someone to step in and save you from yourself.* So true.

"Anyway, thanks. I won't go back to his class until this is taken care of."

Gavin turned to Sarah. "Will you be all right for a little while?"

"Of course." She smiled. "This will give Kaylynn and me a chance to get to know each other a little better."

Kaylynn grinned through a sheen of tears. "I've got stories."

"Oh . . . do tell."

CHAPTER TWENTY-EIGHT

October

Sarah stood in the doorway of her empty apartment and drew in a deep breath. "Bye, Mom," she whispered.

"Anything else?" Gavin asked, coming up the steps. Sweat dripped from his temples in spite of the cool October air.

She turned. "No. Thank you for helping."

"Of course. Are you sure about this?"

"It's time. Your sister was right when she said sometimes we need someone to step in and save us from ourselves. I had people who tried to do that. Dustin, Caden, Brooke . . . all of them. And you. And I suppose my father too, even though it's harder to see it that way. But I need to deal with the past and Brooke is going to help me do that." She shot him a small smile. "She just doesn't know it yet."

He wrapped his arms around her and

kissed the top of her head. "I'm here for you."

"I know. I'd be in a puddle on the floor if you weren't." She patted his cheek. "You're a good man, Gavin Black."

"I try."

"So, how'd it go with Kaylynn's professor?"

"He's facing charges of sexual harassment and will lose his tenure at the university. Kaylynn didn't want to tell our father about what was going on because she was afraid he'd do something he'd regret. But she's told my parents, the school, and the police everything. She also said she plans to testify if he decides to plead not guilty and force a trial."

"She's a brave girl. One who's very blessed to have you looking out for her."

He straightened. "I see someone who wants to look out for you."

She drew back and frowned at him. Then looked over her shoulder. "What's he doing here?" Her father walked slowly, his hand pressed to his shoulder.

"General?"

"Sarah."

He'd called her Sarah. Hope sprung. She sighed. "I just want you to know I'm glad you're not dead."

"I'm glad you're not dead too." His gruff voice held a lot of emotion that wasn't reflected on his face.

"Mom lived here before she met you," she blurted.

He blinked. Realization dawned in his eyes. "And that's why you wanted to live here."

"I told myself that, but I wonder if it was more that it made you mad. And I'm sorry for that. I'm sorry for a lot of things."

He cleared his throat. "So am I."

Sarah nearly fell over.

Her father glanced at Gavin, then back at her. "I wish I'd done things different, but I can't go back and redo them."

"No one can," she said. "I figured that out a while ago."

He rubbed his chin, then stuffed his hand in his pocket. "But we can make changes going forward, can't we? I'd like to try anyway."

It was all Sarah could do not to let her jaw drop to her chest. "So would I. That's why I'm giving up the apartment and moving in with Caden for now. As much as I love some of the residents, it's time for me to leave."

The general nodded and a smile glimmered in his eyes. "You just want to live

450

with Caden because he keeps ice cream in his freezer."

He knew she liked ice cream. And he'd made a joke. Tears gathered and she swallowed the lump that refused to completely go away. "Yeah, he does."

"So do I."

Surprise and joy grabbed her and she nodded. "I'll have to come visit."

"I'd like that. Sarah."

"Me too. Dad."

Her father cleared his throat again. "Right. Right. Uh . . . one more thing." He reached into an inner pocket of his dress coat and pulled out an envelope. "I need to say something and it's not easy, but I'm learning that the things worth fighting for don't come easy. I never told you this, but my father basically paid me off to join the Army. I took the money and never looked back." A pause. "Okay, I looked back in moments of weakness." He let his gaze run over her. Sarah stood still, sensing he wasn't done and not wanting to miss a minute of whatever else he had to say. He waved the envelope at her. "I realize I never really knew how to be a father. I knew how to be a general and a leader, but not a father. However, I promise, everything I ever did for you, I had your best interests in mind —

not that it appeared that way to you. I get that."

He looked away for a moment and cleared his throat. "Anyway, as hard as it is, I have to accept that you're a grown woman who can make her own decisions." He handed her the envelope. "I pulled some strings and got your psychiatric record saying you were suicidal discarded. Since the psychiatrist who made the diagnosis has been arrested and will spend a very long time in prison, it wasn't that difficult to do. You're now free to be reinstated to your old position should you desire to return to it."

Tears dripped down her cheeks and she swiped them away. Gavin's arm came around her and squeezed.

"Thank you, Dad," she whispered. "Thank you."

He nodded, hesitated. "I'm sorry, Sarah. For everything. I really am."

Sarah slipped from Gavin's arms into her father's. "I'm sorry too. For everything."

His hug healed so many wounds. She finally let him go and he stepped back. "I'm going to head home now. We'll talk later."

"Okay. Thank you."

He left and Sarah leaned her forehead against Gavin's chest. He rubbed her back while she gathered her emotions into something manageable.

"I've been meaning to tell you something," he said.

She didn't look up. "What?"

"He tried to save you."

"I know he thought he was doing what was best for me. I didn't like it then and I still don't, but I'm coming to terms with it."

"No, not that. When you were unconscious and on the floor at the lab. Your father dove for McClain trying to protect you and that's how he got shot."

She simply stared at him. "Why didn't you tell me?"

"I thought he might, and I didn't want to take that away from him if he wanted to. But I guess he's not going to say anything."

More tears slipped down her cheeks. "I really didn't think he cared. How could I have been so blind?"

"Well, give yourself some slack. He didn't exactly make it easy for you to see."

"You saw it."

He shrugged. "I'm a guy."

A sob slipped out. "Why am I so weepy? Are you sure you want to be stuck with me and my baggage?"

"Hey, you helped me with mine. I can jump out of planes again. I owe you."

She jerked and glared. "You do not owe me *anything.*"

"Sarah, I was kidding. I didn't mean it that way. I'm with you because I want to be with you. I thought we covered that ground already."

"You're right. I'm sorry. I guess I'm not going to stop being insecure overnight."

He cupped her face and met her gaze. "You're one of the strongest people I know. You've got this. And I've got you."

A tear slipped down her cheek. "Thank you," she whispered.

He kissed her, then pulled her close. "So . . ."

"Yeah," she mumbled against his shirt.

"What are we going to do with ourselves? Reenlist or be civilians for the rest of our days?"

She stilled. "The rest of our days is a long time."

"And thanks to Heather and her genius inspiration, we're going to have that time."

She nodded. "I have something else I need to tell you."

"Do I need to be sitting down for this?"

A laugh slipped from her. "No, I don't think so. Owen Grant and Jefferson Wyatt both offered me a job. Like in a very normal, professional way. Separately. Each one comes with a very nice package, so it's just a matter of choosing which one I want."

"Wow. Both of them? Are you interested?"

"Yes, actually."

"What about the Army?"

She frowned. "The Army was exactly what I needed at that time in my life. I loved what I did. I made a difference in a lot of people's lives and I'd never want to change that. But now? Now I'm at a different place in my life. You're here and . . ."

He tensed. "And?"

"And I don't want to be over there if it means being away from you."

He swallowed and looked away. The sheen of tears appeared, then faded. "I'm glad. If you ever change your mind, I won't hold you back."

"That goes both ways. If you ever decide you want to reenlist, I'll support that." She paused. "Since my father got everything reversed — and the doctor who incorrectly diagnosed me is now in prison — I'll have to finish out my tour, but I only have four months left."

He hugged her and kissed the top of her head. "I can do four months." He paused. "Maybe."

"We can make it. Once I get out, we can take things slow."

"I think we're going to make an awesome team."

"It won't be perfect every day. I'm still me. Stubborn, opinionated, sad that I can't change the decisions I made in high school . . . and too insecure for my own good."

"And I'm . . . well . . . I'm . . . I can't think of anything." He shot her a teasing grin and she punched him in the bicep. Then he sobered. "I'm not perfect either. I'm a lot of those things you listed. And more. Your high school days are gone. The decisions you made back then don't have to define your future. I won't let them define it."

A tear slid down her cheek. "I don't deserve you," she whispered, "but if you're sure, we'll make it work. Together."

"Which brings us back to that whole rest-of-our-days thing." She smiled. "So it does."

"Only if you want to."

"Oh, I want to. I want to, Gavin. More than anything."

"Thank God." He lowered his head and kissed her.

She wrapped her arms around his neck and sent up a silent prayer of agreement.

ACKNOWLEDGMENTS

As always, the list of people to thank is long. For this book, I have to thank my brainstorming team. So many brainstormers! Thank you to Colleen Coble, Carrie Stuart Parks, Pam Hillman, Robin Carroll, Karen Solem, Lynn H. Blackburn, Edie Melson, Alycia Morales, and DiAnn Mills. I could NOT have come up with this story without you.

Thanks once again to Vincent Davis for providing his expertise on military matters. If I got anything wrong, that's on me! ☺

Thank you to Tamela Hancock Murray for being such an amazing agent.

And thanks to my incredible editors, Andrea Doering and Barb Barnes. You guys are amazing, and I'm beyond grateful for you and the whole Revell team.

Thank you to my family. I really couldn't do what I do without your encouragement and support.

And, of course, I have to thank the readers. I REALLY couldn't do this without you! Thank you for reading and loving the stories.

Mostly, I thank Jesus, who allows me to create stories that, hopefully, bring glory and honor and praise to him.

ABOUT THE AUTHOR

Lynette Eason is the bestselling author of *Protecting Tanner Hollow,* as well as the Blue Justice, Women of Justice, Deadly Reunions, Hidden Identity, and Elite Guardians series. She is the winner of three ACFW Carol Awards, the Selah Award, and the Inspirational Reader's Choice Award, among others. She is a graduate of the University of South Carolina and has a master's degree in education from Converse College. Eason lives in South Carolina with her husband and two children. Learn more at www.lynetteeason.com.

The employees of Thorndike Press hope you have enjoyed this Large Print book. All our Thorndike, Wheeler, and Kennebec Large Print titles are designed for easy reading, and all our books are made to last. Other Thorndike Press Large Print books are available at your library, through selected bookstores, or directly from us.

For information about titles, please call:
  (800) 223-1244

or visit our website at:
  gale.com/thorndike

To share your comments, please write:
  Publisher
  Thorndike Press
  10 Water St., Suite 310
  Waterville, ME 04901

461